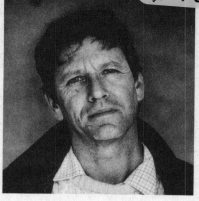

AMOS OZ
My Michael

Amos Oz was born in Jerusalem in 1939. He served in the Israeli Army during the 1967 Six-Day War and again during the 1973 Yom Kippur War. Since the Six-Day War he has published numerous articles on the Arab-Israeli conflict, and since 1977 he has been one of the leaders of Israel's "Peace Now" movement, campaigning for the peaceful co-existence of Israelis and Palestinians on the West Bank and Gaza. He has been a Visiting Fellow at St. Cross College, Oxford, Author-in-Residence at Hebrew University in Jerusalem, and is currently Professor of Hebrew Literature at Ben Gurion University of the Negev. Among his other works are *Where the Jackals Howl*; *Elsewhere, Perhaps*; *Unto Death*; *Touch the Water, Touch the Wind*; *The Hill of Evil Counsel*; *Soumchi*; *In the Land of Israel*; *Black Box*; and *The Slopes of Lebanon*, the latter three of which are available in Vintage. His most recent novel is *To Know a Woman*. He lives with his wife and three children in Arad, Israel.

VINTAGE

INTERNATIONAL

OTHER BOOKS BY AMOS OZ

To Know a Woman
The Slopes of Lebanon
Black Box
A Perfect Peace
In the Land of Israel
Where the Jackals Howl and Other Stories
Soumchi
The Hill of Evil Counsel
Unto Death
Touch the Water, Touch the Wind
Elsewhere, Perhaps

My Michael

My
Michael

AMOS OZ

Translated from the Hebrew by Nicholas de Lange
in collaboration with the author

VINTAGE INTERNATIONAL • VINTAGE BOOKS

A DIVISION OF RANDOM HOUSE, INC. • NEW YORK

The Israeli background is unfamiliar, but not, I hope, unintelligible. The calendar is, of course, the Jewish calendar, dominated by the Sabbath, which begins and ends at sunset. As for the urban landscape of Jerusalem, which is so prominent in the story, and the interplay of the various factions of the population, Jews and Arabs, Europeans and Orientals, religious and "enlightened" Jews, I cannot hope to add anything to Hannah's own vivid and penetrating commentary.

A few specific points which may be helpful or interesting: It was pointed out by Israeli critics that Michael's surname, Gonen, means "protector," and it is only fair to offer this information, for what it is worth, to the English reader. I have kept several non-Hebrew words and phrases in their original languages; where they are not self-explanatory I have occasionally inserted the translation. ("*Cholera,*" on p. 257, is not a diagnosis, but a common Polish curse.) One or two of the names have affectionate diminutive forms—"Hannah," for example, becomes "Hannele" (in Yiddish) or "Hanka" (in Russian). The *Palmach* was the striking-force of the *Haganah,* the Jewish defense organization set up in Palestine during the British Mandate. In transliterating the Hebrew and Arabic names I have aimed at a certain consistency, basing myself on the current pronunciation, but I have sometimes surrendered to the claims of familiar usage. *Ch, kh* and frequently *h* are to be pronounced like the *ch* in *loch.*

Finally, although I have enjoyed and benefited from the close collaboration of the author, any shortcomings in the translation are mine, not his, and I take full responsibility for them.

Cambridge　　　　　　　　　　　　　　　　　　　N. de L.
November, 1971

My Michael

held me I could feel the warmth of his fingers through the sleeve of the blue woolen dress my mother had knitted me. It was winter in Jerusalem.

He asked me whether I had hurt myself.

I said I thought I had twisted my ankle.

He said he had always liked the word "ankle." He smiled. His smile was embarrassed and embarrassing. I blushed. Nor did I refuse when he asked if he could take me to the cafeteria on the ground floor. My leg hurt. Terra Sancta College is a Christian convent which was loaned to the Hebrew University after the 1948 war when the buildings on Mount Scopus were cut off. It is a cold building; the corridors are tall and wide. I felt distracted as I followed this young stranger who was holding on to me. I was happy to respond to his voice. I was unable to look straight at him and examine his face. I sensed, rather than saw, that his face was long and lean and dark.

"Now let's sit down," he said.

We sat down, neither of us looking at the other. Without asking what I wanted he ordered two cups of coffee. I loved my late father more than any other man in the world. When my new acquaintance turned his head I saw that his hair was cropped short and that he was unevenly shaven. Dark bristles showed, especially under his chin. I do not know why this detail struck me as important, in fact as a point in his favor. I liked his smile and his fingers, which were playing with a teaspoon as if they had an independent life of their own. And the spoon enjoyed being held by them. My own finger felt a faint urge to touch his chin, on the spot where he had not shaved properly and where the bristles sprouted.

Michael Gonen was his name.

He was a third-year geology student. He had been born and brought up in Holon. "It's cold in this Jerusalem of yours."

"My Jerusalem? How do you know I'm from Jerusalem?"

4

He was sorry, he said, if he was wrong for once, but he did not think he was wrong. He had learned by now to spot a Jerusalemite at first sight. As he spoke he looked into my eyes for the first time. His eyes were gray. I noticed a flicker of amusement in them, but not a cheerful flicker. I told him that his guess was right. I was indeed a Jerusalemite.

"Guess? Oh, no."

He pretended to look offended, the corners of his mouth smiling: No, it was not a guess. He could see that I was a Jerusalemite. "See?" Was this part of his geology course? No, of course not. As a matter of fact, it was something he had learned from cats. From cats? Yes, he loved watching cats. A cat would never make friends with anyone who was not disposed to like him. Cats are never wrong about people.

"You seem to be a happy sort of person," I said happily. I laughed, and my laugh betrayed me.

Afterwards Michael Gonen invited me to accompany him to the third floor of Terra Sancta College, where some instructional films about the Dead Sea and the Arava were about to be shown.

On the way up, as we passed the place on the staircase where I had slipped earlier, Michael took hold of my sleeve once again. As if there were a danger of slipping again on that particular step. Through the blue wool I could feel every one of his five fingers. He coughed drily and I looked at him. He caught me looking at him, and his face reddened. Even his ears turned red. The rain beat at the windows.

"What a downpour," Michael said.

"Yes, a downpour," I agreed enthusiastically, as if I had suddenly discovered that we were related.

Michael hesitated. Then he added:

5

CHAPTER

2

 My late father often used to
say: Strong people can do almost anything they want to do,
but even the strongest cannot choose what they want to do. I
am not particularly strong.

Michael and I arranged to meet that same evening in Cafe
Atara in Ben Yehuda Street. Outside an absolute storm was
raging, beating down furiously on the stone walls of Jerusalem.

Austerity regulations were still in force. We were given
ersatz coffee and tiny paper bags of sugar. Michael made a joke
about this, but his joke was not funny. He is not a witty man
—and perhaps he could not tell it in an amusing way. I enjoyed his efforts; I was glad that I was causing him some
exertion. It was because of me that he was coming out of his
cocoon and trying to be amused and amusing. When I was
nine I still used to wish I could grow up as a man instead of a
woman. As a child I always played with boys and I always read
boys' books. I used to wrestle, kick, and climb. We lived in

Kiryat Shmuel, on the edge of the suburb called Katamon. There was a derelict plot of land on a slope, covered with rocks and thistles and pieces of scrap iron, and at the foot of the slope stood the house of the twins. The twins were Arabs, Halil and Aziz, the sons of Rashid Shahada. I was a princess and they were my bodyguard, I was a conqueror and they my officers, I was an explorer and they my native bearers, a captain and they my crew, a master spy and they my henchmen. Together we would explore distant streets, prowl through the woods, hungry, panting, teasing Orthodox children, stealing into the woods around St. Simeon's Convent, calling the British policemen names. Giving chase and running away, hiding and suddenly dashing out. I ruled over the twins. It was a cold pleasure, so remote.

Michael said:

"You're a coy girl, aren't you?"

When we had finished drinking our coffee Michael took a pipe out of his overcoat pocket and put it on the table between us. I was wearing brown corduroy trousers and a chunky red sweater, such as girls at the University used to wear at that time to produce a casual effect. Michael remarked shyly that I had seemed more feminine that morning in the blue woolen dress. To him, at least.

"You seemed different this morning, too," I said.

Michael was wearing a gray overcoat. He did not take it off the whole time we sat in Cafe Atara. His cheeks were glowing from the bitter cold outside. His body was lean and angular. He picked up his unlit pipe and traced shapes with it on the tablecloth. His fingers, playing with the pipe, gave me a feeling of peace. Perhaps he had suddenly regretted his remark about my clothes; as if correcting a mistake, Michael said he thought I was a pretty girl. As he said it he stared fixedly at the pipe.

9

garten in Kerem Avraham. In the afternoons I attended lectures on Hebrew literature. But I was only a first-year student. "Student rhymes with prudent." Straining to be witty in his anxiety to avoid pauses in the conversation, Michael resorted to a play on words. But the point was not clear, and he tried to rephrase it. Suddenly he stopped talking and made a fresh, furious attempt at lighting his obstinate pipe. I enjoyed his discomfiture. At that time I was still repelled by the sight of the rough men my friends used to worship in those days: great bears of *Palmach*-men who used to tackle you with a gushing torrent of deceptive kindness; thick-limbed tractor drivers coming all dusty from the Negev like marauders carrying off the women of some captured city. I loved the embarrassment of the student Michael Gonen in Cafe Atara on a winter's night.

A famous scholar came into the cafe in the company of two women. Michael leaned toward me to whisper his name in my ear. His lips may have brushed my hair. I said:

"I can see right through you. I can read your mind. You're saying to yourself: 'What's going to happen next? Where do we go from here?' Am I right?"

Michael reddened suddenly like a child caught stealing sweets:

"I've never had a regular girlfriend before."

"Before?"

Thoughtfully Michael moved his empty cup. He looked at me. Deep down, underneath his meekness, a suppressed sneer lurked in his eyes.

"Till now."

A quarter of an hour later the famous scholar left with one of the women. Her friend moved over to a table in a corner and lit a cigarette. Her expression was bitter.

Michael remarked:

"That woman is jealous."

"Of us?"

"Of you, perhaps." He tried to cover up. He was ill at ease, because he was trying too hard. If only I could tell him that his efforts did him credit. That I found his fingers fascinating. I could not speak, but I was afraid to keep silent. I told Michael that I adored meeting the celebrities of Jerusalem, the writers and scholars. It was an interest I had inherited from my father. When I was small my father used to point them out to me in the street. My father was extremely fond of the phrase "world-famous." He would whisper excitedly that some professor who had just vanished into a florist's shop was world-famous, or that some man out shopping was of international fame. And I would see a diminutive old man cautiously feeling his way like a stranger in an unfamiliar city. When we read the Books of the Prophets at school, I imagined the Prophets as being like the writers and scholars my father had pointed out to me: men of refined features, bespectacled, with neatly trimmed white beards, their pace troubled and hesitant, as if they were walking down the steep slope of a glacier. And when I tried to imagine these frail old men thundering against the sins of the people, I smiled; I thought that at the height of their fury their voices would dry up and they would merely emit a high-pitched shriek. If a writer or university professor came into his shop in Jaffa Road, my father would come home looking as if he had seen a vision. He would repeat solemnly casual words they had spoken, and study their utterances as if they were rare coins. He was always looking for hidden meanings in their words, because he saw life as a lesson from which one had to learn a moral. He was an attentive man. Once my father took me and my brother Emanuel to the Tel Or Cinema on a Saturday morning to hear Martin Buber and Hugo Bergmann speak at a meeting sponsored by a pacifist organization. I still remember a curious episode. As we were leaving the auditorium Professor Bergmann stopped in front of my father and said, "I really did not expect to see you in our midst today, my dear Dr. Liebermann. I beg your pardon—you are not Professor Liebermann? Yet I feel certain we have met. Your face, sir, seems very familiar." Father stuttered. He blanched as if he had been accused of some foul deed. The professor, too, was confused, and apologized for his mistake. Perhaps on account of his embarrassment the scholar touched my shoulder and said, "In any case, my dear sir, your daughter—your daughter? —is a very pretty girl." And beneath his mustache a gentle smile spread. My father never forgot this incident as long as he lived. He used to recount it again and again, with excitement and delight. Even when he sat in his armchair, clad in a dressing gown, his glasses perched high on his forehead and his mouth drooping wearily, my father looked as if he were silently listening to the voice of some secret power. "And you know, Michael, still, to this day, I sometimes think that I shall marry a young scholar who is destined to become world-famous. By the light of his reading lamp my husband's face will hover among piles of old German tomes; I shall creep in on tiptoe to put a cup of tea down on the desk, empty the ash-tray, and quietly close the shutters, then leave without his noticing me. Now you'll laugh at me."

CHAPTER
3

Ten o'clock.

Michael and I each paid our own checks, as students do, and went out into the night. The sharp frost seared our faces. I breathed out, and watched my breath mingle with his. The cloth of his overcoat was coarse, heavy, and pleasant to touch. I had no gloves, and Michael insisted I wear his. They were rough, worn leather gloves. Streams of water ran down the gutter toward Zion Square, as if something sensational was happening in the center of town. A tightly wrapped couple walked past, their arms round each other. The girl said:

"That's impossible. I can't believe it."

And her partner laughed:

"You're very naïve."

We stood for a moment or two, not knowing what to do. We only knew that we did not want to part. The rain stopped and the air grew colder. I found the cold unbearable. I shivered. We watched the water running down the gutter. The road was shiny. The asphalt reflected the broken yellow glare of car headlights. Disjointed thoughts flashed through my mind— how to keep hold of Michael for a little longer.

Michael said:

"I'm plotting against you, Hannah."

I said:

"Be careful. You might find yourself hoist on your own petard."

"I'm plotting dark deeds, Hannah."

His trembling lips betrayed him. For an instant he looked like a big, sad child, a child with most of its hair shaved off. I wanted to buy him a hat. I wanted to touch him.

Suddenly Michael raised his arm. A taxi screeched to a sodden halt. Then we were together inside its warm belly. Michael told the driver to drive wherever he felt like taking us, he didn't mind. The driver shot me a sly glance, full of filthy pleasure. The panel lights cast a dim red glow on his face, as if the skin had been peeled off and his red flesh laid bare. That taxi driver had the face of a mocking satyr. I have not forgotten.

We drove for about twenty minutes, with no idea where we were going. Our warm breath misted up the windows. Michael talked about geology. In Texas people dig for water and suddenly an oil well gushes up instead. Perhaps there are untapped supplies of oil in Israel too. Michael said "lithosphere." He said "sandstone," "chalk bed." He said "Pre-Cambrian," "Cambrian," "metamorphic rocks," "igneous rocks," "tectonics." For the first time then I felt that inner tension which I still feel whenever I hear my husband talking his strange language. These words relate to facts which have meaning for me, for me alone, like a message transmitted in code. Beneath the surface of the earth, opposed endogenic and exogenic forces are perpetually at work. The thin sedimentary rocks are in a continuous process of disintegration under the force of pressure. The lithosphere is a crust of hard rocks. Beneath the crust of hard rocks rages the blazing nucleus, the siderosphere.

I am not absolutely certain that Michael used these exact words during that taxi ride, in Jerusalem, at night, in the winter of 1950. But some of them I heard from him for the first time that night, and I was gripped. It was like a strange, sinister message, which I could not decipher. Like an unsuccessful attempt to reconstruct a nightmare which has faded from memory. Elusive as a dream.

Michael's voice as he spoke these words was deep and restrained. The dashboard lights glared red in the darkness. Michael spoke like a man weighed down with a grave responsibility, as if accuracy was at that moment of supreme importance. If he had taken my hand and pressed it in his I should not have withdrawn it. But the man I loved was carried away on a subdued tide of enthusiasm. I had been wrong. He could be very strong when he wanted to be. Much stronger than I. I accepted him. His words lulled me into that mood of tranquillity which I experience after a siesta; the tranquillity of waking to twilight, when time seems soft and I am tender and things around are tender.

The taxi passed through drenched streets which we could not identify because the windows were misted up. The windshield wipers caressed the windshield. They beat in twin, steady rhythm, as if in obedience to some inviolable law. After twenty minutes' drive Michael told the driver to stop, because he was not rich and our trip had already cost him the price of five lunches in the student restaurant at the end of Mamillah Road.

We got out of the taxi in a place which was unfamiliar: a steep alleyway paved with dressed stones. The paving stones were rain-lashed, for in the meantime the rain had started again. A fierce wind beat at us. We walked slowly. We were soaked to the skin. Michael's hair was drenched. His face was amusing; he had the look of a crying child. Once he stretched out a single finger and wiped away a drop of rain which was clinging to the tip of my chin. Suddenly we were in the square in front of the Generali Building. A winged lion, a rain-soaked, frozen lion, gazed down on us from above. Michael was ready to swear that the lion was laughing under his breath.

"Can't you hear him, Hannah? Laughing! He's looking at us and laughing. And I for one am inclined to agree with him."

I said:

"Maybe it's a pity that Jerusalem is such a small city that you can't get lost in it."

Michael accompanied me along Melisanda Street, the Street of the Prophets, and then along Strauss Street, where the medical center is. We did not meet a living soul. It was as if the inhabitants had abandoned the city and left it to the two of us. We were lords of the city. When I was a child I used to play a game I called "Princess of the City." The twins acted the part of submissive subjects. Sometimes I made them act rebellious subjects, and then I would humble them relentlessly. It was an exquisite thrill.

In winter, at night, the buildings of Jerusalem look like gray shapes against a black backcloth. A landscape pregnant with suppressed violence. Jerusalem can sometimes be an abstract city: stones, pine trees, and rusting iron.

Stiff-tailed cats crossed the deserted streets. The alley walls reflected a counterfeit echo of our footsteps, making them dull and long. We stood outside the door of my house for about five minutes. I said:

"Michael, I can't invite you up to my room for a hot glass of tea, because my landlord and his wife are religious people. When I took the room I promised them not to entertain men there. And it's half past eleven now."

When I said "men" we both smiled.

"I didn't expect you to invite me up to your room now," Michael said.

I said:

"Michael Gonen, you're a perfect gentleman, and I'm grateful to you for this evening. All of it. If you were to invite me to share another evening like it with you, I don't suppose I should refuse."

He bent over me. Forcefully he gripped my left hand in his right. Then he kissed my hand. The movement was abrupt and violent, as if he had been rehearsing it all along the way, as if he had mentally counted to three before he bent over to kiss me. Through the leather of the glove he had lent me when we left the cafe a strong, warm wave entered me. A moist breeze stirred the treetops and fell quiet. Like a duke in an English film Michael kissed my hand through his glove, only Michael was drenched and he forgot to smile and the glove was not white.

I took off both gloves and handed them to him. He hurriedly put them on while they were still warm from the heat of my body. An invalid coughed wretchedly behind the closed shutters on the first floor.

"How strange you are today," I smiled.

As if I had known him on other days, too.

CHAPTER

4

I have fond memories of an attack of diphtheria I suffered as a child of nine. It was winter. For several weeks I lay on my bed opposite the south-facing window. Through the window I could see a gloomy expanse of fog and rain: South Jerusalem, the shadow of the Bethlehem hills, Emek Refaim, the rich Arab suburbs in the valley. It was a winter world without details, a world of shapes in an expanse ranging in color from light to dark gray. I could see the trains, too, and I could follow them with my eyes a long way along Emek Refaim from the soot-blackened station as far as the curves at the foot of the Arab village of Beit Safafa. I was a general on the train. Troops loyal to me commanded the high ground. I was an emperor in hiding. An emperor whose authority was undiminished by distance and isolation. In my dreams the southern suburbs were transformed into the St. Pierre and Miquelon islands, which I had come across in my brother's stamp album. Their name had caught my fancy. I used to carry my dreams over into the world of waking. Night and day were one continuous world. My high fever

20

contributed to this effect. Those were dizzy, multicolored weeks. I was a queen. My cool mastery was challenged by open rebellion. I was captured by the mob, imprisoned, humiliated, tortured. But a handful of loyal supporters in dark corners were plotting to rescue me. I had confidence in them. I relished my cruel sufferings because out of them rose pride. My returning authority. I was reluctant to recover. According to the doctor, Dr. Rosenthal, there are some children who prefer to be ill, who refuse to be cured, because illness offers, in a sense, a state of freedom. When I recovered, at the end of the winter, I experienced a feeling of exile. I had lost my powers of alchemy, the ability to make my dreams carry me over the dividing line between sleeping and waking. To this day I feel a sense of disappointment on waking. I mock at my vague longing to fall seriously ill.

After saying good night to Michael I went up to my room. I made some tea. For a quarter of an hour I stood in front of the paraffin heater warming myself and thinking of nothing in particular. I peeled an apple, sent to me by my brother Emanuel from his kibbutz, Nof Harim. I recalled how Michael had tried three or four times to light his pipe without success. Texas is a fascinating place: A man digs a hole in his garden to plant a fruit tree, and suddenly a jet of oil gushes out. This was a whole dimension I had never considered before, the hidden worlds which lie beneath every spot I tread. Minerals and quartzes and dolomites and all that kind of thing.

Then I wrote a short letter to my mother and my brother and his family. I told them all that I was well. In the morning I must remember to buy a stamp.

In the literature of the Hebrew Enlightenment there are

frequent references to the conflict between light and darkness. The writer is committed to the eventual triumph of light. I must say that I prefer the darkness. Especially in summer. The white light terrorizes Jerusalem. It puts the city to shame. But in my heart there is no conflict between darkness and light. I was reminded of how I had slipped on the stairs that morning in Terra Sancta College. It was a humiliating moment. One of the reasons why I enjoy being asleep is that I hate making decisions. Awkward things sometimes happen in dreams, but some force always operates which makes decisions for you, and you are free to be like the boat in the song, with all the crew asleep, drifting wherever the dream carries you. The soft hammock, the sea gulls, and the expanse of water which is both a gently heaving surface and also a maelstrom of unplumbed depths. I know that the deep is thought of as a cold place. But it is not always so, and not entirely. I read in a book once about warm streams and underwater volcanoes. At a point deep below the freezing ocean depths there is sometimes a warm cave hidden. When I was small I read and reread my brother's copy of Jules Verne's *Twenty Thousand Leagues Under the Sea*. There are some rich nights when I discover a secret way through the watery depths and the darkness among green and clammy sea-creatures until I beat at the door of the warm cavern. That is my home. There a shadowy captain waits for me surrounded by books and pipes and charts. His beard is black, his eyes hold a hungry gleam. Like a savage he seizes me, and I soothe his raging hatred. Tiny fish swim through us, as if we were both made of water. As they pass through they impart minute flickers of searing pleasure.

I read two chapters of Mapu's *Love of Zion* for the next day's seminar. If I were Tamar I would make Amnon crawl to me on his knees for seven nights. When he finally confessed the torments of his love in scriptural language I would order him to transport me in a sailing ship to the isles of the archipelago, to that faraway place where Red Indians turn into delectable sea-creatures with silver spots and electric sparks, and sea gulls float in blue space.

Sometimes at night I see a bleak Russian steppe. Frozen plains coated with a crust of bluish frost which reflects the flickering light of a wild moon. There is a sledge and a bear-skin rug and the black back of a shrouded driver and furiously galloping horses and wolves' eyes glowing in the darkness round about and a solitary dead tree stands on the white slope and it is night within night on the steppe and the stars keep sinister watch. Suddenly the driver turns toward me a heavy face carved by some drunken sculptor. Icicles hang from the ends of his tangled mustache. His mouth is slightly open, as if it is he who is producing the howl of the biting wind. The dead tree which stands all alone on the slope on the steppe is not there by chance, it has a function which on waking I cannot name. But even when I wake I remember that it has a function. And so I return not entirely empty-handed.

In the morning I went out to buy a stamp. I posted the letter to Nof Harim. I ate a roll and yoghurt and drank a glass of tea. Mrs. Tarnopoler, my landlady, came into my room to ask me to buy a can of paraffin on my way home. While I drank my tea I managed to read another chapter of Mapu. At Sarah Zeldin's kindergarten one of the girls said:

"Hannah, you're as happy as a little girl today!"

I put on the blue woolen dress and tied a red silk kerchief round my neck. When I looked in the mirror I was delighted to see that with the neckerchief I looked like a daring girl who is suddenly likely to lose her head.

Michael was waiting for me at midday at the entrance to

Terra Sancta, by the heavy iron gates with their dark metal ornaments. He was carrying a box full of geological specimens in his arms. Even if it had occurred to me, say, to shake hands with him, I could not have.

"Oh, it's you, is it?" I said. "Who do you think you're waiting for? Did anyone tell you to wait here?"

"It's not raining now and you're not soaking wet," Michael said. "When you're wet you're much less bold."

Then Michael drew my attention to the sly, leering smile of the bronze statue of the Virgin on top of the building. Her arms were outstretched as if she were trying to embrace the whole city.

I went downstairs to the library basement. In a narrow, gloomy passage, lined with dark, sealed boxes, I met the kindly librarian, a short man who wore a skullcap. I was in the habit of exchanging greetings and witticisms with him. He too, as if making a discovery, asked me:

"What has come over you today, young lady? Good news? If you will permit me to say so, 'bright joy illumines Hannah in a most amazing manner.' "

In the Mapu seminar the lecturer related a typical anecdote, a story about a fanatically orthodox Jewish sect who claimed that ever since Abraham Mapu had published *Love of Zion* there had been more benches in the houses of ill fame, Heaven forbid.

What has got into everyone today? Have they been talking to each other?

Mrs. Tarnopoler, my landlady, had bought a new stove. She beamed benignly at me.

CHAPTER
5

That evening the sky brightened a little. Blue patches drifted eastward. The air was damp. Michael and I arranged to meet outside the Edison Cinema. Whichever of us arrived first would buy two tickets for the film, which starred Greta Garbo. The heroine of the film dies of unrequited love after sacrificing her body and her soul for a worthless man. Throughout the film I suppressed an overpowering desire to laugh. Her suffering and his worthlessness seemed like two terms in a simple mathematical equation, which I was not tempted to try to solve. I felt full to overflowing. I laid my head on Michael's shoulder and watched the screen sideways, until the pictures turned into a capering succession of different tones graded between black and white, but mainly various shades of light gray.

As we came out Michael said:

"When people are contented and have nothing to do, emotion spreads like a malignant tumor."

"What a trite remark," I said.

Michael said:

"Look here, Hannah, art isn't my subject. I'm just a humble scientist, as they say."

I refused to relent:

"That's also trite."

Michael smiled:

"Well?"

Whenever he cannot answer he smiles, just like a child who notices grownups doing something ridiculous—an embarrassed, embarrassing smile.

We strolled down Isaiah Street toward Geula Street. Sharp stars glittered in the Jerusalem sky. Many of the street lamps of the British Mandate period were destroyed by shell-fire during the War of Independence. In 1950 most of them were still shattered. Shadowy hills showed in the distance at the ends of the streets.

"This isn't a city," I said, "it's an illusion. We're crowded in on all sides by the hills—Castel, Mount Scopus, Augusta Victoria, Nebi Samwil, Miss Carey. All of a sudden the city seems very insubstantial."

Michael said:

"When it's been raining Jerusalem makes one feel sad. Actually, Jerusalem always makes one feel sad, but it's a different sadness at every moment of the day and at every time of the year."

I felt Michael's arm round my shoulder. I buried my hands in the pockets of my warm corduroy trousers. Once I took one hand out and touched him under the chin. He was clean-shaven today, not like the first time we had met, in Terra Sancta. I said he must have shaved especially to please me.

Michael was embarrassed. He just happened, he lied, to have bought a new razor that day. I laughed. He hesitated a moment, then decided to join in.

In Geula Street we saw an Orthodox woman, wearing a

26

white kerchief, open a second-floor window and squeeze half her body out as if she were about to throw herself down into the street. But she merely closed the heavy iron shutters. The hinges groaned as if with despair.

When we passed the playground of Sarah Zeldin's kindergarten I told Michael that I worked there. Was I a strict teacher? He imagined I was. What made him think that? He didn't know what to answer. Just like a child, I said, starting to say something and not knowing how to finish. Expressing an opinion and not daring to defend it. A child.

Michael smiled.

From one of the yards, on the corner of Malachi Street, came the sound of cats screeching. It was a loud, hysterical shriek, followed by two strangled wails, and finally a low sob, faint and submissive, as if there were no sense, no hope.

Michael said:

"They're crying out in love. Did you know, Hannah, that cats are most in heat in winter, on the coldest days? When I'm married I shall keep a cat. I always wanted to have one but my father wouldn't let me. I'm an only child. Cats cry out in love because they're not bound by any constraint or convention. I imagine that a cat in heat feels as if it's been grabbed hold of by a stranger and is being squeezed to death. The pain is physical. Burning. No, I didn't learn that in geology. I was afraid you'd make fun of me talking like this. Let's go."

I said:

"You must have been a very spoiled child."

"I was the hope of the family," Michael said. "I still am. My father and his four sisters, they all bet on me as if I was their racehorse and as if my university education was a steeplechase. What do you do in the morning in your kindergarten, Hannah?"

"What a funny question. I do exactly what any other kindergarten teacher does. Last month, at Hanukah, I glued together paper tops and cut out cardboard Maccabees. Sometimes I sweep the dead leaves from the paths in the yard. Sometimes I tinkle on the piano. And I often tell the children stories, from memory, about Indians, islands, travels, submarines. When I was a child I adored the books my brother had by Jules Verne and Fenimore Cooper. I thought that if I wrestled and climbed trees and read boys' books I'd grow up to be a boy. I hated being a girl. I regarded grown-up women with loathing and disgust. Even now I sometimes long to meet a man like Michael Strogoff. Big and strong, but at the same time quiet and reserved. He must be silent, loyal, subdued, but only controlling the spate of his inner energies with an effort. What do you mean? Of course I'm not comparing you to Michael Strogoff. Why on earth should I? Of course not."

Michael said:

"If we had met as children you would have sent me sprawling. I used to get knocked down by the stronger girls when I was in the lower grades. I was what you'd call a good boy: a bit lethargic, but hard-working, responsible, clean, and very honest. Nowadays I'm not at all lethargic, though."

I told Michael about the twins. I used to wrestle with them furiously. Later on, when I was twelve, I was in love with both of them. I called them Halziz—Halil and Aziz. They were beautiful boys. A pair of strong, obedient seamen from Captain Nemo's crew. They hardly ever spoke. They either kept quiet, or else emitted guttural sounds. They didn't like words. A pair of gray-brown wolves. Alert and white-fanged. Wild and dark. Pirates. What can you know about it, little Michael?

Then Michael told me about his mother:

"My mother died when I was three. I remember her white

28

hands, but I can't remember her face. There are a few photographs, but it's hard to make them out. I was brought up by my father. My father brought me up as a little Jewish socialist, with stories about Hasmonean children, *shtetl* children, children of illegal immigrants, children on kibbutzim. Stories about starving children in India, in the October Revolution in Russia. D'Amicis' *The Heart*. Wounded children saving their towns. Children sharing their last crust. Exploited children, fighting children. My four aunts, my father's sisters, were quite different. A little boy should be clean, work hard, study hard, and get on in the world. A young doctor, helping his country and making a name for himself. A young lawyer, valiantly pleading before British judges, being reported in all the newspapers. On the day that independence was declared, my father changed his name from Ganz to Gonen. I am Michael Ganz. My friends in Holon still call me Ganz. But don't you call me Ganz, Hannah. You must go on calling me Michael."

We passed the wall of Schneller Barracks. Many years ago there was a Syrian orphanage here. The name reminded me of some ancient sadness, the reason for which I could not recall. A distant bell kept ringing from the east. I tried not to count its strokes. Michael and I had our arms round each other. My hand was frozen, Michael's was warm. Michael said jokingly:

"Cold hands, warm heart."

I said:

"My father had warm hands *and* a warm heart. He had a radio and electrical business, but he was a bad businessman. I remember him standing doing the washing-up with my mother's apron round him. Dusting. Beating bedspreads. Expertly making omelettes. Absently blessing the Hanukah lights. Treasuring the remarks of every good-for-nothing. Always trying to please. As if everyone was judging him, and he, exhausted, was forever being forced to do well in some endless examination, to atone for some forgotten shortcoming."

Michael said:

"The man you marry will have to be a very strong man."

A light drizzle began to fall, and there was a thick gray fog. The buildings looked weightless. In the district of Mekor Baruch a motorcycle went past us, scattering showers of droplets. Michael was sunk in thought. Outside the gate of my house I stood on tiptoe to kiss his cheek. He smoothed and dried my forehead. Timidly his lips touched my skin. He called me a cold, beautiful Jerusalemite. I told him I liked him. If I were his wife I would not let him be so thin. In the darkness he seemed frail. Michael smiled. If I were his wife, I said, I would teach him to answer when he was spoken to, instead of just smiling and smiling as if words didn't exist. Michael choked back his resentment, stared at the handrail of the crumbling steps and said:

"I want to marry you. Please don't answer immediately."

Drops of freezing rain began to fall again. I shivered. For an instant I was glad I did not know how old Michael was. Still, it was his fault I was shivering now. I could not invite him up to my room, of course, but why couldn't he suggest we go to his place? Twice after we had come out of the cinema Michael had tried to say something, and I had cut him short, saying, "That's trite." What it was that Michael had been trying to say I could not remember. Of course I would let him keep a cat. How peaceful he makes me feel. Why will the man I marry have to be very strong?

CHAPTER

6

A week later we went on a visit together to Kibbutz Tirat Yaar in the Jerusalem hills.

Michael had a school friend in Tirat Yaar, a girl from his class who had married a boy from the kibbutz. He begged me to go with him. It meant a lot to him, he said, to introduce me to his old friend.

Michael's friend was tall and lean and acid. With her gray hair and her pursed lips she looked like a wise old man. Two children of uncertain ages huddled in a corner of the room. Something in my face or in my dress made them collapse periodically into bursts of muffled laughter. I felt confused. For two hours Michael engaged in animated conversation with his friend and her husband. I was forgotten after the first three or four polite phrases. I was entertained with lukewarm tea and dry biscuits. For two hours I sat and glowered, fastening and unfastening the catch of Michael's briefcase. What had he brought me here for? Why had I allowed myself to be talked into coming? What sort of a man had I landed myself with? Hard-working, responsible, honest, neat—and utterly boring.

And his pathetic jokes. Such a dull man shouldn't be forever trying to be amusing. But Michael did everything he could to be witty and gay. They exchanged boring stories about boring schoolteachers. The private life of a gym teacher called Yehiam Peled reduced Michael and his friend to howls of vicious schoolboy laughter. There then followed an angry argument about a meeting between King Abdullah of Transjordan and Golda Meir on the eve of the War of Independence. Michael's friend's husband thumped on the table, and even Michael raised his voice. When he shouted his voice was frail and tremulous. It was the first time I had seen him in the company of other people. I had been wrong about him.

Afterwards we walked in the dark to the main road. Tirat Yaar was connected to the main Jerusalem road by a lane lined with cypresses. A cruel wind nipped me all over. In the afterglow of sunset the Jerusalem hills seemed to be plotting some mischief. Michael walked beside me, silent. He could not think of a single thing to say to me. We were strangers to each other, he and I. For one strange moment, I remember, I was overcome by a sharp feeling that I was not awake, or that the time was not the present. I'd been through all this before. Or else someone, years before, had warned me against walking in the dark along this black lane next to an evil man. Time was no longer a smooth, even flow. It had become a series of abrupt rushes. It may have been when I was a child. Or in a dream, or a frightening story. All of a sudden I was terrified of the dim figure walking silently beside me. His coat collar was turned up to hide the lower part of his face. His body was thin as a wraith. The rest of his features were hidden by a black leather student's hat pulled down over his eyes. Who is he? What do you know about him? He's not your brother, no relation at all,

32

not even an old friend, but a strange shadow, far from human habitation, in the dark, late at night. Maybe he's planning to assault you. Maybe he's ill. You have heard nothing about him from anyone responsible. Why doesn't he talk to me? Why is he all wrapped up in his own thoughts? Why has he brought me here? What is he up to? It's night. In the country. I'm alone. He's alone. What if everything he has told me was a deliberate lie. He isn't a student. His name isn't Michael Gonen. He has escaped from an institution. He's dangerous. When did all this happen to me before? Somebody warned me, a long time ago, that this was how it would happen. What are those long-drawn-out sounds in the dark fields? You can't even see the light of the stars through the curtain of cypresses. There is a presence in the orchard. If I scream and scream, who will hear me? A stranger, walking with fast, clumsy steps, heedless of my pace. I fall back a little, deliberately. He doesn't notice. My teeth are chattering with cold and fear; the winter wind howls and bites. That silhouette doesn't belong to me; it's distant, wrapped up in itself, as if I were just a figment of its thoughts, with no reality of my own. I'm real, Michael. I'm cold. He didn't hear me. Maybe I wasn't speaking aloud.

"I'm cold, and I can't run this fast," I shouted as loud as I could.

Like a man distracted from his thoughts Michael hurled back his reply:

"Not long to go now. We're almost at the bus stop. Be patient."

As soon as he had spoken, he vanished once more into the depths of his great overcoat. A lump rose in my throat, and my eyes filled. I felt insulted. Humiliated. Frightened. I wanted to hold his hand. I only knew his hand. I didn't know him. At all.

. . .

33

The cold wind spoke to the cypresses in a hushed, hostile tongue. There was no happiness in the world. Not in the crumbling pathway, not in the darkling hills around.

"Michael," I said, despairing. "Michael, last week you said you liked the word 'ankle.' Tell me this, for heaven's sake: Do you realize that my shoes are full of water and my ankles hurt as if I were walking barefoot through a field of thorns? Tell me, who's to blame?"

Michael turned round sharply, frighteningly. He glared at me in confusion. Then he put his wet cheek against my face, and pressed his warm lips to my neck like a suckling child. I could feel every bristle on his cheek against the skin of my neck. I enjoyed the feel of the rough cloth of his coat. The cloth was a warm, quiet sigh. He unbuttoned his coat and drew me inside. We were together. I breathed in his smell. He felt very real. So did I. I was not a figment of his thoughts, he was not a fear inside me. We were real. I took in his pent-up panic. I reveled in it. "You're mine," I whispered. "Don't ever be distant," I whispered. My lips touched his forehead and his fingers found the nape of my neck. His touch was cautious and sensitive. Suddenly I was reminded of the spoon in the cafeteria in Terra Sancta, and how it had enjoyed being held in his fingers. If Michael had been an evil man, then surely his fingers, too, would have been evil.

CHAPTER

7

A fortnight or so before the wedding Michael and I went to see his father and his aunts in Holon, and my mother and my brother's family at Kibbutz Nof Harim.

Michael's father lived in a cramped and gloomy two-room flat in a "Workers' Dwelling" housing project. Our visit coincided with a power failure. Yehezkel Gonen introduced himself to me by the light of a sooty paraffin lamp. He had a cold, and refused to kiss me out of fear I might catch it from him just before my wedding. He was clad in a warm dressing gown, and his face was sallow. He told me he was entrusting a precious burden to my care—his Michael. Then he was embarrassed and regretted what he had said. He tried to pass it off as a joke. Anxiously, shyly, the old man enumerated all the illnesses Michael had had as a child. He lingered only on a very bad fever which had nearly proved fatal to Michael when he was ten. He stressed, finally, that Michael had not been ill since he was fourteen. Despite everything, our Michael, though not one of the strongest, was a decidedly healthy young man.

I recalled that when my father was selling a second-hand radio he used to talk to the customer in the same tones: frankness, fairness, a reserved familiarity, a quiet eagerness to please.

While Yehezkel Gonen addressed me in this tone of courteous helpfulness, with his son he barely exchanged two words. He merely said that he had been amazed to receive his letter, with the news it contained. He regretted that he could not make us some tea or coffee, as the electricity was cut off and he did not have a paraffin stove or even a gas ring. When Tova, God rest her, was alive—Tova was Michael's mother . . . if only she could have been with us on this occasion, everything would have been more festive. Tova had been a remarkable woman. He wouldn't talk about her now because he didn't want to mingle sorrow with gladness. One day he would tell me a very sad story.

"What can I offer you instead? Ah, a chocolate."

So, feverishly, as if he had been accused of neglecting his duty, he rummaged in his chest of drawers and produced an ancient box of chocolates, still in its original gift wrapping. "Here you are, my dears, help yourselves. Please.

"I am sorry, I didn't quite catch what it is you are studying at the University. Ah yes, of course, Hebrew literature. I shall remember in future. Under Professor Klausner? Yes, Klausner is a great man, even though he doesn't approve of the Labor Movement. I have a copy somewhere of one of the volumes of his *History of the Second Temple*. I'll find it to show you. In fact, I'd like to give you the book as a gift. It will be more useful to you than to me: Your life is still ahead of you, mine is behind me now. It won't be easy to find it with the electricity not working, but for my daughter-in-law nothing is too much trouble."

While Yehezkel Gonen was bending down, wheezing, to look for the book on the bottom shelf of the bookcase, three of the four aunts arrived. They, too, had been invited to meet me. In the confusion caused by the power failure the aunts had been late, and had not managed to find Aunt Gitta and bring her with them. That was why only the three of them had come. In my honor, and in honor of the occasion, they had taken a taxi all the way from Tel Aviv to Holon so as to be on time. It had been pitch dark all the way.

The aunts turned to me with a slightly exaggerated sympathy, as if they saw through all my schemes but had decided to forgive me. They were delighted to make my acquaintance. Michael had written such nice things about me in his letter. How glad they were to discover for themselves that he had not been exaggerating. Aunt Leah had a friend in Jerusalem, a Mr. Kadishman, who was a cultured and influential man, and at Aunt Leah's request he had already made inquiries about my family. So the aunts, all four of them, knew that I came from a good home.

Aunt Jenia asked if she could have a few words with me in private. "I'm sorry, I know it's not very nice to whisper in company, but there's no need to insist on strict politeness in the family circle, and I suppose from now on you're one of the family."

We went into the other room, and sat down on Yehezkel Gonen's hard bed in the dark. Aunt Jenia switched on a flashlight, as if the two of us were outside alone together at night. With every movement our shadows executed a wild dance on the wall, and the flashlight shook in her hand. I was struck by the grotesque idea that Aunt Jenia was about to ask me to get undressed. Perhaps because Michael had told me that she was a pediatric specialist.

37

She started in a tone of resolute affection: "Yehezkele's—I mean, Michael's father's financial position is not particularly good. Not at all good, in fact. Yehezkele is a petty clerk. There's no need to explain to a bright girl like you what a petty clerk is. Most of his salary goes on Michael's education. What a burden that is there's no need for me to tell you. And Michael won't give up studying. I must tell you quite clearly, definitely, and unambiguously that the family will on no account consent to his giving up his studies. There's no question of it.

"We discussed the matter on the way here, my sisters and I, in the taxi. We propose making a great effort and giving you, say, five hundred pounds each. Perhaps a bit more or a bit less. Aunt Gitta will certainly contribute too, even though she couldn't manage to be here this evening. No, there's no need to thank us. We are a very familiar family, if you can say that. Very much so. When Michael is a professor you can repay us the money, ha ha.

"It doesn't matter. The point is that even with that you won't have enough to set up a home just yet. I find the monstrous rise in prices these days absolutely appalling. Money itself drops in value every day. What I mean to say is, is your decision to get married in March final? Couldn't you put it off for a while? Let me ask another question, perfectly frankly, as one member of the family to another: Has anything happened which would prevent you putting off the date of the wedding? No? Then what's the hurry? I'll have you know that I was engaged for six years, in Kovno, before I married my first husband. Six years! I realize, of course, that in our modern age there's no question of a long engagement, no six years. But what about, say, a year? No? Oh well. But I don't suppose you manage to save very much from your work in the kindergarten? There will be expenses for housekeeping and expenses for studying. You must realize one thing, that financial difficulties at the outset can well ruin a couple's married life. And I'm speaking from experience. Someday I'll tell you a shocking story. Allow me to speak frankly, as a doctor. I admit that for a month, two months, half a year, your sexual life will overcome all other problems. But what will happen after that? You're a bright girl, and I beg you to consider the question rationally. I have heard that your family is living in some kibbutz . . . What's that? You inherit three thousand pounds under your father's will on your wedding day. That's good news. Very good news. You see, Hannele, Michael forgot to tell us that in his letter. By and large, our Michael still has his head in the clouds. He may be a scientific genius but when it comes to real life he's nothing more than a child. Well then, so you've decided on March? March let it be. It's wrong for the older generation to force its ideas on the young. Your lives are still ahead of you, ours are behind us. Each generation must learn from its own mistakes. Good luck to you. One last thing: If ever you want any help or advice, you must be sure to come to me. I've had more experience than ten ordinary women. Now let's go back and join the others. *Mazel tov*, Yehezkele. *Mazel tov*, Micha. I wish you health and happiness."

At Kibbutz Nof Harim in Galilee my brother Emanuel welcomed Michael with a bear hug and hearty slaps on the shoulder, as if he had found a long-lost brother. In an energetic twenty-minute tour he showed him the whole of the kibbutz.

"Were you in the *Palmach*? No? So what? Never mind. The others did plenty of important work, too."

Half-seriously Emanuel urged us to come and live at Nof

Harim. What's wrong? An intelligent lad can make himself useful and lead a satisfying life just as well here as in Jerusalem. "I can see at a glance that you're no ravening lion. From the physical point of view, that is. But so what? We're not a football team, you know. You could work in the henhouse, or even in the office. Rinele, Rinele, run and get that bottle of brandy we won in the Purim party raffle. Hurry up, our fine new brother-in-law is waiting. And what about you, Hannutchka—why so silent? The girl's going to get married and you'd think from her face she'd just been widowed. Michael, old chap, have you heard why they disbanded the *Palmach*? No, don't rack your brains—all I meant was, do you know the joke? No? You're all behind the times in Jerusalem. Listen then, I'll tell you."

And finally, Mother.

My mother cried when she spoke to Michael. She told him in broken Hebrew about my father's death, and her words were lost in her tears. She asked if she could measure Michael. Measure? Yes, measure. She wanted to knit him a white sweater. She would do everything she could to have it ready in time for the wedding. Had he got a dark suit? Would he like to wear poor, dear Yosef's suit for the ceremony? She could easily alter it to fit him. There wouldn't be much to do. It wasn't much too big and it wasn't much too small. She begged him. For sentimental reasons. It was the only present she could give him.

And in a heavy Russian accent my mother repeated over and over again, as if desperately seeking his confirmation: "Hannele is a fine girl. A very fine girl. She's got a lot of pain. You should know that too. And also—I don't know how you say . . . She's a very fine girl. You should know that too."

8

My late father occasionally used to say: It is impossible for ordinary people to tell a thoroughgoing lie. Deception always gives itself away. It is like a blanket which is too short: When you try to cover your feet your head is left uncovered, and when you cover your head your feet stick out. A man produces an elaborate excuse so as to conceal something, not realizing that the excuse itself reveals some unpleasant truth. Pure truth, on the other hand, is thoroughly destructive and leads nowhere. What can ordinary people do? All we can do is silently stand and stare. Here that is all we can do. Silently stand and stare.

Ten days before our wedding we took an old two-room apartment in the district called Mekor Baruch, in northwest Jerusalem. The people who lived in this neighborhood in 1950 were, besides the Orthodox families, mostly petty clerks in the government service or in the Jewish Agency, textile retailers, cashiers in the cinemas or in the Anglo-Palestine Bank. The area was even then in decline. Modern Jerusalem was reaching out toward the south and southwest. Our apartment was rather gloomy, and the plumbing was antiquated, but the rooms were very tall, which I liked. We discussed plans for painting the walls in bright colors and growing plants in pots. We did not know then that in Jerusalem potted plants never flourish, perhaps because of the large amounts of rust and chemical purifiers in the tap water.

We spent our spare time wandering around Jerusalem buying essentials: basic items of furniture, a few brushes and brooms and kitchen utensils, some clothes. I was surprised to discover that Michael knew how to haggle without being undignified. I never saw him lose his temper. I was proud of him. My best friend Hadassah, who had recently married a promising young economist, summed him up thus:

"A modest and intelligent boy. Not too brilliant, perhaps, but steady."

Old family friends, long-established Jerusalemites, said:

"He makes a good impression."

We walked around arm in arm. I strained to catch in the face of every acquaintance we met his inner judgment of Michael. Michael spoke little. His eyes were alert. He was pleasant and self-restrained in company. People said, "Geology? That's surprising. You'd think he was in the humanities."

In the evening I would go to Michael's room in Mousrara, where we were storing our purchases for the time being. I would sit most of the evening embroidering flowers on pillowcases. And on the clothes I embroidered our name, Gonen. I was good at embroidery.

I would sit back in the armchair we had bought to stand on the balcony of our apartment. Michael sat at his desk, working on a paper on geomorphology. He was trying hard to have the work finished and to present it before the wedding. He had promised himself that he would. By the light of his reading lamp I saw his long, lean, dark face, his close-cropped hair. Sometimes I thought he looked like a pupil in an Orthodox boarding school, or like one of the boys from the Diskin orphanage whom I used to watch crossing our street on their way to the railway station when I was a child. Their heads were shaved and they walked in twos, holding hands. They were sad and resigned. But behind their air of resignation I could sense a suppressed violence.

Michael started shaving casually again. Dark bristles sprouted under his chin. Had he lost his new razor? No, he admitted that he had lied to me on our second evening together. He hadn't bought a new razor. He had shaved especially thoroughly to please me. Why had he lied? Because I had made him feel embarrassed. Why had he gone back now to shaving only every other day? Because now he didn't feel ill at ease in my presence. "I hate shaving. If only I were an artist instead of a geologist, I might consider growing a beard."

I tried to visualize the picture, and burst out laughing.

Michael looked up at me in amazement. "What's so funny?"

"Are you offended?"

"No, I'm not offended. Not in the slightest."

"Then why are you looking at me like that?"

"Because at last I've managed to make you laugh. Time and time again I've tried to make you laugh, and I've never seen you laughing. Now, without trying, I've succeeded. It makes me happy."

Michael's eyes were gray. When he smiled the corners of his mouth quivered. He was gray and self-restrained, my Michael.

.   .   .

Every two hours I would make him a glass of lemon tea, which he liked. We rarely spoke, because I did not want to interrupt his work. I liked the word "geomorphology." Once I got up quietly and tiptoed over barefoot to stand behind him as he bent over his work. Michael didn't know I was there. I could read a few sentences over his shoulder. His handwriting was neat and well rounded, like a tidy schoolgirl's. But the words made me shudder: Extraction of mineral deposits. Volcanic forces pressing outwards. Solidified lava. Basalt. Consequent and subsequent streams. A morphotectonic process which began thousands of years ago and is still continuing. Gradual disintegration, sudden disintegration. Seismic disturbances so slight that they can be detected only by the most sensitive instruments.

Once again I was startled by these words. I was being sent a message in code. My life depended on it. But I didn't have the key.

Then I went back to the armchair and carried on with my embroidery.

Michael raised his head and said:

"I've never known a woman like you."

And then immediately, hastening to forestall me, he added:

"How very trite."

I should like to record that until our wedding night I kept my body from Michael.

A few months before his death my father called me into his room and locked the door behind us. His face was already ravaged by his illness. His cheeks were sunken and his skin was dry and sallow. He looked not at me but at the rug on the floor in front of him, as if he were reading off the rug the words he was about to utter. Father told me about wicked men

44

who seduce women with sweet words and then abandon them to their fate. I was about thirteen at the time. Everything he told me I had already heard from giggling girls and spotty-faced boys. But my father uttered the words not as a joke but on a note of quiet sadness. He formulated his remarks as if the existence of two distinct sexes was a disorder which multiplied agony in the world, a disorder whose results people must do everything in their power to mitigate. He concluded by saying that if I thought of him in moments of difficulty I might prevent myself from taking a wrong decision.

I do not think that this was the real reason why I kept my body from Michael until our wedding night. What the real reason was I do not want to record here. People ought to be very careful when they use the word "reason." Who told me that? Why, Michael himself. When he put his arms round my shoulders Michael was strong and self-restrained. Perhaps he was shy, like me. He didn't plead with words. His fingers entreated, but they never insisted. He would run his fingers slowly down my back. Then he would remove his hand and look first at his fingers, then at me, at me and at his fingers, as if cautiously comparing one thing with another. My Michael.

One evening before I took my leave of Michael to go back to my room (I had less than a week left to live with the Tarnopoler family in Achva) I said:

"Michael, you'll be surprised to learn that I know something about consequent and subsequent streams which perhaps even you don't know. If you're a good boy, one day I'll tell you what I know."

Then I ruffled his hair with my hand: what a hedgehog! What it was I had in mind I don't know.

One of the last nights, two days before the wedding, I had a frightening dream. Michael and I were in Jericho. We were shopping in the market, between rows of low mud huts. (My father, my brother, and I had been on an outing together to Jericho in 1938. It was during the Feast of Succot. We went on an Arab bus. I was eight. I have not forgotten. My birthday is during Succot.)

Michael and I bought a rug, some pouffes, an ornate sofa. Michael didn't want to buy these things. I chose them and he paid up quietly. The *suk* in Jericho was noisy and colorful. People were shouting wildly. I walked through the crowd calmly, wearing a casual skirt. There was a terrible, savage sun in the sky, such as I have seen in paintings by Van Gogh. Then an army jeep pulled up near us. A short, dapper British officer leaped out and tapped Michael on the shoulder. Michael suddenly turned and dashed off like a man possessed, upsetting stalls as he ran till he was swallowed up in the crowd. I was alone. Women screamed. Two men appeared and carried me off in their arms. They were hidden in their flowing robes. Only their eyes showed, glinting. Their grasp was rough and painful. They dragged me down winding roads to the outskirts of the town. The place looked like the steep alleys behind the Street of the Abyssinians in the east of new Jerusalem. I was pushed down a long flight of stairs into a cellar lit by a dirty paraffin lamp. The cellar was black. I was thrown to the ground. I could feel the damp. The air was fetid. Outside I could hear muffled, crazed barking. Suddenly the twins threw off their robes. We were all three the same age. Their house stood opposite ours, across a patch of wasteland, between Katamon and Kiryat Shmuel. They had a courtyard surrounded on all sides. The house was built round the yard. Vines grew up the walls of the villa. The walls were built of the reddish stone which was popular among the richer Arabs in the southern suburbs of Jerusalem.

I was afraid of the twins. They made fun of me. Their teeth were very white. They were dark and lithe. A pair of strong gray wolves. "Michael, Michael," I screamed, but my voice was taken from me. I was dumb. A darkness washed over me. The darkness wanted Michael to come and rescue me only at the end of the pain and the pleasure. If the twins remembered our childhood days, they gave no sign of it. Except their laughter. They leaped up and down on the floor of the cellar as if they were freezing cold. But the air was not cold. They leaped and bounced with seething energy. They effervesced. I couldn't contain my nervous, ugly laughter. Aziz was a little taller than his brother and slightly darker. He ran past me and opened a door I had not noticed. He pointed to the door and bowed a waiter's bow. I was free. I could leave. It was an awful moment. I could have left but I didn't. Then Halil uttered a low, trembling groan and closed and bolted the door. Aziz drew out of the folds of his robe a long, glinting knife. There was a gleam in his eyes. He sank down on all fours. His eyes were blazing. The whites of his eyes were dirty and bloodshot. I retreated and pressed my back against the cellar wall. The wall was filthy. A sticky, putrid moisture soaked through my clothes and touched my skin. With my last strength I screamed.

In the morning my landlady, Mrs. Tarnopoler, came into my room to tell me that I had cried out in my sleep. If Miss Greenbaum cries out in her sleep two nights before her marriage, that is surely a sign of some great trouble. In our dreams we are shown what we must do and what we are forbidden to do. In our dreams we are made to pay the price of all our misdeeds, Mrs. Tarnopoler said. If she were my mother—she had to say it even if it made me angry with her—she would not permit me suddenly to marry some man I happened to have met in the street. I might have chanced to meet someone entirely different, or no one at all! Where would it all lead? To disaster. "You people get married at the spin of a bottle, like in the Purim game. I was married by a *shadchan* who knew how to bring about what is written in heaven because he knew both the families well and he had examined carefully what the bridegroom was made of and what the bride was made of. After all, your family is what you are. Parents, grandparents, aunts and uncles, brothers and sisters. Just as the well is the water. Tonight, before you go to bed, I'll make you a glass of mint tea. It's a good remedy for a troubled soul. Your worst enemies should have such dreams before their wedding night. All this has come upon you, Miss Greenbaum, because you people get married just like the idolators in the Bible: A maiden meets a strange man without knowing what he is made of and arranges the terms with him and sets the date for her own wedding as if people were alone in the world."

As Mrs. Tarnopoler said the word "maiden" she smiled a worn-out smile. I did not speak.

CHAPTER

9

Michael and I were married in the middle of March. The ceremony took place on the roof terrace of the old Rabbinate building in Jaffa Road, opposite Steimatsky's foreign bookshop, under a cloudy sky of dark gray shapes massed against a bright gray background.

Michael and his father both wore dark gray suits, and each had a white handkerchief in his top pocket. They looked so alike that twice I mistook one for the other. I addressed my husband Michael as Yehezkel.

Michael crushed the traditional glass with a hard stamp. As it broke the glass made a dry sound. A low rustle went through the congregation. Aunt Leah wept. My mother also wept.

My brother Emanuel had forgotten to bring a head-covering. He spread a checkered handkerchief over his unruly hair. My sister-in-law Rina held me firmly, as though I were likely to faint suddenly. I have not forgotten a thing.

In the evening there was a party in one of the lecture rooms in the Ratisbone Building. Ten years ago, at the time of our wedding, most of the university departments were housed in wings of Christian convents. The university buildings on Mount Scopus had been cut off from the city as a result of the War of Independence. Long-established Jerusalemites still believed that this was a temporary measure. Political speculation was rife. There was still a great deal of uncertainty.

The room in the Ratisbone Convent in which the party was held was tall and cold, and the ceiling was sooty. The ceiling was covered with faded designs in peeling paint. With difficulty I could make out various scenes in the life of Christ, from the Nativity to the Crucifixion. I turned my gaze away from the ceiling.

My mother wore a black dress. It was the dress she had made herself after my father's death in 1943. On this occasion she had pinned a copper brooch on the dress, to mark the distinction between grief and joy. The heavy necklace she was wearing glittered in the light of the ancient lamps.

There were some thirty or forty students at the party. Most of them were geologists, but a few were first-year literature students. My best friend Hadassah came with her young husband, and gave me a reproduction of a popular painting of an old Yemenite woman as a present. Some of my father's old friends joined together to give us a check. My brother Emanuel brought seven young friends from his kibbutz. Their gift was a gilt vase. Emanuel and his friends tried hard to be the life and soul of the party, but the presence of the students disconcerted them.

Two of the young geologists stood up and read out a very long and tiresome duologue based on the sexual connotations of geological strata. The piece was full of bawdy insinuations and double entendres. They were trying to amuse us.

Sarah Zeldin from the kindergarten, looking ancient and

wrinkled, brought us a tea set. Every piece had a picture of a pair of lovers dressed in blue, and a gold line round the rim. She embraced my mother and they kissed each other. They conversed in Yiddish and their heads nodded up and down continuously.

Michael's four aunts, his father's sisters, stood round a table laden with sandwiches and chatted busily about me. They did not trouble to lower their voices. They did not like me. All these years Micha had been a responsible and well-organized boy, and now he was getting married with a haste which was bound to cause vulgar gossip. Six years Aunt Jenia had been engaged in Kovno, six years before she had finally married her first husband. The details of the vulgar gossip which our haste would cause, the four aunts discussed in Polish.

My brother and his friends from the kibbutz drank too much. They were noisy. They sang rowdy variations on a well-known drinking song. They amused the girls until their laughter lapsed into shrieks and giggles. A girl from the Geology Department, Yardena by name, with bright blond hair and sequins all over her dress, kicked off her shoes and started dancing a furious Spanish dance on her own. The other guests accompanied her with a rhythmic handclap. My brother Emanuel smashed a bottle of orange juice in her honor. Then Yardena got up on a chair and, holding a full liqueur glass, sang a popular American song about disappointed love.

There is another incident I must record: At the end of the party my husband tried to deliver a surprise kiss on the back of my neck. He crept up on me from behind. Perhaps his fellow students had put the idea into his head. At that moment I happened to be holding a glass of wine which my brother had thrust into my hand. When Michael's lips touched my neck I jumped, and the wine was spilled on my white wedding dress.

Some also fell on Aunt Jenia's brown suit. What is so important about this detail? Ever since the morning when my landlady, Mrs. Tarnopoler, had spoken to me after I cried out in my sleep I had been beset by hints and signs. Just like my father. My father was an attentive man. He went through life as if it were a preliminary course in which one learns a lesson and stores up experience.

10

At the end of the week my professor came up to me to congratulate me. It was in the lobby of Terra Sancta College, during the break in the middle of his weekly Mapu lecture. "Mrs. . . . ah yes, Mrs. Gonen, I have just heard the good news and I must hasten to congratulate you on your, ah, nuptials. I sincerely hope that your home will be at once thoroughly Jewish and thoroughly, ah, enlightened. Having said which, I believe I have wished you every possible happiness. May I inquire as to the discipline of your thrice-fortunate bridegroom? Ah, geology! What a very symbolic conjunction of subjects. Both geology, on the one hand, and the study of literature, on the other, delve down into the depths, as it were, in quest of buried treasures. May I ask, Mrs. Gonen, whether you intend to continue with your present studies? Good, I am delighted. As you know, I take an almost paternal interest in the fortunes of my pupils."

My husband bought a large bookcase. He had few books as yet, some twenty or thirty volumes, but in time they would multiply. Michael envisaged a whole wall lined with books. In the meantime the bookcase was almost empty. I brought home from the kindergarten a few figures I had made from twisted wire and colored raffia, to make the empty shelves seem less bare. For the time being.

The hot water system broke down. Michael tried to mend it himself. When he was young, he said, he often used to mend taps for his father or his aunts. This time he failed. He may even have made the damage worse. The plumber was sent for. He was a good-looking North African boy, who managed to put the trouble right easily. Michael was ashamed of his failure. He stood sulking like a child. I enjoyed his discomfiture.

"What a charming young couple," said the plumber. "I won't charge you very much."

The first nights I could only get to sleep with the help of sleeping pills. When I was eight my brother had been given a bedroom of his own, and ever since then I had always slept alone. It seemed odd to me for Michael to close his eyes and go to sleep. I had never seen him asleep till we were married. He would pull the covers over his head and vanish. At times I had to remind myself that the rhythmic hissing sound was simply his breathing, and that from now on there was no man on earth closer to me than he. I tossed and turned till dawn in the second-hand double bed which we had bought for next to nothing from the previous occupants of the flat. The bed was heavily decorated with arabesque carvings, stained shiny brown. It was quite unnecessarily wide, like most old furniture. It was so wide that once I awoke and thought that Michael had got up and left. He was far away, wrapped in his cocoon. Almost tangibly they came to me at dawn. Came sensuous and violent. They appeared, dark and lithe and silent.

I had never wanted a wild man. What had I done to deserve this disappointment? When I was a girl I always thought deep down that I would marry a young scholar who was destined to become world-famous. On tiptoe I would creep into his severely furnished study, put a glass of tea down on one of the heavy German tomes scattered on his desk, empty the ashtray and close the shutters silently, then without his noticing me creep out on tiptoe. If my husband had attacked me like a man dying of thirst I should have been ashamed of myself. If Michael approached me as if I were a delicate instrument, or like a scientist handling a test tube, why was I upset? At night I recalled the warm, rough overcoat he had worn that night when we walked from Tirat Yaar to the bus stop on the Jerusalem road. And the spoon his fingers had toyed with in the Terra Sancta cafeteria came back to me on those first nights.

The coffee cup shook in my hands as I asked my husband one of those mornings, my eyes fixed on a cracked tile in the floor, if I was a good woman. He thought for a moment, then answered, in a rather scholarly way, that he could not judge because he had never known another woman. His answer was frank; why did my hands still shake, so that the coffee spilled on the new tablecloth?

Each morning I would fry a double omelette. Make coffee for us both. Michael sliced the bread.

I enjoyed putting on a blue apron and arranging each vessel and utensil in its new place in my kitchen. The days were quiet. At eight o'clock Michael would leave for his lectures, carrying a new briefcase, a large black briefcase which his father had bought him as a wedding present. I said goodbye to him on the corner of the street and turned toward Sarah Zeldin's kindergarten. I had bought myself a new spring dress, a light cotton print with yellow flowers. But spring held back and the winter continued. The winter was long and hard in Jerusalem in 1950.

Thanks to the sleeping pills I dreamed all day. Old Sarah Zeldin eyed me knowingly through her gold-rimmed spectacles. Perhaps she was imagining wild nights. I wanted to put her right, but I was lost for words. Our nights were quiet. Sometimes I thought I felt a vague expectancy creeping up my spine. As if a decisive event had not yet taken place. As if it were all a preface, a rehearsal, a preliminary. I was learning a complicated part which I should soon have to play. An important event would soon take place.

I should like to record a curious fact about Peretz Smolenskin.

The professor had completed his series of lectures on Abraham Mapu, and had moved on to a discussion of Smolenskin's *The Wanderer in Life's Paths*. He spoke in detail of the author's travels and his emotional difficulties. At that time scholars still believed that the writer himself is bound up in his book.

I remember moments when I was overcome by a strong feeling that I knew Peretz Smolenskin personally. Possibly the portrait printed in his books reminded me of someone I knew. But I do not think that was the real reason. I felt that I had heard from him as a child things which affected my life, and that I should soon meet him again. I must, must formulate in my mind the right questions, so that I would know what to ask Peretz Smolenskin. All I had to do, in fact, was to consider the influence of Dickens on Smolenskin's stories.

Every afternoon I sat at my usual desk in the reading room in Terra Sancta and read *David Copperfield* in an old English edition. Dickens' orphan, David, resembled Joseph, the orphan from the town of Madmena in Smolenskin's story. They both suffered various kinds of hardship. Both writers, since they felt

pity for the orphans, had no pity on society. I would sit peacefully for two or three hours, reading about suffering and cruelty
as if I were reading about long-extinct dinosaurs. Or as if I
were confronted with meaningless fables of which the moral
was unimportant. It was a detached acquaintance.

At that time there worked in the basement of Terra Sancta
a short, elderly librarian who wore a skullcap, and who knew
me by my maiden as well as my married name. He is certainly
no longer alive. I felt glad when he said to me: "Mrs. Hannah
Greenbaum-Gonen: Your initials spell the Hebrew for 'festival';
I pray that all your days may be festive."

March ended. Half of April passed. The winter was long and
hard in Jerusalem in 1950. At dusk I would stand at the
window and wait for my husband's return. I would breathe on
the glass and draw a heart pierced by an arrow, clasped hands,
the letters HG and MG and HM. Sometimes other shapes, too.
As Michael's form appeared at the end of the street I hurriedly
wiped them all off with my hand. From the distance Michael
thought I was waving to him, and he waved back. When he
came in my hand would be wet and frozen from wiping the
windowpane. Michael liked to say: "Cold hands, warm heart."

From Kibbutz Nof Harim a parcel arrived containing two
sweaters knitted by my mother. A white one for Michael, and
one for me in blue-gray wool like the color of his calm eyes.

CHAPTER

11

One blue Saturday, a sudden spring struck the hills, and we set out to walk from Jerusalem to Tirat Yaar. We left the house at seven o'clock and walked down the road to Kfar Lifta. Our fingers were intertwined. It was a blue-steeped morning. The outline of the hills against the blue sky was painted with a fine brush. In the clefts of the rocks wild cyclamens nestled. Anemones blazed on the hillside. The earth was moist. Rainwater still lay in the hollows of the rocks, and the pines were washed clean. A solitary cypress stood breathing ecstatically below the ruins of the abandoned Arab village of Colonia.

Several times Michael paused to point out geological features and to mention their names. Did I know that the sea had once covered these hills, hundreds of thousands of years ago?

"At the end of time the sea will cover Jerusalem again," I stated with conviction.

Michael laughed.

"Is Hannah also among the prophets?"

He was lively and cheerful. From time to time he picked up

a stone and addressed it sternly, reprovingly. As we climbed up to Castel a large bird, an eagle or a vulture, came and circled high above our heads.

"We're not dead yet," I exclaimed happily.

The rocks were still slippery. I slipped deliberately, in memory of the stairs at Terra Sancta. I told Michael, too, what Mrs. Tarnopoler had said to me the day before the wedding, that people like us get married like the idolators in the Bible, like in a Purim game. A maiden fixes her eye on some man she has met by chance, when she might have happened to meet someone entirely different.

Then I picked a cyclamen and laced it through Michael's buttonhole. He took my hand. My hand was cold between his warm fingers.

"I'm thinking of a trite saying," Michael said with a laugh. I have not forgotten a thing. To forget means to die. I do not want to die.

Liora, my husband's friend, had Saturday duties and could not be free to entertain us. She merely asked if we were well and returned to the kitchen. We had lunch in the dining hall. Afterwards we sprawled on the lawn, my husband's head in my lap. I was on the verge of telling Michael about my pain, about the twins. A gnawing fear restrained me. I kept quiet.

Later we walked to the spring of Aqua Bella. Near us, at the edge of the small wood, sat a party of boys and girls who had bicycled from Jerusalem. One of them was mending a puncture. Snatches of conversation reached us.

"Honesty is the best policy," the boy with the puncture said. "Yesterday I told my father I was going to the club, and instead I went to see *Samson and Delilah* at the Zion Cinema.

Who do you think was sitting behind me? My father in person!"

A few moments later we overheard a conversation between two girls.

"My sister Esther married for money. I shall only marry for love. Life isn't a game."

"As a matter of fact, I don't mind telling you I'm not entirely opposed to a little free love. Otherwise how can you know at twenty whether your love will last till you're thirty? I heard one of the youth leaders giving a talk once, and he said that love between modern people ought to be something completely simple and natural, like drinking a glass of water. Still, I don't think one should wallow in it. Moderation in all things. Not like Rivkele, who changes boys every week. But then not like Dalia, either. If a man so much as goes up to her to ask her the time, she blushes and runs away as if they all wanted to rape her. In life one ought to follow the middle path, and avoid both extremes. Anyone who lives without restraint will die young—that's what Stefan Zweig says in one of his books."

We went back to Jerusalem on the first bus after the end of the Sabbath. That evening a strong northwesterly wind arose. The sky clouded over. The morning's spring had been a false alarm. It was still winter in Jerusalem. We abandoned our plan of going into town to see *Samson and Delilah* at the Zion Cinema. We went to bed early, instead. Michael read the weekend supplement of the newspaper. I read Peretz Smolenskin's *A Donkey's Burial* for the next day's seminar. Our house was very quiet. The shutters were closed. The bedside lamp cast shadows that I did not like to look at. I could hear water dripping from the tap into the kitchen sink. I absorbed the rhythm.

Later on, a group of youngsters went past, on their way home from a religious youth club. As they passed our house, the boys sang

> *Girls are all the brood of Satan;*
> *Apart from one I swear I hate 'em,*

and the girls let out shrill shrieks.

Michael put down his paper. He asked whether he could interrupt me for a moment. He wanted to ask me something. "If we had the money we could buy a radio, and then we could listen to a concert at home. But we owe a small fortune in debts, and so we won't be able to afford a radio this year. Perhaps stingy old Sarah Zeldin will give you a raise next month. By the way, the plumber who mended the hot-water system was very pleasant and charming, but it's broken down again."

Michael put out the light. His hand groped for mine in the dark. But his eyes had not yet adjusted to the meager light which filtered through the shutters, and his arm collided violently with my chin so that I let out a groan of pain. He begged my pardon. He stroked my hair. I felt tired and vacant. He put his cheek against mine. We'd had such a nice, long walk today, and that was why he hadn't managed to find time to shave. The bristles scratched my skin. There was a bad moment, I recall, when I suddenly reminded myself of a bride in a vulgar joke, an old-fashioned bride who completely misunderstood her husband's advances. Wasn't the double bed easily big enough for the two of us? It was a humiliating moment.

That night I dreamed of Mrs. Tarnopoler. We were in a town on the plain, perhaps Holon, perhaps in my father-in-law's flat. Mrs. Tarnopoler made me a glass of mint tea. It tasted bitter and revolting. I was sick, and spoiled my white wedding dress. Mrs. Tarnopoler laughed coarsely. "I warned you," she boasted. "I warned you beforehand, but you *would* insist on ignoring all the hints." An evil bird pounced with sharp, hooked claws. Claws scratched at my eyelids. I woke in a panic and flung off Michael's arm. He stirred irritably, mumbling, "You're out of your mind. Leave me alone. I need to sleep. I've got a hard day ahead of me." I took a pill. An hour later I took another. Eventually I fell into a stunned sleep. Next morning I had a slight temperature. I did not go to work. At lunchtime I quarreled with Michael, and hurled abuse at him. Michael stifled his feelings and kept quiet. In the evening we made peace. Each of us blamed himself for starting the row. My friend Hadassah and her husband called. Hadassah's husband was an economist. The conversation turned to the austerity policy. According to Hadassah's husband, the government's action was based on ridiculous assumptions—as if the whole of Israel were one great youth movement. Hadassah said that the officials' only concern was for their own families, and she cited an appalling case of corruption which was going the rounds in Jerusalem. Michael thought for a while, then gave it as his opinion that it was a mistake to demand too much from life. I was not sure whether he was defending the government or agreeing with our guests. I asked him what he meant. Michael smiled at me as though the only reply I had expected of him was his smile. I went out to the kitchen to make tea and coffee and to put out some cakes. Through the open doors I could hear my friend Hadassah talking. She was praising me to my husband. She told him I was the best pupil in my class. Then the discussion turned to the Hebrew University. Such a young university, yet being guided along such conservative lines.

CHAPTER
12

In June, three months after the wedding, I found I was pregnant.

Michael was not at all pleased when I told him. Twice he asked me if I was certain. Once, before we were married, he had read in a medical handbook that it is very easy to make a mistake, especially the first time. Perhaps I had misinterpreted the symptoms.

At that I got up and left the room. He stayed where he was, in front of the mirror, passing his razor over the sensitive skin between his lower lip and his chin. Perhaps I had chosen the wrong moment to talk to him, just when he was shaving.

Next day Aunt Jenia, the pediatrician, arrived from Tel Aviv. Michael had telephoned her in the morning and she had dropped everything and come running.

Aunt Jenia spoke sternly to me. She accused me of irresponsibility. I would ruin all Michael's efforts at getting on and achieving something in life. Didn't I realize that Michael's progress was my own destiny? And right before his final examinations, too!

"Like a child," she said. "Just like a child."

She refused to stay the night. She had dropped everything and come rushing to Jerusalem like a fool. She regretted having come. She regretted a lot of things. "The whole thing is just a simple matter of a twenty-minute operation, no worse than having your tonsils out. But there are some complicated women who won't understand the simplest things. As for you, Micha, you sit there like a dummy as if it's none of your business. Sometimes I think there's no point in the older generation sacrificing itself for the sake of the young. I'd better shut up now and not say everything I've got on my mind. Good day to you both."

Aunt Jenia snatched up her brown hat and stormed out. Michael sat speechless with his mouth half-open, like a child who has just been told a frightening story. I went into the kitchen, locked the door, and cried. I stood by the dresser, grated a carrot, sprinkled sugar on it, added some lemon juice and cried. If my husband knocked on the door, I did not answer. But I am almost certain now that he did not knock.

Our son Yair was born at the end of the first year of our marriage, in March 1951, after a difficult pregnancy.

In the summer, early on in my pregnancy, I lost two ration books in the street. Michael's and my own. Without them it was impossible to buy essential foodstuffs. For weeks I showed signs of vitamin deficiency. Michael refused to buy so much as a grain of salt on the black market. He had inherited this principle from his father, a fierce, proud loyalty to the laws of our state.

Even when we got new ration books I continued to suffer from various troubles. Once I had a dizzy spell and collapsed in the playground of Sarah Zeldin's kindergarten. The doctor forbade me to go on working. This was a difficult decision for us because our financial position was critical. The doctor also prescribed injections of liver extract and calcium tablets. I had a permanent headache. I felt as if I were being stabbed in the right temple with a splinter of ice-cold metal. My dreams became tormented. I would wake up screaming. Michael wrote to his family telling them that I had had to stop working and also mentioning my mental condition. Thanks to the help of my best friend Hadassah's husband, Michael succeeded in getting a modest loan from the Students' Assistance Fund.

At the end of August a registered letter arrived from Aunt Jenia. She had not seen fit to write us a single line, but in the envelope we found a folded check for three hundred pounds. Michael said that if my pride compelled me to return the money he was willing to give up studying and look for a job, and that I was free to send back Aunt Jenia's money. I said I didn't like the word "pride," and that I accepted the money gratefully. In that case, Michael asked me always to remember that he had been willing to give up his studies and look for a job.

"I shall remember, Michael. You know me. I don't know how to forget."

I stopped attending lectures at the university. I would never study Hebrew literature again. I recorded in my exercise book that a quality of desolation pervades the works of the poets of the Hebrew renaissance. Where this quality of desolation came from, what it consists in, I would never know.

The housework, too, was neglected. I would sit for most of the morning alone on our little balcony, which overlooked a deserted backyard. I would rest on the deck-chair, throwing crumbs of bread to the cats. I enjoyed watching the neighbors' children playing in the yard. My father occasionally used to use the phrase "silently stand and stare." I stand and stare silently, but far from the silence, far from the staring to which my father probably referred. What point do the children in the yard see in their eager, panting competition? The game is tiring and the victory is hollow. What does victory hold in store? Night will fall. Winter will return. Rains will fall and eradicate all. Strong winds will blow again in Jerusalem. There may be a war. The game of hide-and-seek is absurdly futile. From my balcony I can see them all. Can anyone really hide? Who tries? What a strange thing excitement is. Relax, tired children. Winter is still far off, but already he is gathering his forces. And the distance is deceptive.

After lunch I would collapse onto my bed, exhausted. I could not even read the newspaper.

Michael left at eight o'clock in the morning and came home at six in the evening. It was summer. I could not breathe on the window and draw shapes on the glass. To make things easier for me, Michael resumed his old routine and lunched with his student friends in the student canteen at the end of Mamillah Road.

December was the sixth month of my pregnancy. Michael took the examinations for his first degree. He got an upper second. I was unmoved by his success. Let him celebrate by himself and leave me alone. My husband had already started studying for his second degree in October. In the evening, when he came home tired, he would volunteer to go out to the grocer, the greengrocer, the druggist. On one occasion he absented himself on my account from an important experiment, because I had asked him to go to the clinic for me and collect the result of a test.

That evening Michael broke his mental vow of silence. He tried to explain to me that his life was not so easy these days, either. I shouldn't imagine that he was living in a bed of roses, as it were.

"I didn't imagine you were, Michael."

Then why did I make him feel guilty?

Did I make him feel guilty? He must realize that I couldn't be romantic at a time like this. I didn't even have a maternity dress. Every day I wore my ordinary clothes, which didn't fit and weren't comfortable. So how could I look pretty and attractive?

No, that wasn't what he wanted of me. It wasn't my beauty which he missed. What he did ask, what he implored, was that I should stop being so stiff and so hysterical.

Indeed, during this time there was a kind of uneasy compromise between us. We were like two travelers consigned by fate to adjacent seats on a long railway journey. Bound to show consideration for each other, to observe the conventions of politeness, not to impose and not to intrude on each other, not to presume on their acquaintance. To be courteous and considerate. To entertain each other, perhaps, from time to time with pleasant, superficial chatter. Making no demands. Even displaying restrained sympathy at times.

But outside the carriage window there stretches a flat and gloomy landscape. A parched plain. Low scrub.

If I ask him to close a window, he is delighted to be of service.

It was a kind of wintry balance. Cautious and laborious, like going down a flight of steps slippery from the rain. Oh, to be able to rest and rest.

I admit it: It was often I who upset the balance. Without Michael's firm grasp I should have slipped and fallen. I deliberately sat for whole evenings in silence as if I were alone in the house. If Michael asked how I felt I would answer:

"What do you care?"

If he took offense and did not ask how I felt next morning, I would snarl that he didn't ask because he didn't care.

Once or twice, early in the winter, I embarrassed my husband by my tears. I called him a brute. I accused him of insensitivity and indifference. Michael rebutted both charges mildly. He spoke calmly and patiently, as if it were he who had given offense and I was to be placated. I resisted like a rebellious child. I hated him till a lump rose in my throat. I wanted to shake him out of his calm.

Coolly and thoroughly Michael washed the floor, wrung out the cloth, and dried the floor twice. Then he asked me if I felt better. He warmed me some milk and removed the skin, which I hated. He apologized for making me angry, in my special condition. He asked me to explain what exactly he had done to make me angry, so that he could avoid making the same mistake again. Then he went out to fetch a can of paraffin.

In the last months of my pregnancy I felt ugly. I did not dare look in the mirror; my face was disfigured with dark blotches. I had to wear elastic stockings because of my varicose veins. Perhaps now I looked like Mrs. Tarnopoler or old Sarah Zeldin.

"Do you find me ugly, Michael?"

"You're very precious to me, Hannah."

"If you don't find me ugly, why don't you hold me?"

"Because if I do you'll burst into tears and say that I'm just pretending. You've already forgotten what you said to me this morning. You told me not to touch you. And so I haven't."

When Michael was out of the house I experienced a return of my old childhood yearning, to be very ill.

CHAPTER

13

Michael's father composed a letter in verse congratulating his son on his examination success. He rhymed "resounding success" with "my joy to express" and "Hannah's great happiness." Michael read the letter out loud to me and then admitted that he had hoped to receive some small token from me too, such as a new pipe, to mark his success in his first final examination. He said this with an embarrassed, embarrassing smile. I was angry with him for what he had said, and his smile also made me angry. Hadn't I told him a thousand times that my head ached as if it were being stabbed with ice-cold steel? Why did he always think of himself and never of me?

Three times Michael declined on my account to go on important geological expeditions in which all his fellow students took part. One was to Mount Manara, where iron ore deposits had been discovered, another to the Negev, and the third to the potash works at Sodom. Even his married friends went on these expeditions. I did not thank Michael for his sacrifice. But one evening there happened to run through my head two half-forgotten lines from a well-known nursery rhyme about a boy called Michael:

Little Michael danced five years, but then he heard the bell;
He went to school, and tearfully bid his pet dove farewell.

I burst out laughing.

Michael stared at me in subdued amazement. It wasn't often, he said, that he saw me happy. He would very much like to know what it was that had suddenly made me laugh.

I looked at his startled eyes, and laughed louder still.

Michael was sunk deep in thought for a few moments. Then he started to tell me a political joke he had heard that day in the student canteen.

My mother arrived from Kibbutz Nof Harim in Upper Galilee to stay with us till the birth and to look after the housework. Since my mother had moved to Nof Harim after my father's death in 1943 she had never had a chance to manage a household. She was disastrously enthusiastic and efficient. After the first lunch, which she cooked as soon as she arrived, she said to Michael that she knew he didn't like eggplant, but that he had just eaten three dishes made with eggplant without realizing it. It was wonderful, the miracles you could work in the kitchen. Had he really not noticed the taste of the eggplant? Not even a bit?

Michael answered politely. No, he hadn't noticed it at all. Yes, it was wonderful what miracles you could do in the kitchen.

My mother sent Michael on one errand after another. She made his life miserable with her vigorous insistence on strict hygiene. He must always wash his hands. Never put money on the table when people were eating. Take the mesh screens out of the window frames to clean them properly. "What do you think you're doing? Not there on the balcony, if you don't mind—the dust will all come flying back into the room. Not on the balcony; downstairs, outside in the yard. Yes, that's right, that's better."

She knew that Michael had been brought up an orphan, without a mother, and that was why she didn't get angry with him. But still, she couldn't understand him: educated, enlightened, a university man—didn't he realize the world was full of germs?

Michael submitted obediently like a well brought-up child. What can I do to help? Allow me. Am I in your way? No, I'll go and get it. Of course I'll ask the greengrocer. All right, I'll try to come home early. I'll take the shopping basket with me. No, I won't forget; look, I've already made a list. He agreed to give up his idea of buying the first volumes of the new *Encyclopaedia Hebraica*. It was not essential. He knew now that we must both save as much as we possibly could.

In the evenings Michael worked at a part-time job, helping the librarian of the departmental library, which brought in a little money. "Nowadays I don't have the honor of Your Excellency's presence in the evenings either," I grumbled. Michael even gave up smoking his pipe in the house because my mother could not bear the smell of tobacco and was also convinced that the smoke would harm the baby.

When he found it hard to contain himself my husband would go down into the street and stand smoking for a quarter of an hour under a lamppost like a poet in search of inspiration. Once I stood at the window and watched him for a while. By the light of the street lamp I could see the close-cropped hair on the back of his head. Rings of smoke curled around him, as if he were a spirit called up from the dead. I remembered some words Michael had spoken long before: Cats are never wrong about people. He always liked the word "ankle." I was a cold, beautiful Jerusalemite. He was an ordinary young man, in his opinion. He had never had a regular girlfriend before he met me. In the rain the stone lion on the Generali Building laughs under his breath. Emotion becomes a malignant tumor when people are contented and have nothing to do. Jerusalem makes one feel sad, but it is a different sadness at every moment of the day, at every time of the year. That was all a long time ago. Michael must have forgotten it all by now. Only I refused to abandon so much as a crumb to the icy claws of time. I wonder, what is the magical change which time works on trivial words? There is a kind of alchemy in things, which is the inner melody of my life. The youth leader who told the girl we saw by Aqua Bella that love in our modern age should be as simple as drinking a glass of water was wrong. Michael was quite right when he told me that night in Geula Street that my husband would have to be a very strong man. At that moment I felt that, although he had to stand there smoking under a lamppost like a child in disgrace, yet he had no right to blame me for his suffering, because I should soon be dead, and so I need show no consideration for him. Michael knocked out his pipe and started walking back. I hurriedly lay down on the bed and turned my face to the wall. My mother asked him to open a can for her. Michael replied that he would be delighted. An ambulance siren sounded in the distance.

One night, after we had turned out the light in silence, Michael whispered to me that he had the feeling, sometimes, that I

73

didn't love him any more. He said this calmly, as if reciting the name of some mineral.

"I'm depressed," I said, "that's all."

Michael was understanding. My condition. My poor health. Difficult circumstances. He may have used the words "psycho-physical," "psychosomatic." All the winter a wind stirs the tops of the pine trees in Jerusalem, and when it dies away it leaves not a trace on the pines. You are a stranger, Michael. You lie next to me at night, and you are a stranger.

CHAPTER

14

Our son Yair was born in
March 1951.

My late father's name, Yosef, had been given to my brother
Emanuel's son. My son was given two names, Yair and Zalman,
in memory of Michael's grandfather, Zalman Ganz.

Yehezkel Gonen came up to Jerusalem on the day after the
birth. Michael brought him to see me in the maternity ward
of Shaare Zedek Hospital, a dark and depressing place built in
the last century. The plaster on the wall opposite my bed was
peeling, and as I stared at the wall I discovered weird shapes,
a jagged mountain range or dark women frozen in hysterical
convulsions.

Yehezkel Gonen, too, was dark and depressing. He sat for a
long time by my bedside, holding Michael's hand and tediously
recounting his troubles: How he had come from Holon to
Jerusalem, how from the bus station he had gone by mistake
to Mea Shearim instead of Mekor Baruch. There were corners
of Mea Shearim, among the twisted stairways and sagging

washlines, which had reminded him of the poor areas of Radom in Poland. We couldn't possibly imagine, he said, how great was his pain, his longing, how deep his sadness. Well, he got to Mea Shearim, and he asked, and they told him, and he asked again, and they misdirected him again—he wouldn't have believed that Orthodox children were capable of such tricks, or perhaps there's a deceptive quality in the side streets of Jerusalem. Finally, tired and worn out, he had managed to find the house, and even that had been more by chance than anything else. "Still, all's well that ends well, as they say. That's not the point. The point is that I want to kiss your forehead—so—to give you my best wishes and also those of Michael's aunts, to hand over this envelope—there's a hundred and forty-seven pounds in it, the rest of my savings—flowers I'm sorry but I've forgotten to bring you, and I beg and implore you to call my grandson Zalman."

When he had finished speaking, he fanned himself with his battered hat to refresh his weary face and sighed with relief at having finally rolled the great stone from the mouth of the well.

"The reason for the name Zalman I should like to explain to you briefly, in a few words. I have a sentiment about it. Does all this talking tire you, my dear? Well then, I have a sentiment. Zalman was the name of my father, our dear Michael's grandfather. Zalman Ganz was a remarkable man in his way. It is your duty to honor his memory, as good Jews should. Zalman Ganz was a teacher, and a very fine teacher indeed. One of the best. He taught natural sciences in the Hebrew teachers college in Grodno. It was from him that Michael received his aptitude for science. Well then, to come straight to the point. I am begging you. I have never asked you for anything before. By the way, when will they let me see the baby? So. I've never asked you for anything before. I have always given you everything I've had to offer. And now, my dear children, I am asking you for a favor, a very special favor. It means a great deal to me . . . Please will you name my grandson Zalman."

Yehezkel rose and left the room so that Michael and I could discuss the matter. He was a considerate old man. I didn't know whether to laugh or to scream. "Zalman"—what a name!

Michael very cautiously put forward the suggestion that the birth certificate should carry the double name "Yair-Zalman." He suggested, but he did not insist. The final decision was mine. Until the child grew up, Michael proposed that we should keep his second name a secret, so as not to make our son's life a misery.

How wise you are, my Michael. How very wise.

My husband stroked my cheek. He asked what extra things I wanted him to buy on the way home. Then he said goodbye and went outside to announce the compromise to his father. I imagine that my husband praised me to his father for consenting readily to an arrangement which any other woman, and so on.

I was not present at the circumcision ceremony. The doctors discovered a slight complication in my condition, and confined me to my bed. In the afternoon I received a visit from Aunt Jenia, Dr. Jenia Ganz-Crispin. She swept through the ward like a hurricane and burst into the doctors' office. She bellowed in German and Polish. She threatened to carry me off in a private ambulance to the hospital in Tel Aviv where she held the post of first assistant in the pediatric department. She was severely critical of the doctor in charge of me. In the presence of the other doctors and the nurses she accused him of culpable negligence. "It's monstrous," she exclaimed. "Just like some Asiatic hospital, God forbid."

I have no idea what the point at issue between Aunt Jenia and the doctor was, or why she was so furious. She only spent a moment at my bedside. She brushed my cheek with her lips and her downy mustache, and ordered me not to worry. "I'll do all the worrying. I won't hesitate to make a scene in the highest places, if necessary. If you ask me, our Micha lives in an ivory tower. Just like his father, *der selber chuchem*."

While Aunt Jenia spoke, she placed her hand on my white blanket. I saw a short-fingered, masculine hand. Aunt Jenia's fingers were tense, as if she was fighting to hold back her sobs while her hand rested on my bed.

Aunt Jenia had suffered a lot in her youth. Michael had told me part of her life story. Her first husband had been a gynecologist by the name of Lipa Freud. This Freud had left Aunt Jenia in 1934 and run off to Cairo after a Czech woman athlete. He had hanged himself in a bedroom in Shepheard's Hotel, then the foremost hotel in the Near East. During the Second World War Aunt Jenia had married an actor named Albert Crispin. This husband had had a nervous breakdown, and when he recovered had been stricken with a total and complete apathy. For the last ten years he had been kept in a boardinghouse in Nahariya, where he did nothing except sleep, eat, and stare. Aunt Jenia supported him at her own expense.

I wonder why other people's sufferings sound to us like the plot of an operetta. Is it perhaps precisely because they are other people's? My father occasionally used to say that even the strongest people cannot choose what they want. As she left, Aunt Jenia said, "You'll see, Hannah; that doctor will rue the day he met me. What a villain. Wherever you turn these days you find scoundrels and imbeciles. Get well soon, Hannah."

"You too, Aunt Jenia. I'm grateful to you. You haven't spared any effort, and all for my sake."

"Nothing of the sort. Don't talk such nonsense, Hannah. People should be human beings, not wild beasts. Don't let them give you any medicines, apart from calcium tablets. Tell them I said so."

CHAPTER

15

That night in the maternity
ward an Oriental woman cried and cried forlornly. The night
nurse and the doctor on duty spoke to her comfortingly and
tried to quiet her. They begged her to tell them what was
wrong so that they could help her. The Oriental woman cried
rhythmically and monotonously, as if there were no words and
no people in the world.

The medical staff spoke to the woman as if they were interrogating a crafty criminal. Now they spoke harshly, now
kindly. They alternately threatened her and assured her that
all would be well.

The Oriental did not react to what they were saying. Perhaps
a stubborn pride prevented her. By the faint light of the night
lamp I could see her face. There was no expression of weeping. Her face was smooth and free of wrinkles. But her voice
was piercing and her tears trickled slowly down.

At midnight the medical staff held a conference. The nurse
brought the weeping woman her baby, although it was not
strictly the permitted time. From under her blanket the woman

drew out a hand like some small animal's paw. She touched the baby's head, then immediately withdrew her hand as if she had touched a red-hot iron. They put the baby down in her bed. Still the woman cried. Even when they took the baby away there was no change. Finally the nurse seized the thin arm and thrust a hypodermic needle into it. The woman slowly nodded her head up and down, bemused, as if mystified by these clever people who cared for her constantly. Didn't they realize that nothing in the world mattered any more?

All night long she kept up her piercing wail. I gradually lost sight of the dingy ward and the faint night light. I saw an earthquake in Jerusalem.

An old man was walking down Zephaniah Street. He was heavy and grim, and he was carrying a large sack. The man stopped on the corner of Amos Street. He started shouting, *"Pri-mus stoves, pri-mus."* The streets were deserted. There was no breeze. The birds had disappeared. Then stiff-tailed cats emerged from the courtyards. They were lean, arched, elusive. They sprang to the trunks of the trees planted along the pavement and clambered among the highest leaves. From here they peeped down, bristling and hissing spitefully, as though an evil dog was passing through the district of Kerem Avraham. The old man put his sack down in the middle of the road. There was nothing moving in the streets, because the British army had imposed a complete curfew. The man scratched his neck, and the gesture suggested rage. In his hand he held a rusty nail, which he dug into the asphalt. He made a little crack. The crack quickly widened and spread like a railway network in an educational film, where processes are shown speeded up. I bit my fist so as not to let out a terrified scream. There was a slight rattle of gravel down Zephaniah Street toward the Bokharian Quarter. The gravel as it touched me caused me no pain. Like tiny balls of wool. But there was a nervous quiver in the air, like the quivering and bristling of a cat before it pounces. Slowly the huge boulder slid down from Mount Scopus, cut through the district of Beit Yisrael as if the houses were built of dominoes, and rolled up Prophet Ezekiel Street. I felt that a huge boulder had no right to roll uphill, that it ought to head down the slope—otherwise it wouldn't be fair. I was afraid that my new necklace would be torn off my neck and be lost, and that I would be punished. I turned to run, but the old man spread his sack across the road and stood on it and I could not move the sack because the man was heavy. I pressed myself against a fence although I knew I would dirty my favorite dress and then the huge boulder covered me and the huge boulder was also like wool and not at all hard. Buildings tottered and crumbled row on row, turned slowly and collapsed like fine heroes in an opera, splendidly slain. The debris did not hurt. It covered me like a warm eiderdown, like a pile of feathers. It was a gentle, halfhearted embrace. Tattered women rose among the ruins. One of them was Mrs. Tarnopoler. They wailed an Oriental melody like the hired mourners I had seen at my father's funeral outside the mortuary at Bikur Holim Hospital. Hundreds and thousands of boys, Orthodox boys, thin boys with sidecurls and black gabardines, poured in streams silently from Achva, Geula, Sanhedriya, Beit Yisrael, Mea Shearim, Tel Arza. They settled on the ruins, scrabbled, scrabbled insidiously, teeming and fervid. It was hard to look at them and not be one of them. I was one of them. One boy dressed up as a policeman hovered high on a crumbling balcony at the top of a free-standing façade. The boy laughed out loud for joy to see me lying as I was in the road. He was a vulgar boy. Collapsed in the road I saw an olive-green British armored car moving slowly on. Over the loudspeaker on its turret a Hebrew voice spoke. The voice was calm and masculine and it sent a pleasant shudder down to the soles of my feet. It announced the regulations for the curfew. Anyone found out of doors would be shot without warning. Doctors stood around me because I had collapsed in the road and could not get up. The doctors spoke Polish. "Risk of an outbreak of plague," they said. The Polish was Hebrew but not our Hebrew. The Scottish redcaps waited for blood-red-capped reinforcements from the two British destroyers *Dragon* and *Tigress*. Suddenly the boy in policeman's clothes sailed down head first from the balcony, sailed down slowly toward the pavement as if the High Commissioner for Palestine General Cunningham had suspended every law of gravity, sailed down slowly toward the ruined pavement, sailed down and I could not scream.

Shortly before two o'clock the night nurse woke me. On a squeaking trolley they brought me my son to be fed. The nightmare was still with me and I cried and cried, even more than the Oriental woman who was still sobbing. Through my tears I begged the nurse to explain to me how it was that the baby was still alive, how my baby had survived the disaster.

CHAPTER

16

Time and memory favor trivial words. They treat them with particular kindness. They surround them with the tender glow of twilight.

I cling to memory and to words as one clings to a railing in a high place.

For example, the words of an old nursery rhyme to which my memory clings relentlessly:

> *Little clown, little clown, will you dance with me?*
> *Pretty little clown will dance with everyone.*

I should like to observe the following: There is a reply in the second half of this rhyme to the question posed in the first, but the reply is a disappointing one.

Ten days after the birth the doctors allowed me to leave the hospital, but I had to stay in bed and avoid any form of strain. Michael was patient and indefatigable.

When I arrived home with my baby in a taxi, a bitter quarrel broke out between my mother and Aunt Jenia. Aunt Jenia had taken another day off from her work in the hospital to come to Jerusalem and give Michael and me her instructions. She wanted to persuade me to behave rationally.

Aunt Jenia instructed Michael to place the baby's cradle against the south wall of the room, so that the shutters could be opened without the sun striking the baby. My mother instructed Michael to put the cradle by my bedside. She wouldn't dispute medicine with doctors, certainly not. But people have souls as well as bodies, said my mother, and only a mother can understand a mother's soul. A mother and her baby need to be close together. To feel each other. A home is not a hospital. This was a question of feeling, not of medicine. My mother spoke these words in rather broken Hebrew. Aunt Jenia did not look at her. She looked toward Michael and said, "One can understand Mrs. Greenbaum's feelings, but at least you and I are rational people."

There ensued a venomous but amazingly polite conflict, in which both women withdrew their objections and insisted that the matter was not worth quarreling about, but each refused to accept the other's surrender.

Michael stood silent in his gray suit. The baby was asleep in his arms. Michael's eyes pleaded with the women to take the baby from him. He had the look of a man who is desperately struggling to hold back a sneeze. I smiled at him.

The two women took hold of each other's arms and pushed each other gently, addressing each other as "Pani Greenbaum" and "Pani Doktor." The argument lapsed into gabbled Polish.

Michael stammered, "There's no point, there's no point," but he did not specify which of the two opinions he considered pointless.

Finally Aunt Jenia, as if hit by a brainstorm, suggested letting the parents choose for themselves.

Michael said, "Hannah?"

I was tired. I accepted Aunt Jenia's suggestion, because that morning when she arrived in Jerusalem she had bought me a blue flannel housecoat. I could not hurt her feelings when I was wearing the pretty housecoat she had bought me.

Aunt Jenia was all smiles. She patted Michael's shoulder like a fine lady congratulating a young jockey who had just ridden her horse to victory. My mother said, in a sickly voice, "*Gut, gut. Azoy wie Hannele will. Yo.*"

But that evening, shortly after Aunt Jenia's departure, my mother, too, decided to leave next day for Nof Harim. There was nothing she could do here. She didn't want to be in the way. And she was badly needed up there. It would all be all right. When Hannele was a baby it had been even worse. It would all be all right.

After the two women had left our house I realized that my husband had learned how to warm milk in a bottle inside a saucepan of boiling water, to feed his child, and to lift him up from time to time to make him burp so that the wind should not be trapped inside him.

The doctor had forbidden me to breastfeed the baby because a new complication had arisen. The new complication was not particularly serious; it caused me occasional pain and a certain discomfort.

Between periods of sleep the baby would open his eyelids and display islands of pure blue. I felt that this was his inner color, that the peepholes of his eyes revealed mere droplets of the radiant blue which filled the baby's body underneath his skin. When my son looked at me I remembered that he could not see yet. The thought frightened me. I did not trust nature to repeat successfully the established sequence of events. I knew nothing of the natural bodily processes. Michael could not offer much help. "Broadly speaking," he said, "the physical world is governed by constant rules. I am not a biologist, but as a natural scientist I can't see any point in your persistent questions about the nature of causality. The term 'causality' always produces difficulties and misunderstandings."

I loved my husband when he spread a white napkin over his gray jacket, washed his hands, and carefully lifted his son.

"You're very hard-working, Michael," I laughed faintly.

"There's no need for you to make fun of me," Michael said in an even voice.

When I was a child my mother often used to sing me the pretty song about a good boy called David:

> *Little David was so sweet,*
> *Always tidy, always neat.*

I do not recall how it goes on. If I had not been unwell I should have gone into town and bought Michael a present. A new pipe. A brightly colored toiletry set. I am dreaming.

At five in the morning Michael would get up, boil some water, and wash the baby's diapers. Later I would open my eyes to see him standing over me, silent and submissive. He would hand me a cup of warm milk and honey. I was drowsy. Sometimes I did not even reach out to take the cup from him because I thought that I was simply dreaming Michael, that he was unreal.

There were nights when Michael did not even get undressed. He sat at his desk till morning reading his books. He chewed on the mouthpiece of his empty pipe. I have not forgotten that tapping sound. He might doze off for half an hour or an hour, sitting with his arm stretched out on the table and his head resting on his arm.

If the baby cried in the night Michael would pick him up and carry him backwards and forwards across the room, from the window to the door and back again, whispering in his ear facts which he had to learn by heart. Poised between waking and sleeping I would hear at night the dim watchwords "Devonian," "Permian," "Triassic," "lithosphere," "siderosphere." In one of my dreams the professor of Hebrew literature was admiring the linguistic synthesis of the writer Mendele and happened to utter some of these words. "Miss Greenbaum," he said to me, "would you be so kind as to describe briefly the inherent ambiguity of the situation?" How that ancient professor smiled at me in my dream. His smile was tender and kind, like a caress.

Michael wrote a long essay during those nights about an ancient conflict between neptunist and plutonist theories of the origin of the earth. This dispute preceded the Kant–La Place nebular theory. I found a certain fascination in the expression "nebular theory."

"How did the earth really originate, Michael?" I asked my husband.

Michael merely smiled, as if that were the only answer I had expected of him. And, indeed, I had not expected any answer. I was withdrawn. I was ill.

During those summer days of 1951 Michael told me that he cherished a dream of expanding his essay and publishing it in a few years' time as a short piece of original research. Could I imagine, he asked, how glad his old father would be? I could not find a single word of encouragement to offer him. I was contracted, withdrawn into myself as though I had lost a tiny jewel on the sea bed. I was lost for hours on end in sea-green twilight. Pains, depression, and frightening dreams by day and by night. I hardly noticed the dark bags which appeared under Michael's eyes. He was desperately tired. He had to stand for hours in the line for free food for nursing mothers with my ration book in his hand. He never uttered a word of complaint. He simply joked in his usual dry way, and said that it was he who deserved the allowance, since he was feeding the baby.

CHAPTER

17

Little Yair began to resemble my brother Emanuel, with a broad, healthy face, a fleshy nose, and high cheekbones. I was not pleased by this resemblance. Yair was a greedy and lusty baby. He grunted as he drank and in his sleep he produced a contented gurgling. His skin was pink. The islands of pure blue turned into small, inquisitive gray eyes. He was prone to mysterious fits of violent rage, in which he would beat the air around him with his clenched fists. It occurred to me that had his fists not been so tiny it would have been dangerous to go near him. At such times I called my son "The Mouse That Roared," after the well-known film. Michael preferred the nickname "Bearcub." At the age of three months our son had more hair than most babies.

Sometimes, when the baby cried and Michael was out, I would get up barefoot and violently rock the cradle, calling my baby in an ecstasy of pain "Zalman-Yair," "Yair-Zalman." As if my son had wronged me. I was an indifferent mother during the early months of my son's life. I remembered Aunt

Jenia's distasteful visit at the beginning of my pregnancy, and at times I imagined perversely that it was I who had wanted to get rid of the baby and Aunt Jenia who had forced me not to. I also felt that I should soon be dead and so I owed nothing to anyone, not even to this pink, healthy, wicked child. Yes, Yair was wicked. Often he would scream in my arms and his face would turn as red as that of a furious drunken peasant in a Russian film. Only when Michael took him from my arms and sang to him softly would Yair consent to be quiet. I resented this; it was as if a stranger had shamed me with base ingratitude.

I remember. I have not forgotten. As Michael walked backwards and forwards across the room from the window to the door and back again, carrying the child in his arms and whispering sinister words in his ear, I would suddenly observe in both of them, in all three of us, a quality which I can only call melancholy, because I do not know what other term to use.

I was ill. Even when Dr. Urbach announced that he was satisfied that the complication was cleared up, and that I was free to resume a normal life in every way, even then I was still ill. However, I resolved to move Michael's camp-bed out of the room where the cradle was. From now on I took the care of the baby on myself. My husband was to sleep in the living room so that we should no longer distract him from his studies. He would have an opportunity to catch up on the work he had been prevented from doing the previous months.

At eight o'clock in the evening I would feed the child, put him to sleep, lock the door from the inside, and then stretch out by myself on the broad double bed. Sometimes at half past nine or ten o'clock Michael would tap gently on the door. If I opened it he would say:

"I saw a light under the door and I knew you weren't asleep. That's why I knocked."

As he spoke he looked at me with his gray eyes like a thoughtful elder son. Distant and cold, I would answer:

"I'm ill, Michael. You know I'm not well."

He clenched his hand on his empty pipe till the knuckles showed red. "I only wanted to ask if . . . if I'm not disturbing you . . . If there's anything I can do to help, or—do you need me? Not now? Well, you know, Hannah, I'm just in the next room if you want anything . . . I'm not doing anything important, just reading through Goldschmidt for the third time, and . . ."

A long time before, Michael Gonen had told me that cats are never wrong about people. A cat would never make friends with anyone who was not disposed to like him. Well, then.

I would wake before dawn. Jerusalem is a remote city, even if you live there, even if you were born there. I wake and hear the wind in the narrow streets of Mekor Baruch. There are corrugated-iron huts in backyards and on ancient balconies. The wind plays on them. Washing rustles on washlines strung across the road. Garbage men drag cans along the pavement. One of them always curses hoarsely. In some backyard a cock crows angrily. Distant voices clamor on all sides. There is a still, tense fever all around. The howling of cats mad with desire. A single shot in the distant darkness to the north. A motor roaring in the distance. A woman moaning in another flat. Bells singing far off in the east, perhaps from the churches of the Old City. A fresh wind plows the treetops. Jerusalem is a city of pine trees. A taut sympathy reigns between the pine trees and the wind. Ancient pines in Talpiot, in Katamon, in Beit Hakerem and behind the dark Schneller Woods. Now in the low village of Ein Kerem white mists at dawn are envoys of a realm of different colors. The convents are ringed with high walls in the low village of Ein Kerem. Even within the walls are whispering pines. Sinister things are plotting by the blind light of dawn. Plotting as if I were not here to hear them. As if I were not here. The swish of tires. The milkman's bicycle. His light footfall on the landing. His muffled coughing. Dogs barking in the yards. There is a frightening sight out there in the yard and the dogs can see it and I cannot. A shutter wails. They know that I am here awake and trembling. They are conspiring as if I were not here. Their target is me.

Every morning, after doing the shopping and tidying the house, I take Yair for a walk in his carriage. It is summer in Jerusalem. A calm blue sky. We make for Mahane Yehuda market to buy a cheap frying pan or strainer. When I was a child I used to like watching the bare brown backs of the porters in the market. I enjoyed the odor of their sweat. Even now the eddying smells in Mahane Yehuda market give me a feeling of repose. Sometimes I would sit on a bench opposite the railings of the Tachkemoni Orthodox Boys' School, the baby carriage by my side, and follow with my eyes the boys wrestling in the playground in the break between lessons.

Often we went as far as the Schneller Woods. For such an expedition I would prepare a flask of lemon tea, cookies, my knitting, a gray rug, and some toys. We would spend an hour or so in the woods. The wood was small, set on a steep hill and carpeted with dead pine needles. Ever since I was a child I have called this wood "the forest."

I spread out the rug, and put Yair down to play with his

blocks. I sit on a cold rock with three or four other housewives. These women are kindly; they are happy to talk to me about themselves and their families without so much as hinting that I should reveal my own secrets in return. So as not to appear superior or condescending, I discuss with them the advantages of various kinds of knitting needles. I tell them about pretty blouses in lightweight materials on sale at Maayan Stub or at Schwartz's Store. One of the women taught me how to cure a baby's cold by means of inhalations. Sometimes I try to amuse them by telling them a political joke brought home by Michael, about Dov Yosef, the "Minister of Rationing," or about a new immigrant who said such and such to Ben Gurion. But when I turn my head I catch sight of the Arab village of Shaafat dozing beyond the border, bathed in blue light. Red are its rooftiles in the distance and in the nearby treetops birds in the morning sing songs in a language I cannot understand.

I soon grow tired. I return home, feed my child, put him to sleep in his cradle and sink panting onto my bed. Ants have appeared in the kitchen. Perhaps they had suddenly discovered how very weak I am.

In the middle of May I gave Michael my permission to smoke his pipe in the house, except in the room where the baby and I slept. What would happen to us if Michael fell ill, even slightly? He had never had a day's illness since he was fourteen. Couldn't he take a few days' holiday? In another year and a half or so, when he had got his second degree, he would be able to adopt a less rigorous routine, and then we could all have a pleasant holiday together. Was there anything he would like? Could I buy him something to wear? As a matter of fact, he was still saving to buy the parts of the big

Encyclopaedia Hebraica as they appeared; to this end he walked home from the university four times a week instead of taking the bus, and in this way he had already saved about twenty-five pounds.

At the beginning of June the baby showed the first signs of recognizing his father. Michael approached him from the direction of the door and the child gurgled with delight. Then Michael tried approaching him from the other side, and again Yair cried out with joy. I did not like the way the child looked when he was so bursting with joy. I told Michael that I was afraid our son would not turn out to be particularly bright. Michael's jaw dropped in amazement. He started to say something, hesitated, then changed his mind and fell silent. Later he wrote a postcard to his father and his aunts informing them that his son recognized him. My husband was convinced that he and his son were destined to become bosom friends.

"You must have been pampered as a child," I said.

CHAPTER

18

In July the academic year
came to an end. Michael was awarded a modest scholarship,
as a token of approval and encouragement. In a private conversation his professor spoke to him of his prospects: A sound,
hard-working young man would not be overlooked; he would
certainly end up as an assistant lecturer. One evening Michael
invited a few of his fellow students around to drink to his
success. He planned a small surprise party.

We received visitors very infrequently. Every three months
one or other of the aunts called and spent half a day with us.
Old Sarah Zeldin from the kindergarten would pop in for
ten minutes towards evening to give us the benefit of her expert
advice about the baby. Michael's friend Liora's husband came
from Kibbutz Tirat Yaar with a crate of apples. Once my
brother Emanuel burst in at midnight. "Here, take this filthy
chicken. Quick. Are you still alive? Here, I've brought you a
bird—it's still alive, too. Well, all the best. Have you heard the
one about the three airmen? Well, love to the baby. I've got

our truck waiting outside, and they'll start tooting at me any moment."

On Saturdays my best friend Hadassah sometimes came over, with or without her husband. She kept trying to persuade me to go back to the university. Aunt Leah's friend, old Mr. Kadishman, was in the habit of dropping in from time to time to keep an eye on us and to play a game of chess with Michael.

On the night of the surprise party eight students came. One of them was a blonde girl who looked dazzling at first glance but later seemed coarse-featured. Apparently she was the girl who had danced the lively Spanish dance at our wedding party. She called me "sweetie," and Michael she called "genius."

My husband poured the wine and handed round cookies. Then he got up on the table and started mimicking his lecturers. His friends laughed politely. Only the blonde girl, Yardena, was really enthusiastic. "Micha," she cheered, "Micha, you're the greatest."

I was ashamed of my husband because he was not amusing. His gaiety was strained and forced. Even when he told a funny story I could not laugh, because he told it as if he were dictating lecture notes.

After a couple of hours the guests left.

My husband collected the glasses and took them out to the kitchen. Then he emptied the ashtrays. He swept the room. He put on an apron and went back to the sink. As he went down the passage he stopped and looked at me like a scolded schoolboy. He suggested I go to bed and promised not to make any noise. He supposed I was worn out after all the excitement. He had been wrong, he could see now how wrong he had been. He shouldn't have invited strangers in; my nerves were still on edge and I was easily tired. He was surprised at himself for not having thought of that beforehand. By the way, he found that girl Yardena utterly vulgar. Would I forgive him for what had happened?

While Michael was asking me to forgive him for the small party he had arranged I recalled how lost I had felt that night when we came back from our first expedition to Tirat Yaar, and how we had stood between the two rows of dark cypresses, how the cold rain had lashed my face and how Michael had suddenly unbuttoned his rough overcoat and gathered me into his embrace.

Now he stood bent over the sink as if his neck were broken, his gestures very weary. He washed the glasses in hot water, then rinsed them in cold. I crept up behind him on bare feet. I kissed his close-cropped head, threw both my arms round his shoulders, and took hold of his firm, downy hand. I was glad that he could feel my breast against his back, because since the beginning of my pregnancy my husband and I had been distant. Michael's hand was wet from washing the glasses. He had a dirty bandage on one of his fingers. Perhaps he had cut himself and not bothered to tell me. The bandage, too, was wet. He turned his long, thin face towards me, and it seemed more emaciated than it had been on the day we first met in Terra Sancta. I noticed that his whole body was emaciated. His cheekbones stood out. A fine line had begun to show by his right nostril. I touched his cheek. He showed no sign of surprise. As if this was what he had been waiting for all these days. As if he had known in advance that it was this evening that the change would come.

Once upon a time there was a little girl called Hannah, and she was given a new dress, white as snow, to greet the Sabbath. She had a pretty pair of shoes, too, of real suede, and her curls were tied up with a pretty silk scarf, because little Hannah had lovely curly hair. Now Hannah went out, and she saw an old charcoal-seller bowed down under the weight of his black sack. The Sabbath was approaching. Hannah hurried to help the charcoal-seller carry his sack of charcoal, because little Hannele had a kind heart. But then her white dress was covered with charcoal and her suede shoes were filthy. Hannah burst out crying bitterly because little Hannele was a good girl, always tidy, always neat. The kindly moon in the sky heard her crying and sent his beams down to play on her gently and to turn every smudge into a golden flower and every spot into a silvery star. For there is no sadness in the world that cannot be turned into great joy.

I lulled the baby to sleep and went into my husband's room wearing a long, transparent nightdress which came down to my ankles. Michael put a marker in his book, closed it, put down his pipe, and switched off the table lamp. Then he stood up and put his arms around my waist. He did not speak.

Afterwards, I spoke the deepest words that I could find in my heart: Tell me something, Michael—why did you say once that you liked the word "ankle"? I like you for liking the word "ankle." Maybe it's not too late to tell you that you're a gentle and sensitive person. You're rare, Michael. You will write your paper, Michael, and I shall make the fair copy. Your paper will be very thorough, and Yair and I will be very proud of you. It will make your father happy, too. Everything will change. We shall be released. I love you. I loved you when we met in Terra Sancta. Maybe it isn't too late to tell you that your fingers fascinate me. I don't know what words I can use to tell you how much I want to be your wife. How very, very much.

Michael was asleep. Could I blame him? I had spoken to him in my gentlest voice and he had been so desperately tired.

Night after night he had sat at his desk till two or three in the morning, bent over his work, chewing on his empty pipe. For my sake he had taken on the job of marking first-year essays and even translating technical articles from English. With the money he earned he had bought me an electric fire, and an expensive baby carriage for Yair with springs and a colored canopy. He was so tired. My voice was so soft. He had fallen asleep.

I whispered to my absent husband the most tender thing I had in me. About the twins. And about the pent-up girl who was queen of the twins. I hid nothing. All night long I played in the dark with the fingers of his left hand and he buried his head in the bedclothes and felt nothing. Once again I slept beside my husband.

In the morning Michael was his usual self, subdued and efficient. Recently a fine line had begun to show under his left nostril. As yet it was barely visible, but if deeper wrinkles began to spread and cover his face, then my Michael would grow to look more and more like his father.

CHAPTER
19

I am at rest. Events can touch me no more. This is my place. Here I am. As I am. There is a sameness in the days. There is a sameness in me. Even in my new summer dress with its high waistline, I am still the same. I was carefully made and beautifully wrapped, tied up with a pretty red ribbon and put on display, bought and unwrapped, used and set aside. There is a dreary sameness in the days. And especially when summer reigns in Jerusalem.

What I have just written is a weary lie. There was a day, for instance, late in July 1953; a bright blue day full of sounds and sights. Our handsome greengrocer early in the morning, our Persian greengrocer Elijah Mossiah and his pretty daughter Levana. Mr. Guttmann the electrician from David Yelin Street promised to mend the iron within two days, and promised to keep his word. He also offered to sell me a yellow light bulb to keep mosquitoes away from the balcony at night. Yair was two years and three months old. He fell down the stairs, and so he beat them with his tiny fists. Spots of blood appeared on his knees. I dressed the wound without looking at the child's face.

The previous evening we had seen a modern Italian film, *The Bicycle Thief,* at the Edison Cinema. At lunchtime Michael expressed reserved approval. He had bought an evening paper in town which mentioned South Korea and gangs of infiltrators in the Negev. There was a squabble between two Orthodox women in our street. An ambulance siren sounded in Rashi Street or one of the other streets nearby. A neighbor grumbled to me about the high price and poor quality of fish. Michael wore glasses because his eyes hurt. They were only reading glasses. I bought an ice cream for Yair and another for myself in Cafe Allenby in King George Street. I spilled ice cream on the sleeve of my green blouse.

The Kamnitzer family upstairs had a son called Yoram, a dreamy, fair-haired boy of fourteen. Yoram was a poet. His poems were about loneliness. He brought me his manuscripts to read because he had heard that I had studied literature in my youth. I was the judge of his work. His voice trembled, his lips quivered, and a green flicker shone in his eyes. Yoram brought me a new poem, which he had dedicated to the memory of the poetess Rachel. Yoram's poem compared a life without love to a barren wilderness. A solitary wayfarer searches for a spring in the desert, but is led astray by mirages. By the side of the real spring he would finally collapse and die.

"Imagine a well brought up, pious, Orthodox boy like you writing love poems," I laughed.

For an instant Yoram had the strength to join in my laughter, but he had already begun to grip the arms of his chair and his fingers were pale as a girl's. He laughed with me, but suddenly his eyes filled. He snatched up the sheet of paper with the poem on it and crumpled it in his clenched hand. Suddenly he turned and fled from my apartment. By the door he paused.

"I'm sorry, Mrs. Gonen," he whispered. "Goodbye."

Regret.

That evening Aunt Leah's friend, old Mr. Avraham Kadishman, came to visit us. We drank coffee and he criticized the leftist government. Were the days all still the same? Days passed without leaving a trace. I owe myself a solemn duty to record in this journal the passing of every day, every hour, for my days are mine and I am at rest and the days flash past like hills seen from the train on the way to Jerusalem. I shall die Michael will die the Persian greengrocer Elijah Mossiah will die Levana will die Yoram will die Kadishman will die all the neighbors all the people will die all Jerusalem will die and there will be a strange train full of strange people and they like us will stand at the window and watch strange hills flashing past. I cannot even kill an ant on the kitchen floor without thinking of myself.

And I also think of delicate things deep down inside my body. Delicate things which are mine, all mine, like my heart and my nerves and my womb. They are mine, they are my very own, but I shall never be allowed to see them or touch them because everything in the world is distance.

If only I could overpower the engine and be the princess of the train, manipulate two lissom twins as if they were extensions of me, left hand and right hand.

Or if only it could really happen that on the seventeenth of August, 1953, at six o'clock in the morning, a Bokharian taxi driver named Rahamim Rahamimov would finally arrive, powerfully built and smiling, on my doorstep, knock on the door and ask politely if Miss Yvonne Azulai is ready to leave. I would be absolutely ready to drive with him to Lydda Airport to fly Olympic to the snowbound Russian steppes at night in a sledge wrapped in bearskins the silhouette of the driver's massive skull and on the huge icy expanse lean wolves' eyes gleam. The rays of the moon fall on the neck of the solitary tree. Stop, driver, stop a moment, turn your head and let me see your face. His face is a woodcarving, coarse-grained in the soft white light. Icicles hang from the end of his tangled mustache.

And the submarine *Nautilus* existed and still exists, gliding through the depths of the sea, huge, brightly lit and soundless in a gray ocean crisscrossed by warm currents and tangled underwater caverns at the roots of coral reefs in the archipelago, gliding deeper and deeper with powerful thrusts, it knows where it is going and why and is not at rest, unlike a stone, unlike a weary woman.

And off the coast of Newfoundland, beneath the northern lights, the British destroyer *Dragon* patrols watchfully and her crew knows no rest for fear of Moby Dick, the noble white whale. In September *Dragon* will sail from Newfoundland to New Caledonia to carry supplies to the garrison there. Please, *Dragon,* don't forget the port of Haifa and Palestine and far-off Hannah.

All these years Michael has nursed a hope of exchanging our apartment in Mekor Baruch for one in Rehavia or Beit Hakerem. He does not like living here. His aunts, too, wonder insistently why Michael lives surrounded by Orthodox people instead of in a civilized neighborhood. A scholar needs peace and quiet, the aunts maintain, and here the neighbors are noisy.

It was my fault that we had still not managed to save enough even for a deposit on a new apartment, although Michael was considerate enough not to mention this fact to his aunts. Every year, with the return of spring, I am overcome by a mania for shopping. Electrical gadgets, a bright gray curtain to cover a whole wall, lots and lots of new clothes. Before I was married I bought few clothes. As a student I used to wear the same clothes right through the winter, a blue woolen dress my mother had knitted me or else a pair of brown corduroy trousers and a chunky red sweater such as girls at the University used to wear at that time to produce a casual effect. Nowadays I grew tired of new dresses after a few weeks. Every spring I felt a desire for new purchases. I stormed feverishly from shop to shop, as if the big prize was waiting for me somewhere, but always somewhere else.

Michael wondered why I no longer wore the dress with the high waistline. I had been so pleased with it when I had bought it less than six weeks before. He fought back his surprise and silently nodded his head up and down as if expressing an understanding which made my blood boil. Maybe that was why I went into town with the express intention of shocking him with my prodigality. I loved his self-restraint. I wanted to shatter it.

Dreams.

Hard things plot against me every night. The twins practice throwing hand grenades before dawn among the ravines of the Judean Desert southeast of Jericho. Their twin bodies move in unison. Submachine guns on their shoulders. Worn commando uniforms stained with grease. A blue vein stands out on Halil's forehead. Aziz crouches, hurls his body forward. Halil drops his head. Aziz uncurls and throws. The dry shimmer of the explosion. The hills echo and re-echo, the Dead Sea glows pale behind them like a lake of burning oil.

CHAPTER

20

There are old peddlers who wander around Jerusalem. They are not like the poor charcoal-seller in the story of little Hannah's dress. Their faces are not lit by an inner glow. They are enveloped in an icy hatred. Old peddlers. Weird craftsmen wandering about the city. They are weird. I have known them for years, them and their cries. Even when I was five or six I was terrified of them. I shall describe these, too—then perhaps they will stop frightening me at night. I try to decipher their ways, their orbits, to guess beforehand on which day each of them will come to cry his wares in our streets. Surely they, too, are subject to some scheme or regular pattern. *"Gla-zier, gla-zier"*—his voice is hoarse and stark. He carries no tools, no panes of glass, as if resigned to receiving no response to his cry. *"Alte zachen, alte shich"*—a great sack on his shoulder like the burglar in an illustration in a children's story. *"Pri-mus stoves, pri-mus"*—a heavy man with a huge, bony skull like the archetypal blacksmith. *"Mattresses, mattresses"*—the word resounding in his throat with an almost immoral suggestiveness. The knife-grinder carries about with him a wooden wheel worked by a treadle. He has no teeth,

and his ears are hairy and protruding. Like a bat. Old craftsmen, weird peddlers, year after year they wander about the
streets of Jerusalem untouched by time. As if Jerusalem is a
wraiths' castle in the north, and they the avenging spirits lying
in wait.

I was born in Kiryat Shmuel, on the edge of Katamon, during the Feast of Succot in 1930. Sometimes I have a strange
feeling that a bleak wasteland divides my parents' home from
my husband's. I have never revisited the street where I was
born. One Sabbath, in the morning, Michael, Yair, and I went
for a walk to the edge of Talbiyeh. I refused to go any further.
Like a spoiled child I stamped my foot. No, no. My husband
and my child laughed at me, but they gave in.

In Mea Shearim, in Beit Yisrael, Sanhedria, Kerem Avraham,
Achva, Zichron Moshe, Nahalat Shiva live Orthodox people,
Ashkenazim with fur hats and Sephardim with striped robes.
Old women huddle silently on low stools, as if there were
spread out before them not a small town but a broad expanse
of country, whose furthest horizons they must scan daily with
the eyes of a hawk.

There is no end to Jerusalem. Talpiot, a forgotten continent
in the south, hidden amid her ever-whispering pine trees. A
bluish vapor spreads up from the Judean Desert which borders
Talpiot on the east. The vapor touches her small villas, and
even her gardens, overshadowed by the pines. Beit Hakerem, a
solitary hamlet lost beyond the windswept plain, hemmed in
by rocky fields. Bayit Vagan, an isolated hill-fort where a violin
plays behind windows kept shuttered all day, and at night the
jackals howl to the south. Tense silence broods in Rehavia, in
Saadya Gaon Street, after the sun has set. At a lighted window
sits a gray-haired sage at his work, his fingers tapping at the
keys of his typewriter. Who could imagine that at the other
end of this very street stands the district of Shaarei Hesed, full

of barefoot women wandering at night between colored sheets flapping in the breeze, and sly cats slipping from yard to yard? Is it possible that the old man playing tunes on his German typewriter cannot sense them? Who could imagine that beneath his western balcony spreads the Valley of the Cross, an ancient grove creeping up the slope, clutching at the outermost houses of Rehavia as if about to enfold and smother them in its luxuriant vegetation? Small fires flicker in the valley, and long-drawn-out, muffled songs rise out of the woods and reach out towards the windowpanes. At dusk crowds of white-toothed urchins make their way to Rehavia from the outskirts of the city to smash her stately street lamps with small, sharp stones. The streets are still calm: Kimhi, Maimonides, Nachmanides, Alharizi, Abrabanel, Ibn Ezra, Ibn Gabirol, Saadya Gaon. But then the decks of the British destroyer *Dragon* will still be calm after the mutiny has begun dimly to break out below. Towards nightfall in Jerusalem at the ends of the streets you can glimpse brooding hills waiting for darkness to fall on the shuttered city.

In Tel Arza, in the north of Jerusalem, lives an elderly lady pianist. She practices ceaselessly and tirelessly. She is preparing for a new recital of pieces by Schubert and Chopin. The solitary tower of Nebi Samwil stands on a hilltop to the north, stands motionless beyond the border and stares night and day at the elderly pianist who sits innocently at her piano, her stiff back turned to the open window. At night the tower chuckles, the tall, thin tower chuckles, as though whispering to himself "Chopin and Schubert."

One day in August Michael and I went out for a long walk. We left Yair with my best friend Hadassah, in Bezalel Street.

It was summer in Jerusalem. Her streets had a new light. I am thinking of the time between half past five and half past six, the last light of the day. There was a caressing coolness. In the narrow lane which is Pri Hadash Street was a stone-paved yard, detached from the street by a broken-down fence. An ancient tree forced its way up between the unevenly laid paving stones. I do not know what kind of tree it was. When I had passed this way alone in the winter I had wrongly imagined that the tree was dead. Now new shoots had burst out from the trunk, clawing the air with pointed talons.

From Pri Hadash Street we turned left into Josephus Street. A big, dark man wrapped in an overcoat, with a gray cap on his head, stared at me through the lighted window of a fish market. Am I mad, or is my real husband eyeing me furiously, reprovingly, through the lighted window of a fish market, wrapped in an overcoat and wearing a gray cap?

Women had brought out all the substance of their houses onto their balconies: pinks and whites, sheets and quilts. A straight, slender girl stood on one of the balconies in Hashmonaim Street. Her sleeves were rolled up, and her hair wrapped in a scarf. She was beating an eiderdown angrily with a wooden bat, oblivious of our presence. On one of the walls was a faded slogan in red letters from the days of the underground: *Judaea fell in blood and fire, in blood and fire will Judaea rise*. The sentiment was alien to me, but I was moved by the music in the words.

We had a long walk, Michael and I, that evening. We went down through the Bokharian Quarter and along Prophet Samuel Street to the Mandelbaum Gate. From here we took the curving lane through the Hungarian Buildings to the Abyssinian Quarter, to Mousrara and along the end of Jaffa Road to Notre Dame Square. Jerusalem is a burning city.

Whole districts seem to be hanging in the air. But a closer glance reveals an immeasurable weightiness. The overpowering arbitrariness of the intertwining alleys. A labyrinth of temporary dwellings, huts and sheds leaning in smouldering anger against the gray stone that takes on now a blue, now a reddish tinge. Rusting gutters. Ruined walls. A harsh and silent struggle between the stonework and the stubborn vegetation. Waste-plots of rubble and thistles. And, above all, the wanton tricks of the light: if a stray cloud comes for a moment between the twilight and the city, immediately Jerusalem is different.

And the walls.

Every quarter, every suburb harbors a hidden kernel surrounded by high walls. Hostile strongholds barred to passers-by. Can one ever feel at home here in Jerusalem, I wonder, even if one lives here for a century? City of enclosed courtyards, her soul sealed up behind bleak walls crowned with jagged glass. There is no Jerusalem. Crumbs have been dropped deliberately to mislead innocent people. There are shells within shells and the kernel is forbidden. I have written "I was born in Jerusalem"; "Jerusalem is my city," this I cannot write. I cannot know what lurks in wait for me in the depths of the Russian Compound, behind the walls of Schneller Barracks, in the monastic lairs of Ein Kerem or in the enclave of the High Commissioner's palace on the Hill of Evil Counsel. This is a brooding city.

In Melisanda Street, when the street lights had come on, a large and dignified man pounced on Michael, took hold of his coat button as if he was an old acquaintance and thus addressed my husband:

"A curse upon you, O troubler of Israel. May you perish."

Michael, who was not acquainted with the madmen of Jerusalem, was taken aback and went pale. The stranger smiled a friendly smile and added calmly:

"So perish all enemies of the Lord, Amen Selah."

Michael may have been about to try to explain to the stranger that he must have mistaken him for his worst enemy, but the man put an end to the discussion by aiming at Michael's shoes:

"I spit upon you and upon all your descendants forever and ever, Amen."

Villages and suburbs surround Jerusalem in a close circle, like curious bystanders surrounding a wounded woman lying in the road: Nebi Samwil, Shaafat, Sheikh Jarrah, Isawiyeh, Augusta Victoria, Wadi Joz, Silwan, Sur Baher, Beit Safafa. If they clenched their fists the city would be crushed.

Incredibly, in the evening the frail old scholars wander out for a breath of fresh air. They prod the pavement with their sticks like blind wanderers on a snowy steppe. Michael and I encountered a pair of them that evening in Luntz Street, behind Sansur House. They were strolling arm in arm, as if lending each other support in their hostile surroundings. I smiled and greeted them cheerfully. Both of them hastily raised their hands to their heads. One flourished his hat eagerly to return my greeting; the other's head was bare, and he waved in a symbolic or absent-minded gesture.

21

That autumn Michael was appointed to an assistant lectureship in the Geology Department. This time he did not celebrate with a party, but marked the occasion by taking two days off work. We took Yair to Tel Aviv, where we stayed with Aunt Leah. The flat, shimmering city, the brightly colored buses, the sight of the sea and the taste of the salt breeze, the neatly trimmed trees planted along the sidewalks, all these aroused in me a poignant yearning, I knew not why or what for. There was tranquillity and a vague expectancy. We saw three school-friends of Michael's, and went to a couple of productions at the Habima Theatre. We hired a boat and rowed up the Yarkon towards Seven Mills. Reflections of broad eucalyptus trees fell trembling in the water. It was a very tranquil moment.

That autumn, too, I went back to working five hours a day at old Sarah Zeldin's kindergarten. We began to repay the money we had borrowed after our wedding. We even paid back some of the money we had had from Michael's aunts. But we could not begin to save up for a deposit on a new apartment because on Passover Eve I went out without consulting Michael and bought an expensive modern sofa and three matching armchairs at Zuzovsky's.

As soon as Michael received planning permission from the municipality we bricked up the balcony. We called the new room the study. Here Michael put his desk, and his bookshelves were also moved in. I bought Michael the first volume of the *Encyclopaedia Hebraica* as a present on our fourth wedding anniversary. Michael bought me an Israeli-made radio.

Michael sat up late at night working. A glass door separated the new study from my bedroom. Through the glass door the reading lamp threw giant shadows on the wall opposite my bed. At night Michael's shadow intruded on my dreams. If he opened a drawer or moved a book, put on his glasses or lit his pipe, dark shadows lapped the wall facing me. The shadows fell in total silence. At times they took on shapes. I closed my eyes hard, but still the shapes would not relax their grip. When I opened my eyes the whole room seemed to tumble with every movement of my husband at his desk at night.

I was sorry that Michael was a geologist and not an architect. If only he could be poring at night over plans of buildings, roads, strong fortresses, or a naval harbor in which the British destroyer *Dragon* might anchor.

Michael's hand was delicate and steady. What neat diagrams he drew. He drew a geological plan on thin tracing paper, and his lips as he worked were tightly pressed together. He seemed to me like a general or a statesman, taking a fateful decision with icy calm. If Michael had been an architect perhaps I could have come to accept the shadow he cast on my bedroom wall at night. Strange and terrifying at night was the thought that Michael was exploring unknown layers in the depths of the earth. As if he were desecrating and provoking at night an unforgiving world.

Eventually I got up and made myself a glass of mint tea, as I had learned to do from Mrs. Tarnopoler, who was my landlady before I was married. Or else I turned on the light and read until midnight or one o'clock, when my husband would silently lie down beside me, say good night, kiss me on the lips, and pull the bedclothes over his head.

The books I read at night gave no indication that I had once been a student of literature: Somerset Maugham or Daphne du Maurier in English, in paperbacks with glossy covers; Stefan Zweig, Romain Rolland. My taste had become sentimental. I cried when I read André Maurois' *Women Without Love* in a cheap translation. I cried like a schoolgirl. I had not lived up to my professor's expectations. I had never fulfilled the hopes he had expressed for me shortly after my wedding.

When I stood by the kitchen sink I could see down into the garden below. Our garden was neglected, full of mud in the winter and dust and thistles in the summer. Broken dishes rolled around in the garden. Yoram Kamnitzer and his friends had built stone forts whose ruins remained. At the end of the garden stood a broken tap. There is a Russian steppe, there is Newfoundland, there are the isles of the archipelago, and I am exiled here. But at times my eyes are opened and I can see Time. Time is like a police van patrolling the streets at night, a red light flashing rapidly, the wheels moving slowly by comparison. The wheels swish softly. Cautiously moving. Slowly. Menacing. Prowling.

I wanted to imagine that inanimate objects obey a different rhythm because they have no thoughts.

For example, on a branch of the fig tree which sprouted in our garden a rusty bowl had hung suspended for years. Perhaps a long-dead neighbor had once thrown it from the window of the flat above and it had caught in the branches. It was already hanging covered in rust outside our kitchen window when we first arrived. Four, five years. Even the fierce winds of winter had not brought it to the ground. On New Year's Day, however, I stood at the kitchen sink and saw with my own eyes how the bowl dropped from the tree. No breeze stirred the air, no cat or bird moved the branches. But strong forces came to fruition at that moment. The rusty metal crumbled and the bowl clattered to the ground. What I mean to say is this: All those years I had observed complete repose in an object in which a hidden process was taking place, all those years.

CHAPTER

22

Most of our neighbors are Orthodox, with a lot of children. At the age of four Yair sometimes comes out with questions which I cannot answer. I send him with his questions to his father. And Michael, who sometimes speaks to me as if I were an unruly little girl, converses with his son as man to man. The sounds of their conversation reach me in the kitchen. They never interrupt each other. Michael has taught Yair to end whatever he has to say with the words "I have finished." Michael himself sometimes uses this expression when he comes to the end of one of his answers. This was the method my husband chose to teach his son that people should not interrupt one another.

Yair might ask, for instance, "Why does everyone think something different?" Michael would reply, "People are different." Yair would then ask, "Why aren't there two men or two children the same?" Michael would admit that he didn't know the answer. The child would pause for a moment, consider carefully, then say perhaps:

"I think Mummy knows everything, because Mummy never says, 'I don't know.' Mummy says, 'I know but I can't explain.'

I think if you can't explain how can you say you know? I've finished."

Michael, perhaps with a restrained smile, would try to explain to his son the difference between thinking something and saying it.

Whenever I overheard a conversation like this I could not help remembering my late father, who was an attentive man who always scrutinized every utterance he heard, even from a child, for signs or hints of some truth which was denied him, at whose threshold he must prostrate himself all his life.

At the age of four and five Yair was a strong, silent child. Sometimes he displayed a tendency towards extraordinary violence. Perhaps he had discovered how timid the neighbors' children were. His drowsy gestures could even inspire awe in older children. He occasionally came home beaten and bruised by other children's parents. Usually, however, he refused to tell us who was responsible for his wounds. If Michael pressed him, the reply often was:

"I deserved it because I started it. I started fighting first and then they fought me back. I've finished."

"Why did you start it?"

"They made me."

"How did they make you?"

"All sorts of ways."

"Such as?"

"Can't tell. Not saying things—doing things."

"What things?"

"Things."

I noticed a sullen insolence in my son. A concentrated interest in food. In objects. Electrical instruments. The clock. Long silences, as if he was continuously absorbed in some complicated mental process.

Michael never raised his hand against the child, both as a matter of principle and because he himself had been brought up with understanding and had never been beaten as a child. I cannot say as much for myself. I beat Yair whenever he displayed this sullen insolence. I would thrash him, without looking into calm gray eyes, until, panting, I succeeded in wringing the sobs from his throat. His willpower was so strong that it sometimes made me shudder, and when his pride was finally broken he would throw me a grotesque whimper which sounded more like an imitation of a crying child.

Upstairs from us, on the second floor, across the landing from the Kamnitzers, lived an elderly couple with no children. Their name was Glick. He was a pious little haberdasher and she suffered from fits of hysteria. I would be awakened at night by a prolonged low sobbing like that of a young puppy. Sometimes a harsh scream sounded before dawn, to be followed after a pause by a second, muffled as if under water. I would leap out of bed and run in my nightdress to the child's bedroom. Time and again I thought that Yair was screaming, that something terrible was happening to my son.

I hated the nights.

The quarter of Mekor Baruch is built of stone and iron. Iron handrails on flights of steps climbing the outer walls of ancient houses. Dirty iron gates inscribed with the date of erection and the names of the donor and his parents. Battered fences frozen in contorted poses. Rusty shutters hanging on a single hinge, threatening to hurl themselves down into the street. And painted in red on a peeling plaster wall near our house, the slogan "*Judaea fell in blood and fire, in blood and fire will Judaea rise.*" It is not the idea in this slogan which appeals to me, but a certain symmetry. A kind of disciplined balance which I cannot explain, but which is also present with me at night, when the street lights print the shadow of the window-bars on the wall opposite and everything seems to be doubled.

When the wind blows it rattles the corrugated iron structures which people erect on their balconies and roofs. This sound, too, contributes to the depression which continually returns. Silently the pair of them float over the neighborhood at the end of the night. Naked to the waist, barefoot and light they glide outside. Lean fists hammer on the corrugated iron, because they have been ordered to scare the dogs into a frenzy. Towards dawn the dogs' barking dies down to a confused howl. Outside the twins are streaming on. I can sense them. I can hear the padding of their bare feet. They laugh to each other without a sound. They are standing on one another's shoulders and climbing to me up the fig tree which grows in the garden. They have instructions to seize a branch and tap my shutter with it. Not hard. Softly. Once I heard fingernails clawing at the shutters. Once they chose to throw pine cones. They have been sent to wake me. Someone imagines I am asleep. When I was young I was full of the strength to love, and now my strength to love is dying. I do not want to die.

In the course of these years I occasionally asked myself similar questions to those which had passed through my mind as we returned on foot that night from Tirat Yaar three weeks before our wedding. What do you find in this man and what do you know about him? Suppose another man had caught hold of your arm when you slipped on the stairs at Terra Sancta? Are there forces at work, forces perhaps which there is no possibility of identifying, or was Mrs. Tarnopoler right in what she said two days before the wedding?

What my husband thinks I make no attempt to guess. On his face I see repose, as if his wish has been granted and now he stands, vacant and contented, waiting for the bus which will take him home after an enjoyable visit to the zoo, to eat, get undressed, and go to bed. At primary school when we were describing an outing we used to summarize our feelings at the end with the words "tired but happy." That is precisely the expression that Michael has on his face most days.

Michael takes two buses every morning to get to the University. The briefcase which his father had bought him as a wedding present wore out, being a relic of the years of austerity and made of some synthetic material; but he would not let me buy him a new one. He was sentimentally attached, he said, to the old one.

With firm, unerring fingers Time wears down inanimate objects. All things are at his mercy.

In his briefcase Michael carries his lecture notes, which he numbers in roman numerals instead of the usual arabic ones. He also keeps in his briefcase, winter and summer alike, a woolen scarf knitted for him by my mother. And also some tablets to relieve heartburn. Recently Michael has begun to suffer from slight heartburn, especially just before lunch.

In winter my husband wears a bluish-gray raincoat which matches the color of his eyes. And he wears a plastic cover over his hat. In summer he wears a loose mesh shirt, with no tie. His body half-shows through the shirt, lean and hairy. He still insists on wearing his hair cropped short, so that he looks like a sportsman or an army officer. Has Michael ever longed to be a sportsman or an army officer? How little one is permitted to know about another person. Even if one is very attentive. Even if one never forgets a thing.

We do not talk much on an ordinary afternoon: could you pass me, will you hold, hurry up, don't make a mess, where's Yair, supper's ready, would you mind turning out the light in the hall.

In the evening, after the nine o'clock news, we peel and eat fruit, facing each other in our armchairs. Khrushchev will smash Gomulka; Eisenhower won't dare. Does the Government really intend to keep. The King of Iraq is a puppet in the hands of young officers. The elections will not produce many changes.

Then Michael sits down at his desk and puts on his reading glasses. I put the radio on softly and listen to music. Not a concert, but dance music from some far-off foreign station. At eleven I go to bed. There is a water pipe in one of the walls. The sounds of hidden pouring. The coughing. The wind.

Every Tuesday, on his way back from the University, Michael goes through the center of town and buys two movie tickets at Kahana's Agency. We start dressing at eight o'clock and at a quarter past we leave the house. The pale youth Yoram Kamnitzer keeps an eye on Yair while Michael and I are out at the show. In return I help him prepare for his Hebrew literature examinations. It is thanks to him that I have not forgotten everything I learned as a student. We sit and read the essays of Ahad Haam together, and compare Priest and Prophet, Flesh and Spirit, Slavery and Freedom. All the ideas are expressed in symmetrically contrasted pairs. I like this kind of system.

Yoram, too, thinks that prophecy, freedom, and the spirit call on us to liberate ourselves from the bonds of slavery and the flesh. Whenever I admire one of his poems a green flicker passes through Yoram's eyes. Yoram's poems are written with passion. He uses unusual words and phrases. Once I asked him the meaning of the expression "ascetic love" which appeared in one of his poems. Yoram explained that there are some loves which give us no cause for rejoicing. I repeated a remark I had heard a long time before from my husband, that when people are contented and have nothing to do, emotion spreads like a malignant tumor.

Yoram said "Mrs. Gonen," and his voice suddenly broke so that the last syllable sounded like a screech, because he was at the age when boys have difficulty in controlling their voices.

Whenever Michael came into the room when I was sitting with Yoram the boy seemed to experience an inner contraction. He hunched his back and stared at the floor in an uncomfortable sort of way, as if he had spilled something on the rug or knocked over a vase. Yoram Kamnitzer would finish at high school, go to the university, and then teach Hebrew and Bible in Jerusalem. Every New Year he would send us a pretty greeting card, and we would send one back to him. Time would still be there, a tall, transparent presence, hostile to Yoram, hostile to me, boding no good.

One evening in the autumn of 1954 Michael came home carrying a grayish-white kitten in his arms. He had found it in David Yelin Street, by the wall of the Orthodox girls' school.

"Isn't he sweet? Touch him. Look how he lifts up his tiny paw to threaten us, as if he were a leopard or a panther at least. Where's Yair's animal book? Get the book, please, Mummy, and let's show Yair how cats and leopards are cousins."

As Michael took my son's hand and made him stroke the kitten, I noticed a tremor at the corner of the child's mouth, as if the kitten was fragile or as if it was dangerous to stroke it.

"Look, Mummy, he's looking right at me. What does he want?"

"He wants to eat, dear. And to sleep. Go and make him a place to sleep on the kitchen floor. No, stupid, cats don't need blankets."

"Why not?"

"Because they're not like humans. They're different."

"Why are they different?"

"That's the way they're made. I can't explain."

"Daddy, why don't cats use blankets like us?"

"Because cats have warm fur coats, so they can keep warm without blankets."

Michael and Yair played with the kitten all evening. They called him "Snowy." He was only a few weeks old, and still displayed a touching lack of coordination in his movements. He tried hard to catch a moth which was fluttering just below the kitchen ceiling. His leaps were ridiculous because he lacked any sense of height or distance; he would jump a few inches off the floor, opening and closing his little jaws as if he had already reached the moth. We all burst out laughing. The kitten bridled when we laughed and uttered a hiss which was intended to be bloodcurdling.

"Snowy will grow big," Yair said, "and be the strongest cat in the neighborhood. We will teach him to guard the house and catch thieves and infiltrators. Snowy will be our watchcat."

"He needs to be fed," Michael said, "and he also needs to be petted. Every creature needs to be loved. So we will love Snowy and Snowy will love us. There's no need to kiss him, though, Yair. Mummy will be cross with you."

I contributed a green plastic bowl, milk, and cheese. Michael had to rub Snowy's nose in the milk, as the kitten had not yet learned to drink from a bowl. The animal was startled; it spat and shook its wet face vigorously, scattering white droplets. Finally it turned a soggy, pathetic, defeated face towards us. Snowy's color was not snowy, but grayish white. An ordinary cat.

In the night the kitten discovered a narrow opening in the kitchen window. He slipped across the balcony into the bed-room and found our bed. He chose to curl up at my feet, even though it was Michael who had adopted him and played with him all evening. He was an ungrateful kitten. He ignored the person who had been kind to him, and fawned instead on the person who had treated him coldly. Some years before Michael Gonen had said to me, "A cat will never make friends with the wrong sort of person." Now I realized that this had simply been a metaphor and not literally true, and that Michael had said it merely to appear original. The kitten lay curled up at my feet, uttering a low gurgling sound which was both calm and calming. Towards dawn the kitten scratched at the door. I got up and let him out. No sooner had he gone out than he started mewing through the door to be let in again. As soon as he was in he stalked over to the balcony door, yawned, stretched, growled, mewed, and pleaded to be let out. Snowy was a capricious kitten, or else perhaps just very indecisive.

. . .

After five days our new kitten went out and did not return. All evening my husband and my son searched for him in the street, in the neighborhood, and also round the wall of the Orthodox girls' school where Michael had first picked him up the previous week. Yair was of the opinion that we had offended Snowy. Michael, on the other hand, suggested that he had gone home to his mother. My conscience was clear. I mention this because I was suspected of having done away with the kitten. Could Michael really imagine that I was capable of poisoning a kitten?

"I realize," he said, "that I did wrong in deciding to keep a cat without consulting you, as if I lived on my own. Please try to understand me: I only wanted to make the boy happy. And when I was a child I longed to have a cat, but my father wouldn't let me."

"I never touched him, Michael. You've got to believe me. I won't even object if you bring another kitten home. I never touched him."

"I suppose he just went up to heaven in a fiery chariot." Michael smiled a dry smile. "Let's not talk about it any more. I'm only sorry for the boy, though; he was very much attached to Snowy. But let's drop the subject. Must we quarrel over a little kitten?"

"There's no quarrel," I said.

"No quarrel, and no kitten." Again Michael smiled his dry smile.

CHAPTER
23

About this time the flavor of our nights changed. By dint of prolonged and careful attention Michael had learned to make my body glad. His fingers were confident and experienced. They never gave up before I was forced to utter a low groan. Michael persevered with patience and sensitivity in extracting this groan from me. He learned to press his lips to a particular spot in my neck and dwell on it forcefully. To climb with his warm, firm hand right up my back to the nape of my neck, to the roots of my hair, and then return by a different route. By the meager light of the street lamp shining through the slatted shutter Michael saw on my face an expression resembling one of sharp pain. My eyes were always closed in a perpetual effort of concentration. I know Michael's eyes were not closed because he was concentrated and lucid. Lucid and responsible was his touch now. Every movement of his hand was calculated to give me pleasure. When I awoke towards morning I wanted him again. Wild visions came without my wanting them. A hermit wrapped in skins takes me in the Schneller Woods, bites my shoulder, and cries out. A mad workman from the new factory to the west of

Mekor Baruch snatches me up and rushes off towards the hills, bearing me lightly in his grease-stained arms. And the dark ones: their hands are soft but firm, their legs hairy and bronzed. They do not laugh.

Or else war has broken out in Jerusalem, and I dash out of my house in a flimsy nightdress and run crazed along a dark and narrow road. Strong flashlight beams suddenly light up the avenue of cypresses: my child is lost. Stern strangers search for him in the valleys. A tracker. Police officers. Weary volunteers from the surrounding villages. Their sympathy is obvious from their eyes, but how busy they are. Politely but firmly they urge me not to worry. The chances are good. After sunrise their efforts will be redoubled. I wandered in the dim alleyways behind the Street of the Abyssinians. I cried out "Yair, Yair" in a street full of dead cats rolling on the pavement. From one of the courtyards stepped the venerable professor who had taught me Hebrew literature. He was wearing a shabby suit. His smile was the smile of a very tired man. "You too are childless, young lady," he said politely, "and so you will permit me to invite you in." Who is that strange girl in green with her arms round my husband's waist further down the street, as if I were not here? I was invisible. My husband said, "A happy sentiment. A sad sentiment." He said, "They're going to build a very deep harbor at Ashdod."

It was autumn. The trees were not properly joined to the earth. Swaying suspiciously. Obscenely. On a high balcony I saw Captain Nemo. His face was pale and his eyes glittered. His black beard was cropped short. I knew that it was my fault, my fault that they had delayed setting sail. Time is slipping away. I'm ashamed of myself, Captain. Don't look at me so silently.

One day when I was six or seven I was sitting in my father's shop in Jaffa Road when the poet Saul Tchernichovsky came in to buy a table lamp. "Is this lovely girl for sale, too?" the poet asked my father with a laugh. Suddenly he lifted me in his strong arms and his silvery mustache tickled my cheek. A strong, warm odor rose from his body. His smile was mischievous, like that of a high-spirited boy who has managed to provoke the grownups. After he left my father was agitated and excited: "Our great poet spoke to us and behaved just like an ordinary customer. But surely the poet meant something," my father went on in a thoughtful tone, "when he lifted Hannah up in his arms and laughed that great laugh." I have not forgotten. In the early winter of 1954 I dreamt of the poet. And of the city of Danzig. And of a great procession.

Michael had begun collecting stamps. His explanation was that he was collecting for the child's sake, but so far Yair had shown no interest whatever in stamps. One suppertime Michael showed me a rare stamp from Danzig. How had he come by it? That morning he had bought a second-hand foreign book in Solel Street. The book was called *The Seismography of Deep-Water Lakes,* and in among the pages he had found this scarce stamp from Danzig. Michael tried to explain to me about the high value attaching to the stamps of extinct states: Latvia, Lithuania, Estonia, Free Danzig, Schleswig-Holstein, Bohemia and Moravia, Serbia, Croatia. I fell in love with the names as Michael uttered them.

The rare stamp was not exciting to look at: dark colors, a

stylized cross with a crown above, and, in Gothic script, "Freie Stadt." There was no scene at all depicted on the stamp. How could I guess what the city looked like? Broad avenues or high-walled buildings? Sloping steeply down to dip its feet in the water of the harbor, like Haifa, or extending flat over the surface of a marshy plain? A city of towers, surrounded by forests, or perhaps a city of banks and factories, all built on a square plan? The stamp gave no indication.

I asked Michael what the city of Danzig looked like.

Michael replied with a smile, as if the only reply I had expected from him was his smile.

This time I repeated the question. And so, because I had asked twice, he was forced to admit that he was astonished by my question.

"Why on earth do you want to know what Danzig looks like? And how do you expect me to know? After supper I'll look it up for you in the *Encyclopaedia Hebraica*—no, I can't do that, because they haven't got to *D* yet. By the way, if you're so keen on traveling abroad sometime I advise you to cut down on your spending, and not throw away your new dresses when you've only had them a few weeks. What happened to that gray skirt we bought together at Maayan Stub at Succot?"

And so I could discover nothing from Michael about the city of Danzig. After supper, when we were drying the dishes, I spoke to him mockingly. I said he had only pretended to be collecting stamps for the child's sake, that in fact the child was just an excuse for his own infantile desire to play with stamps like a baby. I wanted to defeat my husband in one small argument.

Michael denied me even this meager satisfaction. He is not easily offended. He did not interrupt my stream of provocations, because it is wrong to break in when someone is talking. He went on carefully drying the china plate he was holding. He stood on tiptoe to put the clean plate back in its place, in the cupboard over the sink. Then, without turning his head, he said that there was nothing new in what I had said. You didn't need to know much about psychology to know that even grownups like to play occasionally. He was collecting stamps for Yair in exactly the same way that I cut paper figures out of the magazines for him, even though they didn't interest the child in the least. So what point could I see in poking fun at his sentiment?

After we had put away the plates Michael sat down in an armchair and listened to the news. I sat opposite him and kept silent. We peeled fruit. We passed the peeled fruit to each other. Michael said:

"The electricity bill this month is enormous."

I said:

"Everything's getting more expensive. Milk's just gone up, too."

That night I dreamed of Danzig.

I was a princess. From the tower of my castle I gazed out over the city. Crowds of subjects had gathered at the foot of the tower. I stretched out my arms to greet them. The gesture resembled the attitude of the bronze statue of the Virgin on top of the Terra Sancta Convent.

I saw the dim masses of roofs. In the southeast the skies were darkening over the old parts of the city. Black clouds scudded from the north. There will be a storm. Down the hill I could make out the silhouettes of gigantic derricks in the port, black iron scaffolds. At the top of each derrick glimmered a red warning-light. The daylight turned gradually gray. I heard the siren of a ship leaving the harbor. To the south I could hear the roar of moving trains, but the trains themselves were not visible. I could see a park with leafy spinneys. In the middle of the park was an elongated lake. In the center of the lake was a small, long island. On it stood the statue of a princess. My statue.

The water in the harbor was smeared with black oil from the ships. The street lights came on, and cast strips of cold light on my city. The cool glow beat against the roof of fog, cloud, and smoke. It gathered like a murky halo in the sky above the outlying areas.

A tumultuous hubbub rose from the square. I, the princess of the city, stood at the top of the castle, and it was my duty to speak to the people waiting in the square. I had to say that I loved them, that I forgave them, but that I had been seriously ill for a long time. I could not speak. I was still ill. The poet Saul, whom I had appointed Chamberlain, came and stood at my right hand. He spoke to the people, using soothing words in a language I could not understand. The crowd cheered him. Suddenly I seemed to hear beyond the cheers a vague, angry murmur. The poet uttered four rhyming words, a slogan or catch phrase in another language, and the crowd burst into infectious laughter. A woman started shouting. A child climbed a column and grimaced. A man in a cloak shot out a venomous phrase. The loud cheering swept everything else away. Then the poet slipped a warm coat round my shoulders. I touched his fine, silvery hair with my fingertips. The gesture caused a fervid commotion in the crowd, a swelling din which turned to tumult. An outpouring of love or of rage.

An airplane flew over the city. I ordered it to flash green and red. For an instant it seemed as if the plane were flying among the stars and trailing the weaker ones along behind it. Then an army unit thronged through Zion Square. The men were singing a spirited anthem in honor of the princess. I was borne through the streets in a carriage drawn by four gray horses. With a weary hand I scattered kisses to my people. My subjects thronged in their thousands into Geula Street, in Mahane Yehuda, in Ussishkin Street and Keren Kayemet Street. Every hand held a flag or a flower. It was a procession. I leaned on the arms of my two bodyguards. They were self-restrained, dark, and graceful. I was tired. My subjects threw chrysanthemum wreaths. Chrysanthemums are my favorite flower. It was a feast day. By the Terra Sancta Convent Michael held out his arm and helped me down from the carriage. As usual, he was calm and collected. The princess knew that this was a decisive moment. She felt that she must be regal. A short librarian appeared, wearing a black skullcap. His movements were submissive. It was Yehezkel, Michael's father. "Your Highness." The Master of Ceremonies bowed submissively. "With Your Highness's gracious permission." Behind the submissiveness I seemed to sense a vague sneer. I have never liked old Sarah Zeldin's dry laugh. She has no right to stand there on the landing and laugh at me. I was in the basement of the library. In the half-light I could make out the forms of thin women. The thin women lay on the floor with their legs lewdly spread out, in the narrow passage between the bookcases. The floor was slimy. The thin women all looked alike, with their hair dyed and their breasts obscenely exposed. Not one of them smiled or accorded me respect. Suffering showed frozen on their faces. They were coarse. Those women who hated me touched me yet did not touch me. Their fingers were pointed and menacing. They were loose women from the docks. They mocked out loud. They belched. They were drunk. A rank smell rose from their bodies. "I am the Princess of Danzig," I tried to shout, but my voice was taken from me. I was one of those women. The thought occurred to me, "They are all princesses of Danzig." I remembered that I was due to receive an urgent deputation of citizens and merchants about privileges. I don't know what privileges are. I am tired. I am one of these hard women. Out of the fog, from the distant shipyards, came the lowing of a ship, as from a scene of slaughter. I was a prisoner in the library basement. I was handed over to a mob of repulsive women on the slimy floor. I did not forget that there was a British destroyer named *Dragon,* which knew me, which would be able to single me out from among all the others, which would come and save my life. But the sea would not return to the Free City until the new Ice Age. Until then *Dragon* was far, far way, patrolling night and day off the coast of Mozambique. No ship could reach the city, which had long been abolished. I was lost.

CHAPTER
24

My husband Michael Gonen dedicated his first article in a scientific journal to me. The title was "Processes of Erosion in the Ravines of the Wilderness of Paran." This was also the subject he had been allotted for his doctoral thesis. The dedication was printed underneath the title in italics:

To Hannah, his understanding wife, the author wishes to dedicate this work.

I read the article and congratulated Michael on it: I liked the way he avoided the use of adjectives and adverbs and concentrated instead on nouns and verbs. I also liked his avoidance of long clauses. He had expressed himself throughout in short, concise sentences. I admired his dry and factual style.

Michael seized on the word "dry." Like most people who have no interest in language and who use words in the same way that they use air or water, Michael supposed that I had used the term in an adverse sense. He was sorry, he said, that he wasn't a poet, that he couldn't dedicate a poem to me instead of a dry piece of research. Everyone does what he is capable of. "I know—what a trite sentiment."

"Michael, do you imagine that I'm not grateful to you for the dedication, or that I don't appreciate the article?"

"Well, I don't blame you. The article is intended for specialists in geology and the related subjects. Geology isn't history. It's possible to be perfectly well educated and cultured without knowing the basic rudiments of geology."

Michael's voice pained me, because I had been trying to find a way of sharing in his joy, and unintentionally I had offended him.

"Can you possibly explain to me in simple words what geomorphology is all about?"

Michael reached out thoughtfully, picked up his glasses from the table, and contemplated them with one of his secret smiles. Then he put them down again.

"Yes, I'm willing to explain it to you, provided you really want to know, and aren't asking just to please me.

"No, don't put down your knitting. I enjoy sitting opposite you talking while you knit. I like to see you relaxed. You needn't look at me; I know I have your attention. We're not interrogating each other. Geomorphology is a subject on the border between geology and geography. It deals with the processes by means of which the features on the earth's surface are formed. Most people are of the mistaken opinion that the earth was formed and created once and for all many millions of years ago. In fact, the earth's surface is perpetually coming into being. If we may employ the popular concept of 'creation,' we can say that the earth is continuously being created. Even while we are sitting here talking. Different and even opposed factors cooperate in forming and changing both the visible contours and also the underground features which we cannot perceive. Some of the factors are geological, deriving from the action of the molten nucleus at the earth's center, from its gradual, uneven cooling. Other factors are atmospheric, such as wind, floods, and contrasts of heat and cold succeeding one another in accordance with a set cyclical pattern. Certain physical factors, too, have an effect on geomorphological processes. Incidentally, this simple fact is often overlooked by scientists, perhaps because of its very simplicity; the physical factors are so obvious that even some of the most eminent experts sometimes tend to ignore them. The forces of gravity, for example, and the action of the sun. Several complicated and elaborate explanations have been suggested for phenomena which owe their origin to the simplest natural laws.

"Besides geological, atmospheric, and physical factors, one must also take into account certain concepts from the field of chemistry. Melting, for instance, and fusion. We may conclude by saying that geomorphology is the meeting point of various scientific disciplines. Incidentally, this approach was anticipated by ancient Greek mythology, which seems to ascribe the formation of the world to a perpetual conflict. This principle is accepted by modern science, which makes no attempt, however, to explain the origins of the various factors. In a sense we limit ourselves to a much narrower question than that considered by ancient mythology. Not 'why' but 'how'—that is the only question with which we are concerned. But some modern scientists are occasionally unable to resist the temptation to attempt an over-all explanation. The Soviet school, in particular, so far as one can follow their publications, sometimes makes use of concepts borrowed from the field of the humanities. There is a great temptation for any scientist to be carried away by metaphors and to succumb to the popular illusion that a metaphor can take the place of a scientific explanation. I myself conscientiously avoid using the striking phrases current in certain schools. I am referring to such vague expressions as 'attraction,' 'repulsion,' 'rhythm,' and the like. There is a very slender dividing line between a scientific description and a fairy tale. Far more slender than is usually believed. I make every effort to avoid crossing this line. Perhaps that is why my article creates a rather dry impression."

"Michael," I said, "I ought to try to clear up a misunderstanding. When I used the word 'dry' I was using it as a term of praise."

"It makes me very happy to hear you say so, although I find it hard to believe that we both mean the same thing by the word 'dry.' We are two such very different people. If you can spare me a few hours someday, I shall be happy to show you around my laboratory, and you can attend one of my lectures. then I'll be able to explain everything rather more simply, and perhaps a little less drily."

"Tomorrow," I said. And as I said the word I tried to select one of my prettiest smiles.

"I shall be delighted," said Michael.

Next morning we sent Yair off to the kindergarten with a note of apology to Sarah Zeldin: for urgent personal reasons I had to take a day off from work.

Michael and I traveled on two buses to the geological laboratories. When we arrived, Michael asked the charwoman to make two cups of coffee and bring them up to his room.

"Two cups instead of one today," he said cheerfully, and hastily added: "Matilda, this is Mrs. Gonen. My wife."

Then we went up to Michael's office on the third floor. This was a tiny cubicle at the lighted end of a long corridor, separated from it by a plywood partition. In this cubicle stood a desk which had made its way there from some office of the British administration; a pair of rush chairs; and an empty bookcase adorned with a large shellcase that served as a vase. Under the glass top of the desk was a picture of me on our wedding day, Yair in carnival costume, and a couple of white kittens cut out of a color magazine.

Michael sat down with his back to the window, stretched out his legs, rested his elbows on the desk in front of him, and attempted to adopt an official-looking pose. "Take a seat, please, Madam," he said. "What can I do for you?"

At that moment the door opened, and Matilda came in carrying a tray with two cups of coffee. She might have caught Michael's last words. In his embarrassment my husband repeated:

"Matilda, this is Mrs. Gonen. My wife."

Matilda left the room. Michael asked me to excuse him while he devoted a few minutes to his papers. I sipped my coffee and looked at him, because I guessed that he wanted me to. He noticed me looking at him, and beamed with quiet satisfaction. How little we need to do to make someone else happy.

After a few moments Michael stood up. I stood too. He apologized for the slight delay. "I just had to put my papers in order, as they say. Let's go down to the lab now. I hope you'll find it interesting. I'll be glad to answer any questions you may have to ask."

My husband was clear and polite as he showed me around the geological laboratories. I asked him questions so as to give him the chance to explain. He repeatedly inquired whether I was tired or bored. This time I was very careful in my choice of words.

"No, Michael," I said, "I'm not tired or bored. I want to see lots more. I enjoy listening to your explanation. You have a flair for explaining complicated things in a very clear and precise way. I find everything you are saying utterly new and fascinating."

When I said this, Michael took my hand between his own and held it there for a moment, just as he had done once when we came out of Cafe Atara into the rainy street.

Like many students of the humanities, I had always imagined that every academic subject is a system of relating words and ideas. I now discovered that Michael and his colleagues did not deal with words alone but also searched for buried treasures in the bosom of the earth: water, oil, salts, minerals, raw materials for construction and industry, and even precious stones for women's jewelry.

As we left the laboratory I said:

"I wish I could convince you that when I used the word 'dry' at home I was using it in a favorable sense. If you invite me to come and hear you lecture, I'll sit at the back of the room and be very proud."

That was not enough. I longed to go home with him so that I could stroke and stroke his hair. I racked my brain for some glowing compliment which would bring the reticent glimmer, the beam of satisfaction, back into his eyes.

I found an empty seat in the last row but one. My husband stood leaning with his elbows on the lectern. His body was lean. His pose was relaxed. From time to time he turned and indicated with a pointer one of the diagrams he had drawn on the blackboard before the lecture. The lines which he had chalked on the board were precise and delicate. I thought of his body under his clothes. The first-year students sat hunched over their notebooks. Once a student raised his hand and asked a question. Michael gazed at the student for a moment as if trying to gauge his reason for making the question before he would answer it. And when he did answer, he spoke as if the point which the student had raised was the most crucial one of all. He was quiet and self-restrained. Even when he paused slightly between his sentences he seemed to me to be not so much at a loss as choosing his words carefully out of some inner sense of responsibility. I suddenly recalled the old geology lecturer in Terra Sancta that February five years before. He too had used a pointer to indicate the significant features of the educational film. His voice had been slow and resonant. My husband also had a pleasant voice. Early in the morning while he stood in the bathroom shaving, when he thought I was still asleep, he would hum to himself under his breath. Now, lecturing to his students, Michael would select one word in each sentence and dwell on it with a soft emphasis as if he were dropping a gentle hint for only the most intelligent of his pupils. The features, arm, and pointer of the old lecturer at Terra Sancta had reminded me, by the light of the magic lantern, of the woodcuts in the books I had loved as a child, *Moby Dick* or the stories of Jules Verne. I do not know how to forget. Where will I be, what will I be, on the day when Michael catches up with the shadow of the old lecturer from Terra Sancta?

After the lecture we had lunch together in the University canteen.

"I'd like you to meet my wife," Michael said proudly to some of his acquaintances who happened to be passing. My husband was like a schoolboy introducing his famous father to his headmaster.

We had coffee. Michael ordered me a Turkish coffee. He himself preferred coffee light.

Afterwards Michael lit his pipe. "I can't believe for a moment," he said, "that you found anything interesting in my lecture. *I* felt quite excited, though, even though none of the students was aware of my wife's presence. I felt so excited, in fact, that twice I nearly lost the thread of what I was saying, because I was thinking of you and looking at you. I only regretted that I wasn't lecturing on a literary subject. I should very much have liked to have kept your interest, instead of boring you with such a dry topic."

Michael had just begun writing his doctoral thesis. He looked forward, he said, to the day when his old father could address his weekly letter to "Dr. and Mrs. M. Gonen." Of course, this was a simple sentiment, but surely everyone cherishes some simple sentiments. On the other hand, could one hurry a doctoral thesis? He had to deal with a very complicated subject.

As my husband said the words "complicated subject" a sudden spasm passed across his face, and for an instant I could see just how the tiny lines which had recently appeared around the corners of his mouth would spread in the future.

CHAPTER

25

 In the summer of 1955 we took our son for a week's holiday to Holon, to relax and swim in the sea.

Next to us in the coach sat a frightening man, a war victim perhaps, or a refugee from Europe. His face was battered and one of his eye sockets was empty. His most terrifying feature was his mouth: he had no lips, and so his teeth were completely exposed, as if he were grinning from ear to ear or as if he were an empty skull. When our unfortunate fellow traveler looked at our son, Yair buried his face in my bosom, but every now and again, as if trying to whet his terror, he would peep out at those shattered features. The child's shoulders shook, and his face was white with fear.

The stranger thoroughly enjoyed this game. He did not turn his face away, nor did he take his single eye off our son. As if trying to draw every note of terror out of the boy, he now began to contort his face and bare his teeth until even I was horrified. Slavering, he lay in wait for each sneaking glance from the child, and tried to make a face each time Yair raised his eyes. Yair entered into the grisly game. He would sit up and stare at the stranger for a while, patiently waiting for him to make a new face; then he would burrow his shoulders in my bosom once more and tremble violently. His whole body shook. The game was played without a sound; Yair sobbed with his muscles, with his lungs, but not with his voice.

There was nothing we could do; there were no spare seats in the coach. The man and the boy would not even allow Michael to interpose his body between them, as he tried to do. They peeped and peered at each other behind his back or under his arms.

When we got off the coach at the central station in Tel Aviv, the stranger came up to us and offered Yair a dry cake. His hand was gloved, even though it was summer. Yair accepted the cake and silently slipped it into his pocket.

The man touched the child's face with his finger and said, "What a lovely child. What a sweet little boy." Yair shivered feverishly, but said not a word.

When we were on the bus to Holon the toddler pulled the dry cake out of his pocket, held it in front of him in dismay, and uttered one sentence:

"Someone who wants to die can eat this."

"You shouldn't take presents from strangers," I replied.

Yair fell silent. He started to say something, changed his mind, finally declared firmly, "That man was very bad. Not a Jew at all."

Michael felt obliged to take issue with him. "He was probably very badly wounded in the war. Perhaps he was a hero."

Yair repeated stubbornly, "Not a hero. Not a Jew at all. Bad man."

"Stop prattling, Yair," Michael cut in sharply.

The child raised the dry cake towards his mouth, and again

he trembled all over. "I going to die you," he mumbled. "I going to eat this."

I was about to reply "You shall never die," echoing a beautiful passage I had once read in Gershom Shoffman, but Michael, "before whom there is no merriment and no lightheartedness," anticipated me and pronounced a considered sentence:

"You will die when you are a hundred and twenty. Now kindly stop talking nonsense. I've finished."

Yair obeyed. For a while he kept his lips pressed firmly together. Finally he spoke hesitantly, as if he had just completed some complicated mental process:

"When we come to Grandpa Yehezkel, I not going to eat nothing there. Nothing."

We stayed at Grandpa Yehezkel's for six days. In the mornings we took our son to the beach at Bat Yam. The days were calm.

Yehezkel Gonen had left his job at the municipal water department. Since the beginning of the year he had been living on a modest pension. He did not, however, neglect his duties at the local branch of the Workers' Party. He still went to the club every evening with his bunch of keys in his pocket. He made notes in a little memo book, to send the curtains to the cleaners, to buy a bottle of fruit juice for the speaker, to collect the receipts and file them in order of date.

His mornings he spent studying the basic elements of geology on his own, by means of a correspondence course run by the Institute of Public Education, so that he could conduct a simple scientific conversation with his son. "I find I have free time now in abundance," he said. "A man should never say, 'I have grown too old to derive profit from study.'"

"Please treat this apartment precisely as if it were your own," he said to us. "Ignore my existence. To be forever thinking of me would ruin your holiday. If you wish to rearrange the furniture or leave your beds unmade, you are on no account to feel constrained by considerations of politeness. I want you to have a complete rest.

"You both seem very young to me, my dears; so young that were I not so delighted to see you I should be plunged in self-pity."

Yehezkel repeated this last sentence on several occasions. There was a certain ponderous formality in everything he said, either because he tended to enunciate his words as though he were addressing a small gathering or else because he was inclined to use expressions which are normally employed only on solemn occasions. I was reminded of the remark Michael had made during our conversation in Cafe Atara, that his father used Hebrew phrases in the way that people handle fragile pieces of china. I now realized that Michael had succeeded, quite by chance, in making a very accurate observation.

From the first day a close friendship grew up between grandfather and grandson. They would both get up at six in the morning, taking care not to wake Michael and me, dress and eat a light breakfast, and then go out together to stroll in the deserted streets. Yehezkel took pleasure in initiating his grandson into the mysteries of the municipal services: the ramifications of the electricity lines from the central transformer, the circuit of the water supply, the headquarters of the fire brigade, and the alarms and hydrants disposed at various points around the town, the sanitation department's garbage disposal arrangements, and the network of bus routes. It was a whole new world, with a fascinating logic of its own.

Another amusing novelty was the name Grandpa called the child.

"Your parents may call you Yair, but I shall call you Zalman, for Zalman is your real name."

The child did not reject the new name, but in accordance with a code of fair play known only to himself, he began calling the old man by the very same name, Zalman. At half past eight they would return from their walk, and Yair would announce:

"Zalman and Zalman have come back."

I laughed till my eyes filled. Even Michael could not suppress his smiles.

When Michael and I got up we would find breakfast ready for us on the kitchen table—salad, coffee, and white bread already sliced and buttered.

"Zalman prepared your breakfast with his own hands, clever boy that he is," Yehezkel would declare proudly. Then, so as not to distort the facts, he would add, "I merely offered him a few words of advice."

Afterwards Yehezkel would accompany the three of us to the bus stop, warning us about the currents or about sunburn. Once he ventured to remark, "I would have joined you, but I should not wish to be a burden."

At midday, when we returned from the beach, Yehezkel would make us a vegetarian lunch: fried eggs, vegetables, toast, and fruit. Meat never appeared on his table, out of some principle which he refrained from explaining, for fear of boring us. During the meal he was at pains to entertain us with anecdotes of Michael's childhood, such as something Michael had once said to the Zionist leader Moshe Shertok, who was visiting his primary school, and how Moshe Shertok had suggested publishing Michael's remark in a children's newspaper.

At mealtimes Yehezkel would tell his grandson stories about bad Arabs and good Arabs, Jewish watchmen and armed Arab gangs, heroic Jewish children and British officers maltreating children of illegal immigrants.

Yair turned out to be an attentive and devoted pupil. He did not miss a word or forget the slightest detail. It was as if he combined Michael's thirst for knowledge with my depressing aptitude for remembering everything. The child could be tested on everything he had learned from "Grandpa Zalman": The electricity lines are linked to Reading Station; Hassan Salame's gang was firing into Holon from the hill of Tel Arish; the water supply comes from the spring at Rosh Haayin. Bevin was a bad Englishman, but Wingate was a good one.

Grandpa bought us all little presents. Five ties in a box for Michael, for me Professor Shirman's *Hebrew Poetry in Spain and Provence,* for his grandson he bought a red clockwork fire engine with a siren that really worked.

The days were calm.

Outside, on the grounds of the workers' housing project, ornamental trees were planted around neat, square lawns. Birds sang all day. The town was bright and sun-drenched. Towards evening a breeze blew in off the sea, and Yehezkel would throw the shutters and the kitchen door wide open.

"There's a refreshing wind," he would say. "The sea air is the breath of life."

At ten o'clock, when he came home from the club, the old man would lean over the bed and kiss his sleeping grandson. Then he would join us on the balcony, and we would sit together on the fraying deck-chairs. He refrained from talking to us about the Party, on the grounds that we would probably not be interested in the things which interested him. He mustn't bore us during our short holiday. He steered the conversation instead to topics which he thought would be nearer to our hearts. He spoke about Yosef Hayyim Brenner, who had been killed not far away thirty-four years previously. Brenner, in his opinion, had been a great writer and a great socialist, even though he was looked down on by the professors in Jerusalem as having been too much involved in politics and too little interested in literature for its own sake. "You mark my words," he said, "sooner or later Brenner's greatness will be recognized again even in Jerusalem."

I did not venture to contradict him.

My silence pleased Yehezkel, who took it as further evidence of my good taste. Like Michael, he considered that I was gifted with a sensitive soul. "You must excuse my indulging in sentiment when I say that you are as dear to me as a daughter."

To Michael he would talk about the natural resources of the country. "The day is not far off when oil will be discovered in our land. Of this I entertain not the slightest doubt. I still recall how skeptical the so-called experts were about the verse in Deuteronomy, 'A land whose stones are iron, and out of whose hills you may dig copper.' And now we have Mount Manara and we have Timna: iron and copper. I am quite convinced that soon we shall find oil, too. Its existence is explicitly mentioned in the Tosefta, and the ancient Rabbis were thoroughly practical and realistic men. What they wrote was based on scholarship, not mere sentiment. I believe, my son, that you are not just another unimaginative geologist; your destiny lies, I am convinced of it, among those who seek out and find new things . . .

"But now I must stop wearing you both out with all this chatter. You are supposed to be on holiday, and here am I, foolish old man that I am, jabbering on about things which are part of your work. As if there were not intellectual effort enough waiting for you back in Jerusalem. What a long-winded old nuisance I am. Why don't you both go off to bed now, and wake up in the morning bright and fresh. Good night to you both, my dears. Sleep well, and don't pay any attention to the ramblings of an old man who lives alone and rarely has the chance to talk to anyone."

The days were calm.

In the afternoon we would stroll down to the municipal gardens, where we would meet old friends and neighbors who had all prophesied a great future for Michael and who were now pleased to share in his brilliant success. They were proud to shake hands with his wife and pinch his son's cheek, and tell amusing stories about the days when Michael was a babe in arms.

Every day Michael bought me an evening paper. He also bought me color magazines. We were bronzed by the sun. A sea smell clung to our skins. The town was small, with white-washed houses.

"Holon is a new town," said Yehezkel Gonen. "It has not been restored to some ancient splendor, but sprang clean and pleasant out of the sands. And I, who remember its earliest days, take renewed pleasure in it daily—even though, of course, we haven't a fraction here of what you have in your Jerusalem."

On the last evening the four aunts came from Tel Aviv to see us. They brought presents for Yair. They hugged him roughly and delivered brisk kisses. For once, they were all pleasant; even Aunt Jenia spared us her usual complaints.

Aunt Leah was spokesman:

"On behalf of us all, I think I can say that you haven't disappointed us in our hopes for you, Micha. Hannah, you should be glowing with pride at his success. I still remember how Micha's friends made fun of him after the War of Independence for not going off with them like a numskull to some kibbutz in the Negev. Instead he sensibly chose to go to Jerusalem to study at the University, and to serve his people and his country with his brains, with his talents, and not with his muscles like a beast of burden. And now that our Michael is nearly a doctor, the same friends who made fun of him then are coming to him to ask him to help them with their first steps at the University. The best years of their lives they have wasted like imbeciles, and now they are sick and tired of their kibbutz in the Negev, while our Micha, who was so smart right from the start, is in a position to hire those old braggarts, if he wants to, to move his furniture for him from the old apartment to the new one you're bound to be getting soon."

When she said "kibbutz in the Negev" Aunt Leah screwed up her face; she pronounced the word "Negev" almost like a curse. Her last remark reduced all four aunts to gales of shrill laughter.

"You should never feel scorn for any man," old Yehezkel said.

Michael pondered for a moment, then agreed with his father, adding that in his opinion education does not alter a man's basic worth.

This comment delighted Aunt Jenia. She drew attention to the fact that Michael's success had not gone to his head or affected his modesty.

"Modesty is a very useful commodity. I have always maintained that a wife's duty is to encourage her husband on the road to success. It is only when the husband is a good-for-nothing that his wife is forced to follow the cruel path of fighting a man's fight in a man's world. Such has been my fate. I am glad that Micha has not inflicted a similar lot on his wife. And you too, my dear Hannah, you too should be glad, because in this life there is no greater satisfaction than a determined effort which achieves success, and will bring, I am sure, even greater success in the future. That has always been my creed from childhood on. All the troubles I have experienced have done nothing to weaken my faith; on the contrary, they have strengthened it."

On the morning of our return to Jerusalem Yehezkel did something I shall never forget. He climbed up on a stepladder to a high cupboard and brought down a large box, from which he extracted an old watchman's uniform, faded and crumpled. He also pulled out of the chest the old watchman's hat, the *kolpak,* which he put on his grandson's head. The hat was so big it almost came over the child's eyes. Grandpa himself put on the watchman's uniform, over the pajamas he was wearing.

All that morning, until it was time to leave, the two of them stormed round the apartment enacting battles and maneuvers. They sniped at each other with sticks from entrenched positions behind the furniture. They called out "Zalman" to each other. Yair's face was lit with frenzied joy as he discovered for the first time the delights of power, and the old private obeyed every command with steadfast devotion. Yehezkel was a happy old man on that final morning of our last visit to Holon. For a single searing moment I felt that the scene was familiar, as if I had already seen it long, long before. It was like a blurred copy of a much sharper, much clearer original. I could not remember where or when. A cold shiver ran down my spine, and I felt a strong compulsion to put something into words, to warn my son and my father-in-law perhaps against a danger of fire or electrocution. But there was no suggestion of either of these risks in their game. I felt an urge to suggest to Michael that we leave immediately, that very minute, but I could not bring myself to say this. It would have sounded foolish and rude. What was it that made me feel so uneasy? Several flights of fighters had flown low over Holon that morning. I do not think that was the reason for my feeling of unease. I do not think "reason" is an appropriate word to use in this context. The aircraft engines roared. The windowpanes rang. I felt that this was by no manner of means the first time.

Before we left, my father-in-law Yehezkel kissed me on both cheeks. As he did so, I noticed that his eyes seemed changed, as if the clouded pupils had spread to cover the whites. His face was gray, too, his cheeks drooping and furrowed, and the lips which touched my forehead were not warm. His handshake, by contrast, was amazingly warm; it was firm and almost frantic, as if the old man were trying to give me his fingers as a present. Four days after our return to Jerusalem all this came back to me with a blinding flash when, towards evening, Aunt Jenia arrived to inform us that Yehezkel had collapsed by the bus stop opposite his home.

"Last night still, only just last night poor Yehezkel came home to us to visit," she gabbled apologetically, almost as if to dispel an ugly suspicion. "Only last night he came to visit us and didn't complain of any discomfort. On the contrary. He talked to me about a new medicine for infantile paralysis which has just been discovered in America. He was . . . normal. Quite normal. And then suddenly this morning right in front of the eyes of the Globermans next door he fell on the floor by the bus stop." Suddenly she sobbed, "Micha an orphan!" As she sobbed she curled her lips like an elderly scolded child. She clasped Michael's hand to her shriveled breast, stroked his forehead, then stopped.

"Micha, how can it be that a man suddenly, just like that, for no reason, on the sidewalk, just like a bag or a parcel falls from your hands, just like that on the sidewalk, and . . . it's terrible. It's . . . it's not right. It's disgusting. As if poor Yehezkele was just a bag or a parcel, to fall like that and burst open . . . it's . . . think what it looks like, Micha . . . the shame of it . . . with the Globermans next door sitting back watching from their veranda like in a box in the opera and total strangers coming and lifting by the arms and legs out of the way not to block the traffic and then going and taking up his hat and his glasses and the books he dropped all over the road . . . And you know where he was going anyway?" Aunt Jenia raised her voice to a shrill, outraged wail. "He was only just going out to the library to return some books and he never even meant to take the bus and just by chance he fell down right at the bus stop, opposite the Globermans'. Such a gentle man, such a sweet . . . such a gentle man, and suddenly . . . just like in the circus, I tell you, like in a movie, a man is walking along peacefully in the middle of the road and suddenly someone comes up from behind and with a stick on the head they hit him and he just folds up and collapses like if a man was just a rag doll or something. I tell you, Micha, life is just a filthy heap of dung. Leave the child with the neighbors or somewhere, quick, and come back with me to Tel Aviv. Leahle is left all alone there, Leahle with her two left thumbs, to do all the arrangements. And thousands of formalities. A man passes on and with all the formalities you'd think he was going abroad at least. Bring your coats or something and let's go. I'll just go round to the drugstore in the meantime and call for a taxi, and . . . yes, Micha, please, a dark suit or at least a jacket, and hurry up, both of you, please. Micha what a disaster oh what a terrible disaster Micha."

· · ·

Aunt Jenia left. I could hear her anxious footsteps on the stairs and on the stone-paved yard below. I remained standing just as I was when she walked in, leaning on the ironing board and holding a hot iron. Michael spun around and dashed to the balcony as if he meant to call after her "Auntie Jenia, Auntie Jenia."

A moment later he came in again. He closed the shutters, silently shut the windows, and then went out to lock the kitchen door. As he came along the passage he uttered a low sound. Perhaps he had suddenly caught sight of his face in the mirror by the coatstand. He opened the closet, took out his dark suit, and transferred the trouser belt. "My father has passed on," he said softly, not looking at me. As if I had not been there while his aunt was talking.

I put the iron down on the floor of the closet, put the ironing board away in the bathroom, and went to Yair's room. I stopped him playing, wrote out a note, and sent him with it to the Kamnitzers. "Grandpa Yehezkel is very ill," I told him before he left. A twisted echo of my words came back to me from the stairs, as Yair excitedly proclaimed to all the children in the house: "My Grandpa Zalman is very ill and my parents are going to make him get better soon."

Michael put his wallet in his inside pocket and buttoned up the jacket of the dark suit which had once belonged to my late father, and which my mother had altered to fit him. Twice he buttoned it up wrongly. He put on his hat. By mistake he picked up his battered black briefcase, then put it back with an irritated gesture.

"I'm ready to go," he said. "Perhaps some of the things she said were rather uncalled for, but she's quite right. It shouldn't have happened like that. It's not right. To take an honest, up-right old man, not very strong and his health none too good, and suddenly throw him down on the sidewalk in the middle of town in broad daylight, like a dangerous criminal. It's indecent, I tell you, Hannah, it's cruel, it's . . . cruel. Indecent."

As Michael said the words "cruel, indecent," his whole body began to shake. Like a child waking up in the night in winter and finding, instead of his mother, a strange face peering at him out of the dark.

CHAPTER
26

Michael abstained from shaving during the week following the funeral. I do not think he did this out of respect for religious tradition, or even in deference to his father's wishes (Yehezkel had used to describe himself as a practicing atheist). He may have felt that it would have been degrading to shave during his week of mourning. When we are hemmed in by grief we sometimes find trivial things bitterly degrading. Michael had always hated shaving. Dark bristles covered his jaws and gave him a furious expression.

With his bristles Michael seemed to me like a new man. At times I had the feeling that his body was stronger than it really was. His neck had grown lean. There were wrinkles around his mouth which suggested a cold irony which was not in Michael. There was a tired look in his eyes as if he had been worn out by hard manual labor. My husband in his days of mourning had the look of a grimy laborer from one of the little workshops in Agrippa Street.

Most of the day Michael would sit in an armchair wearing warmly lined slippers and a light gray dressing gown with dark gray checks. When I put the daily paper in his lap he bent over to read it. If the paper fell on the floor he did not trouble to pick it up. I could not tell whether he was pensive or vacant. Once he asked me to pour him a glass of brandy. I did as he asked, but he seemed to have forgotten. He stared at me in surprise and did not touch the drink. And once, after listening to the news, he remarked: "How strange." He said no more. I did not ask. The electric light shone yellow.

Michael was very quiet in the days following his father's death. Our house was quiet, too. At times it seemed as if we were all sitting waiting for a message. If Michael said anything to me or to his son, he spoke softly, as if it were I who was in mourning. At night I wanted him very much. The feeling was painful. All the years we had been married I had never felt how degrading this dependence could be.

One evening my husband put on his glasses and stood leaning over with his hands on his desk. His head was bent, his back drooping. I came into the study and saw Yehezkel Gonen in my husband. I shuddered. With his bent head, his sloping shoulders, his unsteady bearing, Michael seemed to be acting his father. I recalled our wedding day, the ceremony on the roof terrace of the old Rabbinate building opposite Steimatsky's bookshop. Then, too, Michael had looked so much like his father that I had mistaken each for the other. I have not forgotten.

Michael spent his mornings sitting on the balcony, following with his gaze the antics of the cats in the yard below. There was calm. I had never seen Michael in a state of calm before. He had always been rushing to catch up with his work. Pious neighbors came in to express their sympathy. Michael received them with cold politeness. He eyed the Kamnitzer family and Mr. Glick through his glasses like a stern schoolteacher staring at a pupil who has let him down, until their condolences stuck in their throats.

Mrs. Zeldin came in hesitantly. She had come to suggest that Yair should stay with her until the period of mourning was over. A grim smile played round Michael's mouth.

"Why?" he said. "It is not I who have passed on."

"Heaven forbid, perish the thought," said his visitor, startled. "I only thought, perhaps . . ."

"Perhaps what?" Michael cut in sternly.

The old schoolmistress was taken aback. She hurriedly took her leave. As she went out, she apologized as if she had offended us.

Mr. Kadishman arrived, wearing a black serge suit, a solemn expression on his face. He announced that he had enjoyed a slight acquaintance with the deceased through Miss Leah Ganz. Despite a certain difference in their political outlooks, he had always held the deceased in the deepest respect. The deceased had been one of the few honest men in the Labor Movement. Not one of the hypocrites, but one of the misguided. "He is not lost, but gone before," he added.

"He is certainly not lost," Michael agreed coldly. I suppressed a smile.

The husband of Michael's friend from Tirat Yaar appeared at the door. He declined to enter, out of a natural delicacy of feeling. He wished to convey his sympathy. He asked me to tell Michael he had called. On Liora's behalf as well, of course.

On the fourth evening we had a visit from the professor of geology and two assistant lecturers. They sat on the sofa in the living room, facing Michael's armchair. They sat with stiff backs and with their knees together, considering it improper to lean back. I sat on a stool by the door. Michael asked me to make coffee for our three guests and a glass of tea for him, without lemon because of his heartburn. He inquired about a survey of Nahal Arugot in the Negev. When one of the young men started to speak, he turned his face to the window with a sudden, violent spasm, as if a spring in him had broken. His shoulders shook. I was alarmed, because I had a feeling that he was convulsed with laughter which he was unable to suppress. Then he turned his head back again. His face was tired and expressionless. He apologized, and demanded that they resume what they had been saying. "Please don't leave anything out; I want to hear everything." The young man who had been speaking took up his remarks precisely where he had left off. Michael shot me a gray look, as if he were amazed by some detail in my appearance he had never noticed before. A night breeze banged the shutter against the wall of the house. It seemed as if time were taking on visible features. The electric light. The pictures. The furniture. The shadows cast by the furniture. The trembling line between the light patches and the shadows.

The professor suddenly came to life and interrupted his assistant's remarks:

"The outline you drew up for us at the beginning of the month has not proved disappointing, Gonen. The facts agree with your hypothesis. Hence our mixed feelings: we are disappointed at the results of the drilling, but at the same time impressed by your thoroughness."

Then he added an involved observation about the thanklessness of practical as against theoretical research. He stressed the importance of creative intuition for both kinds of research.

Michael observed drily:

"Winter will soon be upon us. The nights are growing longer. Longer and colder."

The two assistants looked at each other, then glanced sideways at the professor. The old man nodded energetically to show that he had grasped their hint. He stood up and said solemnly:

"We all share your grief, Gonen, and we all look forward to your return. Try to be strong, and . . . be strong, Gonen."

The visitors took their leave. Michael accompanied them out into the vestibule. As he hurried forward to help the professor on with his heavy overcoat, he moved somehow clumsily, and was compelled to apologize with a faint smile. From the beginning of the evening up to that moment I had found him impressive, and so his faint smile pained me. His politeness sprang from deference, not from sympathy. He followed his visitors as far as the door. When they had gone he went back into the study. He was silent. His face was towards the dark window and his back towards me. On the fringe of the silence his voice spoke; he did not turn his shoulders. He said:

"Another glass of tea, please, Hannah, and would you mind turning off the main light? When Father asked us to give the child a rather old-fashioned name we ought to have deferred to his wishes. When I was ten I had a very bad fever. All night, night after night, Father sat up by my bedside. He kept putting fresh damp cloths on my forehead, and singing over and over again the only lullaby he knew. He sang out of tune and flat. The song went like this: *Time to sleep, the day is done, In the sea has set the sun. Stars are shining in the sky, Lulla, lulla, lullaby.*

"Have I ever told you, Hannah, that Aunt Jenia used to try by every means she could to find a second wife for Father? She rarely came to visit us without bringing some friend or acquaintance with her. Aging nurses, Polish immigrants, skinny divorcees. The women would begin by advancing on me, with hugs and kisses, boxes of sweets and cooing noises. Father used to pretend not to understand Aunt Jenia's intention. He was polite. He would start talking about the High Commissioner's latest edicts, and such like.

"When I had the fever I had a very high temperature, and the perspiration poured out of me all night long. The bedclothes were soaked. Every two hours Father carefully changed the sheets. He took care not to move me roughly, but he always overdid the caution. I would wake up and cry. Before dawn Father would wash all the sheets in the bath, and then go out in the dark and hang them out to dry on the washline outside our building. The reason I didn't want lemon in my tea was that the heartburn is very bad, Hannah. When the fever abated Father went out and bought me a checkers set at a discount from our next-door neighbor Globerman's shop. He tried to lose every game we played. To make me happy he would groan and hold his head in his hands, and call me 'little genius, little professor, little Grandpa Zalman.' Once he told me the story of the Mendelssohn family, and jokingly compared himself to the middle Mendelssohn, who was the son of one great Mendelssohn and the father of another. He prophesied a great future for me. He made me cup after cup of warm milk and honey, without the skin. If I was stubborn and refused to drink, he resorted to temptations and bribes. He would flatter my common sense. That was how I recovered. If you wouldn't mind, Hannah, could you bring me my pipe? No, not that one, the English one. The smallest one. Yes, that's it. Thank you. I recovered, and Father caught the fever from me and was very ill. He lay for three weeks in the hospital where Aunt Jenia worked. Aunt Leah volunteered to look after me while he was ill. After two months they told me that he had only escaped death by good luck or a miracle. Father himself joked about it a lot. He quoted a proverb which says that great men die young, and he said that fortunately for him he was only a very ordinary man. I swore before the picture of Herzl in the living room that if Father died suddenly I would find some way of dying too, instead of going to an orphanage or to Aunt Leah. Next week, Hannah, we'll buy Yair an electric train. A big one. Like the one he saw in the window of Freimann and Bein's shoestore in Jaffa Road. Yair is very fond of mechanical things. I'll give him the alarm clock which doesn't work. I'll teach him to take it to pieces and put it together again. Maybe Yair will grow up to be an engineer. Have you noticed how the boy is fascinated by motors and springs and machines? Have you ever heard of a child of four and a half who can understand a general explanation of how a radio works? I've never thought of myself as outstandingly brilliant. You know that. I'm not a genius or whatever my father supposed or said he supposed. I'm nothing special, Hannah, but you must try as hard as you can to love Yair. It will be better for you, too, if you do . . . No, I'm not suggesting that you neglect the child. Nonsense. But I have the feeling that you're not wild about him. One's got to be wild, Hannah. Sometimes one even has to lose all sense of proportion. What I'm trying to say is, I'd like you to start . . . I don't know quite how to explain this sort of sentiment. Let's forget it. Once, years ago, you and I were sitting in some cafe, and I looked at you and I looked at myself and I said to myself, I'm not cut out to be a dream-prince or a knight on horseback, as they say. You're pretty, Hannah. You're very pretty. Did I tell you what Father said to me last week in Holon? He said that you seemed to him to be a poetess even though you don't write poems. Look, Hannah, I don't know why I'm telling you all this now. You're not saying anything. One of us is always listening and not saying anything. Why did I tell you all that just now? Certainly not to

162

offend you or hurt you. Look, we shouldn't have insisted on the name Yair. After all, the name wouldn't have affected our regard for the child. And we trampled on a very delicate sentiment. One day, Hannah, I'll have to ask you why you chose me out of all the interesting men you must have met. But now it's late and I'm talking too much and probably surprising you. Will you start getting the beds ready, Hannah? I'll come and help you in a moment. Let's go to sleep, Hannah. Father is dead. I'm a father myself. All this . . . all these arrangements suddenly seem like some idiotic children's game. I remember we used to play once, at the edge of our housing project, on an empty site near where the sands began: we stood in a long line and the first one threw the ball and ran to the end of the line until the first became the last and the last became the first, over and over again. I can't remember what the point of the game was. I can't remember how you won the game. I can't even remember if there were any rules or if there was any method in the madness. You've left the light on in the kitchen."

CHAPTER
27

The days of mourning ended.
Once again my husband and I sat facing each other at breakfast time across the kitchen table, so silent and good-natured
that a stranger might have mistakenly supposed that we were
at peace. I hold out the coffee-pot. Michael passes me two cups.
I pour out the coffee. Michael slices the bread. I put sugar in
the two cups of coffee and stir and stir, until his voice stops me:

"That's enough, Hannah. It's stirred. You're not drilling a
well."

I drink my coffee black. Michael prefers a little milk in his.
I count out four, five, six drops of milk into his cup.

This is how we sit: I rest my back against the side of the
refrigerator and face the bright blue rectangle which is the
kitchen window. Michael's back is towards the window and
his eyes can take in the empty bottles on top of the refrigerator,
the kitchen door, part of the vestibule, and the bathroom doorway.

Then the radio surrounds us with light morning music,
Hebrew songs which remind me of my childhood and remind

Michael that it is getting late. He gets up without a word, stands at the sink, and washes his cup and plate. He goes out of the kitchen. In the vestibule he takes off his slippers and puts on his shoes. Puts on a gray jacket. Takes his hat down from the peg. With his hat on his head and his old black briefcase under his arm he comes back into the kitchen to kiss me on the forehead and say good-bye. I mustn't forget to buy some paraffin at lunchtime: we've almost run out. He himself makes a note in his memo book to call in at the Water Department to pay the water bill and query a possible error.

Michael leaves the house and the tears clutch in my throat. I ask myself where this sadness comes from. From what accursed lair it has come creeping in to spoil my calm blue morning. Like a filing clerk in an office I sort out a heap of crumbling memories. Check every figure in a long column. There is a serious mistake lurking somewhere. Is. it an illusion? Somewhere I thought I spotted a bad mistake. The radio has stopped singing. It suddenly starts talking about outbreaks of unrest in the villages. I start: eight o'clock. Time never rests and never lets one rest. I snatch up my handbag. Unnecessarily hurry Yair, who is ready before me. Hand in hand we walk to Sarah Zeldin's kindergarten.

In the streets of Jerusalem it is a brilliant morning. Bright voices. An old wagon-driver sprawls on his box and sings at the top of his voice. The boys of the Tachkemoni Orthodox School wear berets pulled down on one side. They stand along the sidewalk opposite, making fun of the old driver and provoking him. The driver waves his hand as if returning a greeting, smiles, and carries on singing at the top of his voice. My son starts to explain to me that on the 3B bus route there are two makes of bus, Ford and Fargo. The Ford has a much more powerful engine, the Fargo is weak and sluggish. Suddenly the boy suspects that I have stopped listening to his explanation. He tests me. I am ready for him. I heard every word, Yair. You're a very clever boy. I'm listening.

A clear blue morning reigns in Jerusalem. Even the gray stone walls of Schneller Barracks try hard not to look heavy. And in the plots of wasteland, strong, vigorous vegetation: brambles, convolvulus, squirting cucumber, and a host of other wild plants whose names I do not know and which are generally termed weeds. Suddenly I stop dead with a cold shock:

"Did I lock the kitchen door before we left the house, Yair?"

"Daddy locked the door last night. And today nobody's opened it. What's the matter with you today, Mummy?"

We walk past the heavy iron gates of Schneller Barracks. I have never set foot inside these grim walls. When I was a child the British army was here, and machine guns protruded from the loopholes. Many years ago this fortress was called the Syrian Orphanage, a strange name which threatens me in its own way.

A fair-haired sentry stands before the gates, breathing on his fingers to warm them. As we pass, the young soldier looks down at my legs, at the gap between my skirt and my short white socks. I choose to smile at him. He shoots me a feverish glance, a mixture of shame, desire, longing, and apology. I look at my watch: a quarter past eight. Quarter past eight in the morning, a clear blue day, and already I am tired. I want to sleep. But only on condition that the dreams leave me alone.

Every Tuesday Michael stops in town on his way home from the University to book seats at Kahana's Agency for the second showing at the cinema. While we are out, Yoram, the son of the Kamnitzers upstairs, keeps an eye on the child. Once, when we got back from the cinema, I found a piece of paper in the novel which lay on my bedside table. Yoram had left his latest poem for me to pronounce judgment on it. Yoram's poem described a boy and a girl walking in an orchard at dusk. Suddenly a strange horseman rides past, a black horseman on a black stallion holding a lance of black fire. As he gallops past, a dark veil spreads over the land and over the lovers. In brackets, at the bottom of the page, Yoram explained that the black horseman was Night. Yoram did not trust me.

Next day, when I met Yoram Kamnitzer on the stairs, I told him that I liked his poem and that perhaps he ought to send it to one of the youth magazines. Yoram gripped the bannister tightly. One moment he threw me a panic-stricken glance, and the next he let out a faint, anguished laugh.

"It's all a lie, Mrs. Gonen," he mumbled.

"*Now* you're lying," I smiled.

He turned and bolted up the stairs. Suddenly he stopped, looked back, and muttered a frightened apology, as if he had pushed past me on his way up.

Sabbath Eve. Evening in Jerusalem. At the top of Romema Hill the tall water tower is caught in the flow of sunset. Needles of light filter through the leaves of the trees as if the city is on fire. A low mist spreads slowly eastward, glides palefingered over stone walls and iron railings. It has been sent to appease. There is silent dissolution all around. A seething yearning settles unseen on the city. Huge rocks release their heat and surrender to the cold fingers of the mist. A light breeze blows through the courtyards. It rustles scraps of paper, then abandons them, finding no pleasure in them. Neighbors in Sabbath clothes on their way to their prayers. The caress of a distant motor falls purple on the whispering pines. Stop, driver, stop a moment. Turn your head and let me see your face.

On our table a white tablecloth. A bunch of yellow marigolds in a vase. A bottle of red wine. Michael slices the Sabbath loaf. Yair sings three Sabbath songs he has learned in kindergarten. I serve baked fish. We do not light Sabbath candles, because Michael would consider it hypocritical in people who choose not to follow the ways of religion.

Michael tells Yair a story about the 1936 riots. Yair's pose suggests rapt attention. I, too, hear my husband's voice. There is a pretty little girl, too, in a blue coat and the girl is trying to call to me through the closed window, which is why she is beating on the pane with feeble fists. Her face is full of apprehension. She is not very far from despair. Her lips are saying something and repeating it and I cannot hear and she has stopped talking and while her face still and already the glass. My late father used to pronounce the blessing over wine and bread every Sabbath Eve. We always had Sabbath candles, too. My father did not know what truth there was in the ways of religion. Hence he kept them. It was only when my brother Emanuel joined a socialist youth movement that all the Sabbath observances were abandoned. Our respect for tradition was very frail. Father was an irresolute man.

At the foot of the slope in the German Colony in the south of Jerusalem a weary train is climbing. The engine howls and pants. It collapses into the arms of the deserted platforms. The last puff of steam escapes with a helpless wheeze. One last time the engine bellows against the silence. But the silence is too strong. The engine surrenders, succumbs, grows cold. Sabbath Eve. A vague expectancy. Even the birds are silent. His feet are standing perhaps in the gates of Jerusalem. In the orchards of Siloam or beyond the Hill of Evil Counsel. The city darkens.

"*Shabbat Shalom*. Good Sabbath," I say distantly.

My son and husband laugh. What Michael says is:

"How festive you are tonight, Hannah. And how well your new green dress suits you."

At the beginning of September our hysterical upstairs neighbor, Mrs. Glick, was removed to an institution. Her attacks had grown more and more frequent. In between the attacks she used to wander outside in the yard and in the street with a blank expression on her face. She was a full-bodied woman endowed with that ripe, wanton beauty which sometimes appears in childless women in their late thirties. Her clothes were always carelessly unbuttoned, as if she had just got out of bed. One day she attacked Yoram, that gentle youth, in the backyard, slapped his face, ripped his shirt open, and called him lecher, voyeur, peeping Tom.

One Sabbath Eve at the beginning of September Mrs. Glick snatched up the two candlesticks with the Sabbath lights burning in them and threw them in her husband's face. Mr. Glick took refuge in our apartment. He collapsed into an armchair, his shoulders heaving. Michael put down his pipe, switched off the radio, and went out to the drugstore to telephone the authorities. An hour later the white-coated attendants arrived. They took hold of the patient from either side and gently propelled her towards the ambulance. She went downstairs as if in the arms of her lovers, humming a cheerful Yiddish song all the while. The other tenants stood silently watching from the doors of their apartments. Yoram Kamnitzer came down and stood by my side. "Mrs. Gonen, Mrs. Gonen," he whispered, and his face was deathly white. I reached out for his arm, but stopped halfway and withdrew my hand.

"It's Sabbath today, it's Sabbath today," Mrs. Glick shrieked as she reached the ambulance. Her husband stood in front of her and said in a broken voice:

"Don't worry, Duba, it's nothing, it'll pass, it's just a mood, Duba, everything's going to be all right."

Mr. Glick was wearing a crumpled Sabbath suit on his small body. His thin mustache quivered as if it had a life of its own.

Before the ambulance moved off, Mr. Glick was asked to sign a declaration. It was a tedious, detailed form. By the headlights of the ambulance Michael read out item after item. He even signed in two places for Mr. Glick to keep him from having to desecrate the Sabbath. Then Michael supported him until the street was empty and brought him into our apartment for a cup of coffee.

This may explain how Mr. Glick came to be a regular visitor at our apartment.

"I understand from our neighbors, Dr. Gonen, that you collect stamps. By a fortunate coincidence I have a whole box upstairs full of stamps which I do not need and I should be delighted to make you a present of them . . . I beg your pardon, you are not a doctor? What of it? All Israel is equal in the sight of the Almighty, except for those whom He views with disfavor. Doctor, corporal, artist—we all have a great deal in common, and the differences are negligible. To return to the point: My poor wife Duba has a brother and a sister, one in Antwerp and the other in Johannesburg, and they send many letters and stick pretty stamps on them. God has not seen fit to favor me with children, and so the stamps are of no use to me. I should be happy to make you a free gift of them, Dr. Gonen. In return, I should like to beg you very humbly to permit me to visit your apartment from time to time so that I may read the *Encyclopaedia Hebraica.* Let me explain. I am at present in quest of knowledge, and I have formed the intention of reading through the *Encyclopaedia Hebraica.* Not at a single sitting, of course. A few pages at a time. For my part, I give you my word that I shall not bother you or cause any disturbance, and that I shall not bring mud into the house. I shall wipe my feet thoroughly when I come in."

Thus our neighbor became a frequent visitor in our apartment. In addition to the stamps, he gave Michael the weekend supplements of the Orthodox daily *Hatsofeh,* because they contained a scientific column. From that time on, I enjoyed a special discount at Glick's Haberdashery in David Yelin Street. Zip-fasteners, curtain hooks, buttons, buckles, and embroidery thread, all these Mr. Glick would give me as a gift. And I was unable to refuse his presents.

"All these years I have piously observed the commandments of our faith. And the fact is that now, since my poor wife Duba's calamity, I have been assailed by doubts. Serious doubts. I intend to broaden my knowledge, and to study the encyclopedia. I have already reached the article 'Atlas,' and I have discovered that in addition to denoting a book of maps, Atlas is also the name of a Greek giant who supports the whole world on his shoulders. I have made a great number of new discoveries recently, and whom do I have to thank? Why, whom else but the munificent Gonen family who have been so kind to me. I should like to repay kindness with kindness, and I do not know how else I can express my gratitude if you will not consent to accept this giant-size Animal Lotto which I have bought for your son Yair."

We consented to accept it.

. . .

These were the friends who were in the habit of visiting us:

My best friend Hadassah and her husband, whose name was Abba. Abba was an up-and-coming civil servant in the Ministry of Trade and Industry. Hadassah worked as a telephone operator in the same ministry. They intended to save up enough money to buy an apartment in Rehavia, and only then to bring a child into the world. From them Michael heard snippets of political information which were not published in the newspapers. Hadassah and I exchanged memories of our schooldays and the period of the British Mandate.

Polite assistant lecturers from the Geology Department would come and joke for a while with Michael about how impossible it was to get on in the University unless one of the old men died. There ought to be rules established to ensure fair opportunities for junior academics.

From time to time we had a visit from Liora from Kibbutz Tirat Yaar, either alone or with her husband and daughters. They had come up to Jerusalem to shop or lick an ice cream, and looked in to see if we were still alive. What pretty curtains, what a sparkling kitchen. Could they just peep into the bathroom? They were going to build a new housing project on their kibbutz, and they would like to get an idea and make comparisons. On behalf of the cultural committee they invited Michael to give a Friday evening lecture about the geological structure of the Judean Hills. They admired the life of the scholar. "Academic life is so free from tedious routine," Liora said. "I still remember Michael in the old days in the youth movement. He was an earnest, responsible fellow. Now it won't be long before he's the pride of our class. When he comes to Tirat Yaar to lecture," she added, "you must all come. It was a general invitation. What a lot of memories we have in common."

. . .

Every ten days Mr. Avraham Kadishman came. He was from
a long-established Jerusalem family, owned a well-known shoe
firm, and was an old friend of Aunt Leah's. It was he who had
investigated my family before our marriage and informed the
aunts before they first met me that I came from a good family.

When he arrived at our house he would take off his overcoat
in the hall and smile at Michael as if he brought the breath of
the great world into our home and as if we had been sitting
waiting for this visit ever since the last one. His favorite bever-
age was cocoa. His conversations with Michael centered on the
government. Mr. Kadishman was an active member of the
Jerusalem branch of the right-wing National Party. There was
a perpetually recurrent argument between him and Michael:
the assassinated socialist leader Arlozoroff, the factions in the
anti-British underground movements, the sinking by the government of the *Altalena*. I do not know what it was that
Michael found in Mr. Kadishman's company. Perhaps it was a
common addiction to pipe-smoking, or to chess, or an unwil-
lingness on Michael's part to abandon a desperately lonely old
man. Mr. Kadishman used to compose little rhymes about our
son Yair, such as:

> *Master Yair Gonen*
> *Will be a leader of men.*
> *May he live for many years*
> *And quell his nation's fears.*

or:

> *Our fine Yair is now quite small;*
> *One day he'll free the Wailing Wall.*

173

I made tea, coffee, and cocoa. Pushed the trolley from the kitchen into the living room. The living room was hazy with tobacco smoke. Mr. Glick, my husband, and Mr. Kadishman sat round the table like children at a birthday party. Mr. Glick looked at me out of the corner of his eye and then blinked quickly, as if he suspected I was about to hurl some insult at him. The other two were bent over the chessboard. I cut a cake into slices, and put a slice on each plate. The visitors praise the housewife. On my face is a polite smile that I do not share in. The conversation goes something like this:

"Once upon a time people used to say, 'When the British leave, the Messiah will come,' " Mr. Glick begins hesitantly. "Well, the British have left and still Redemption tarries."

Mr. Kadishman:

"That is because the country is led by little men. Your Alterman says somewhere that Don Quixote fights bravely but it is always Sancho who wins."

My husband:

"There's no point in reducing everything to heroes and villains. There are objective factors and objective trends in politics."

Mr. Glick:

"Instead of being a light to the nations, we have become just one of the nations, and who can say whether it is for better or for worse?"

Mr. Kadishman:

"Because the Third Kingdom of Israel is run by petty party hacks. Instead of the King Messiah we have little kibbutz treasurers. Perhaps when the generation of our fine young friend Yair Gonen grows up, they will give our people self-respect."

As for me, I move the sugar bowl towards one or other of the visitors and utter absent-mindedly some such remark as:

"Where will all these fashionable ideas lead us?"

Or sometimes:

"One has to move with the times."

Or:

"There are two sides to every question."

I say these things so as not to sit silent all evening and seem rude. The sudden pain: Why have I been exiled here? *Nautilus.* *Dragon.* Isles of the Archipelago. Come, O come, Rahamim Rahamimov, my handsome Bokharian taxi driver. Give a loud blast on your horn. Miss Yvonne Azulai is all ready for the journey. Ready and waiting. Doesn't even need to change. Absolutely ready to leave. Now.

CHAPTER

28

The dreary sameness of the days. I cannot forget a thing. I refuse to surrender a crumb to the fingers of cold time. I hate it. Like the sofa, the armchairs, and the curtains, so the days too are subtle variations on a single color theme. A pretty, clever girl in a blue coat, a scaly kindergarten teacher with varicose veins, and in between the two a pane of glass which grows progressively more opaque, despite the frantic polishing. Yvonne Azulai has been left behind. She has been led astray by a base deceiver. My best friend Hadassah told me once about what happened when our headmaster was told that he had cancer. When the doctor broke the news the man expostulated furiously: "I've always paid my medical premiums on time, and during the war I volunteered for the Medical Corps despite my age. And what about the exercises I've been doing all these years? And the dieting? I've never had a cigarette in my mouth all my life. And my book on the elements of Hebrew grammar!"

Pathetic complaints. But the deception is both pathetic and

ugly. I make no excessive demands. Only that the glass should stay transparent. That is all.

Yair is growing. Next year we will send him to school. Yair is a child who never complains of boredom. Michael says he is entirely self-sufficient.

In the sand-pit in the garden Yair and I play at digging tunnels. My hand burrows towards his tiny hand until we meet under the surface of the sand. Then he raises his intelligent head and softly says, "We've met."

Once Yair asked me a question:

"Mummy, suppose I was Aron and Aron was me. How would you know which boy to love?"

Yair could play for an hour, two hours in his room without making a sound. So that suddenly I would be startled by the silence. I rush to his room in a panic. Disaster. Electricity. And he looks up at me calmly and full of cautious surprise: "What's the matter, Mummy?"

A clean and careful child; a balanced child. Sometimes he comes home beaten and bruised. Refuses to explain. Black eyes. Finally he gives way to pleas and threats, and says:

"There was a fight. They quarreled. Me too. I don't care, it doesn't hurt. Sometimes there are quarrels, and that's that."

Outwardly my son resembles my brother Emanuel, with his strong shoulders, his massive head, and his torpid movements. But he has nothing of my brother's open, boisterous enthusiasm. Whenever I kiss him he flinches, as if he has disciplined himself to stand and suffer in silence. Whenever I try to say something that will make him laugh, he fixes me with a searching glance, sidelong, alert, knowing, serious. As if considering what it was that had made me choose that particular joke. He finds objects much more interesting than people or words. Springs, taps, screws, plugs, keys.

The sameness of the days. Michael goes out to work and comes home at three o'clock. Aunt Jenia has bought him a new brief-case, because the one his father gave him as a wedding present has fallen apart. Wrinkles are spreading over the lower part of his face. They suggest an expression of cool, bitter irony which is not in Michael. His doctoral thesis is progressing slowly but surely. Every evening Michael devotes the two hours between the nine o'clock and eleven o'clock news bulletins to his thesis. If we have no visitors and there is nothing interesting on the radio, I ask Michael to read me a few pages of his work. The peacefulness of his even voice. His desk lamp. His glasses. The relaxed pose of his body in the armchair as he talks about volcanic eruptions, about the cooling of the crystalline crust. Those words have come out of the dreams I dream, and into those dreams they shall return. My husband is level and self-restrained. Sometimes I remember a little, grayish-white kitten we called Snowy. The kitten's faltering leaps to catch a moth on the ceiling.

We both begin to suffer from various minor ailments. Michael has never had a day's illness since he was fourteen, and I have not suffered from anything more serious than a slight cold. But now Michael is often troubled by heartburn, and Dr. Urbach has forbidden him to eat fried foods. I suffer from painful constrictions of the throat. Several times I have lost my voice for a few hours.

Occasionally a small row flares up between us. There follows a still calm. For a short while we accuse each other, then suddenly accuse ourselves. Smile like two strangers who have met by chance on an ill-lit staircase; embarrassed but very polite.

We have bought a gas cooker. Next summer we shall have a washing machine. We have already signed the contract and paid the first installment. Thanks to Mr. Kadishman, we shall have the benefit of a considerable discount. We have painted Yair's room blue. Michael has installed more bookshelves in his study, the converted balcony. At the same time we put up two shelves of books in Yair's room.

Aunt Jenia came to spend New Year with us. We entertained her for four days, because the holiday was followed immediately by the Sabbath. She had grown older and harder. An expression like an ugly sob had set on her face. She smoked heavily, despite severe pains around her heart. A doctor's lot is a hard one in a hot and restless country.

Michael and I went walking with Aunt Jenia on Mount Herzl and Mount Zion. We also visited the hill where the new University campus was to be built. Aunt Jenia had brought with her from Tel Aviv a Polish novel with a brown cover, which she read in bed all night.

"Why don't you go to sleep, Aunt Jenia? You ought to make the most of your holiday and get some good, sound sleep."

"You're not asleep either, Hanka. At my time of life it's permissible. At yours it's not."

"I could make you some mint tea. It'll relax you and help you to sleep."

"But I don't get any relaxation from sleep, Hanka. Thank you all the same."

. . .

At the end of the holiday Aunt Jenia asked us:

"If you've made up your minds not to move from this disgusting apartment, why don't you have another child?"

Michael reflected for a moment, then smiled:

"We thought perhaps, when I've finished writing my thesis . . ."

I said:

"No. We haven't given up the idea of moving. We're going to have a lovely new apartment. And we're going to travel abroad, too."

And Aunt Jenia, in an outburst of embittered sadness:

"Well, time flies, you know, time flies. You two live your lives as if time will stand still and wait for you. Let me tell you that time doesn't stand still. Time waits for no man."

A fortnight later, during Succot-week, I had my twenty-fifth birthday. I am four years younger than my husband. When Michael is seventy I shall be sixty-six. My husband bought me a phonograph for my birthday, and three classical records— Bach, Beethoven, Schubert. It was a first step towards a record library. It would do me good, Michael said, to collect records. He had read somewhere that music is relaxing. And collecting is relaxing in itself. He too, after all, collected pipes, and also stamps for Yair. Was he also in need of relaxation, I wanted to ask. I did not want his smile. So I did not ask.

Yoram Kamnitzer heard from Yair that it was my birthday. He came in to borrow the ironing board for his mother. Suddenly he stretched out his hand clumsily and handed me a packet wrapped in brown paper. I opened it: a book of poems by Jacob Fichmann. Before the words of thanks were out of my mouth Yoram had started off upstairs. The ironing board was returned next day by his younger sister.

The day before the holiday I went to the hairdresser's and had my hair cropped very short, like a boy's. Michael said:

"What's got into you, Hannah? I can't understand what's got into you."

My mother sent a parcel from Nof Harim for my birthday. It contained a pair of green tablecloths, each embroidered with mauve cyclamens by my mother. The embroidery was very delicate.

There was a visit during Succot to the Biblical Zoo.

The Biblical Zoo was only ten minutes' walk from our house, yet it seemed like another continent. The zoo stands in a wood on the slope of a rocky hill. At the foot of the slope is a wasteland. Rough wadis meandering at random. The wind rustled the tops of the pines. I saw dark birds soaring into a wilderness of blue. I followed them with my eyes. For an instant I lost my bearings. I imagined that instead of the birds soaring it was I who was falling and falling. An elderly attendant touched my shoulder anxiously: This way, Madam, this way.

Michael explained to his son about the habits of nocturnal animals. He used simple words, and avoided adjectives. Yair asked a question. Michael answered. I missed the words but I didn't miss the sounds, the sound of the wind and the screeching of the monkeys in their cages. In the dazzling daylight the monkeys were absorbed in their lascivious games. I could not remain indifferent to the sight. It aroused an indecent joy in me like the feeling I sometimes experience when strangers abuse me in my dreams. An old man in a gray coat with the collar turned up stood facing the monkeys' cages. His bony hands rested on a carved walking stick. Young and erect in my summer frock, I pass deliberately between him and the cages. The man stares and stares as if I am transparent and the monkeys' mating continues through my flesh. What are you staring at, sir? Why do you ask, young lady? You offend me, sir. You are too sensitive, young lady. Are you leaving, sir? I am going home, young lady. Where is home, sir? Why do you ask? You have no right to ask. I have my place, you have yours. Is something the matter? What do you take me for? Forgive me, sir, I wrongly suspected your motives. My dear, tired young lady, you seem to be talking to yourself. I cannot understand what you are saying. You appear to be unwell. I hear distant music, sir; is it a band playing far away? What is beyond the trees, young lady, I cannot say; it is hard to trust a strange young lady who is unwell. I hear a melody, sir. It is a delusion, my child; it is only the rapturous shrieking of the monkeys, indecent sounds. No, sir, I refuse to believe you. You are deceiving me. A procession is passing beyond the wood and the buildings, in the Street of the Kings of Israel. There our youth march and chant, there are burly policemen on prancing horses, a military band in gleaming white uniforms with gold braid. You are deceiving me, sir. You mean to isolate me until I am empty. I do not belong yet and already I am not the same. I shall not allow you, my good sir, to seduce me with soft words. And if lean, gray wolves stream round and round their cages, lightly padding on gentle paws, their jaws gaping and their noses moist, their fur matted with mud and saliva, then surely it is us they menace, we are the object of their full fury, now, yes, now.

29

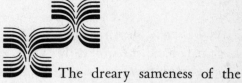

The dreary sameness of the days. Autumn will come. In the afternoon the sun beats through the west-facing window, engraving patterns of light on the rug and on the covers of the armchairs. With every rustle of the treetops outside the patterns of light break into a gentle swaying. The movement is restless and complex. The topmost branches of the fig tree burst into flame afresh each evening. The voices of the children playing outside suggest a distant wilderness. Autumn will come. I remember my father saying once when I was a child that in autumn people seem quieter and wiser.

To be quiet and wise: how dull.

One evening Yardena, Michael's friend from his student days, came to our house. With her she brought an overpowering cheerfulness. She and Michael had begun studying at the same time, and now hard-working Michael had got so far, and here was she, she blushed to tell, still struggling with some wretched paper.

Yardena was heavy-hipped and tall, and she wore a short,

tight skirt. Her eyes, too, were green, and her hair was blond and rich. She had come to ask Michael's help: she was having difficulty with her paper. She had always known how clever Michael was, from the first day she had met him. He must rescue her.

Yardena affectionately called Yair "little brat," and me she addressed as "Sweetie":

"Sweetie, you don't mind if I abduct your husband for half an hour or so, do you? If he doesn't explain this Davis to me right away, I swear I'll jump off the roof. It's driving me crazy."

As she spoke, she stroked his head as if he were hers. With a large pale hand she stroked his head, with sharp-nailed fingers adorned with two huge rings.

My face darkened. Instantly I was ashamed of myself. I tried to answer Yardena in her own language. I said:

"Take him. He's all yours. And your Davis, too."

"Sweetie," Yardena said, and a cruel smile flitted across her face, "Sweetie, don't talk like that, or you'll be very sorry afterwards. You don't look to me like one of those bold women you're trying to sound like."

Michael chose to smile, and as he smiled the corners of his mouth quivered. He lit his pipe and invited Yardena into his study. For half an hour or an hour he sat at his desk with her. His voice was deep and serious. Her voice was perpetually stifling little giggles. Their heads, one blond the other graying, seemed to be floating on clouds of smoke when I wheeled in the trolley to serve them some coffee and cakes.

"Sweetie," Yardena said, "you don't seem to be a bit excited about catching yourself a little genius. If I were in your place I'd gobble him up alive. But you, Sweetie, you don't seem to be the greedy type. No, don't be frightened of me. I may be a bitch, but my bark's worse than my bite. Now if you wouldn't mind excusing us and letting us get on with our lesson, so that we can give you back this clever, spotless lamb. Little brat, that child of yours—standing there quietly in the corner like that and staring at me, just like a little man. He stares just like his dad, shy but sharp. Take that child out of my sight before he drives me wild."

I went out into the kitchen. There were blue curtains on the window. There were flowers printed on the curtains. On the kitchen balcony hung a large washtub. This was the washtub I was doing our washing in, until we got a washing machine. Next summer. On the ledge stood a dead potted plant and a sooty paraffin lamp. There are frequent power failures in Jerusalem. Why did I have my hair cut short, I mutter to myself. Yardena is tall and flashy, her voice is warm and loud. Time to get supper.

I dashed out to the greengrocer. The Persian greengrocer, Elijah Mossiah, was about to close up shop. If I had come two minutes later, he said cheerfully, I would have found him gone. I bought some tomatoes. Cucumbers. Parsley. Green and red peppers. The greengrocer laughed and laughed at the hopeless confusion of my movements. I picked up the basket with both hands and ran home. Suddenly I stopped dead in a cold panic: No key. I've forgotten to bring the key.

But so what? Michael and his visitor are at home. The door isn't locked. And besides, we've left a spare key to the apartment with the Kamnitzers upstairs, in case of emergency.

My haste had been unnecessary. Yardena was already standing on the stairs, repeating her farewells to my husband. She rested a sculpted leg against the bars of the bannister. A confused smell of sweat and perfume filled the staircase. I was short of breath from running and from my panic about the key. Yardena said:

"Your shy husband has cleared up in half an hour a problem that's had me stymied for half a year. I don't know how to thank—you both."

As she spoke she suddenly shot out two well-manicured fingers to pick a flake of skin or a stray hair from my chin.

Michael took off his reading glasses. He smiled calmly. I suddenly took hold of my husband's arm and stood leaning on him. Yardena laughed and left. We went inside. Michael turned on the radio. I made a salad.

The rain held off. A biting chill passed through the city. The electric heater burned all day in our flat. The sun was swathed once more with damp mist. My son draws shapes on the windowpane with his finger. I stand behind him sometimes looking, but I can never make anything out.

On Sabbath Eve Michael got out the stepladder and brought down our winter clothes. He put the summer ones away. I hated all my clothes from last year. The dress with the high waistline seemed to me like an old woman's now.

After the Sabbath I went into town to do some shopping. Hysterically I bought more and more things. I spent a month's earnings in a single morning. I bought myself a green coat, a pair of fur-lined boots, suede shoes, three long-sleeved dresses and a casual cardigan in orange with a zip fastener. For Yair I bought a warm sailor suit of Shetland wool.

Then, as I walked westward along Jaffa Road, I passed the electrical goods shop which had belonged to my father years before. Inside the door I put down my parcels. I stood blindly in front of a strange man. The man asked me what I wanted. His voice was patient, and in my heart I thanked him for that. Even when he was forced to repeat his question the man did not raise his voice. In the dim recesses of the shop I could see the entrance to the low back room which has two steps going down to it. In that room my father used to carry out simple repairs. There I used to sit and read children's books meant for boys, on the days when I visited my father's shop. In that room my father used to brew himself a cup of tea twice a day, at ten o'clock in the morning and at five in the afternoon. For nineteen years my father had brewed his tea there twice a day, at ten and at five, in summer and in winter.

An ugly little girl came out of the back room holding a bald-headed doll. Her eyes were red from crying.

"What can I do for you?" the stranger asked for the third time. There was no surprise in his voice. What I want is a good electric razor, to spare my husband the agony of shaving. My husband shaves like a young man; scraping his skin with the razor till the blood flows, yet leaving bristles under his chin. The best and most expensive electric razor there is. I want to give him a very big surprise.

I stood counting the money I had left in my purse, and suddenly the ugly child's face lit up: she thought she recognized me. Wasn't I Dr. Kopperman from the clinic in Katamon? No, my dear, you've made a mistake. My name is Miss Azulai and I play on the tennis team. Thank you, and good day to you both. You ought to put the heat on. It's cold in here. The shop is damp.

Michael was shocked when he saw all the parcels I had brought home.

"What's got into you, Hannah? I can't understand what's got into you."

I said:

"Surely you remember the story of Cinderella. The prince chose her because she had the tiniest feet in the kingdom, and she wanted him so as to spite her stepmother and the ugly sisters. Don't you agree that the decision of the prince and of Cinderella to set up home together was based on vain and childish considerations? Tiny feet. I tell you, Michael, that prince was an utter fool and Cinderella was out of her mind. Maybe that was why they suited each other and lived happily ever after."

"That's too deep for me," Michael complained with a dry smile. "It's too deep for me, that parable of yours. Literature isn't my subject. I'm not good at interpreting symbols. Please say what you were trying to say again, but say it in simple words. If it's really important."

"No, my dear Michael, it wasn't really important. I'm not sure exactly what it was I was trying to explain. I'm not sure. I bought all these new clothes to be happy and enjoy them, and I bought you the electric razor to make you happy."

"Who says I'm not happy?" Michael asked quietly. "And what about you, Hannah, aren't you happy? What's got into you, Hannah? I can't understand what's got into you."

"There's a pretty nursery rhyme," I said, "in which a girl asks, 'Little clown, little clown, will you dance with me?' And somebody answers 'Pretty little clown will dance with anyone.' Do you think, Michael, that that was a good enough answer to the girl's question?"

Michael began to say something. Changed his mind. Kept silent. He untied the parcels. Put each thing away in its place. He went out to his study, then came back a few moments later, hesitantly. Thanks to me, he said, he would have to ask one of his friends, perhaps Kadishman, for a loan, to enable us to get through the month. And what for, that was what he was trying to understand. What was the reason? Surely some- where, in heaven or on earth, there must be some reason.

"People ought to be very careful when they use the word 'reason.' Wasn't it you yourself who taught me that, Michael, less than six years ago?"

CHAPTER

30

Autumn in Jerusalem. The rain is late. The color of the sky is deep blue, close to the colors of the calm sea. A dry cold bites into the flesh. Stray clouds scud eastward. Early in the morning the clouds come down and roam among the houses like a silent cavalcade. They burst out to darken the freezing stone arches. Early in the afternoon the mist descends on the city. By five, or a quarter past, darkness reigns. The street lamps are not numerous in Jerusalem. Their light is yellow and feeble. In the alleyways and courtyards fallen leaves dance. An obituary notice in flowery prose is pasted up in our street: *Nahum Hanun, father of the Bokharian community, has gone to his eternal rest in the fullness of years.* I found myself brooding on the name Nahum Hanun. On fullness of years. And on death.

Mr. Kadishman appeared, dark, agitated, and wrapped in a Russian fur coat. He said:

"There is going to be a war. This time we shall conquer Jerusalem, Hebron, Bethlehem, and Nablus. The Almighty has wrought justly, in that, while He has denied our so-called leaders common sense, He has confounded the wits of our enemies. What He takes away with one hand, as it were, He restores with the other. The folly of the Arabs will bring about what the wisdom of the Jews has failed to achieve. There is going to be a great war, and the Holy Places will once again be ours."

"Since the day the Temple was destroyed"—Michael repeated a favorite saying of his father's—"since the day the Temple was destroyed, the power of prophecy has been granted to men like you or me. If you want to know my opinion, the war we are about to fight will not be over Hebron or Nablus but over Gaza and Rafah."

I laughed and said:

"Gentlemen, you are both out of your minds."

Stone-strewn yards are carpeted with dead pine needles. The autumn is stiff and thick. A wind sweeps dry leaves from yard to deserted yard. Towards dawn in the district of Mekor Baruch the sheets of corrugated iron on the balconies play a melody. The movement of abstract time resembles a substance sizzling in a test tube: pure, radiant, and lethal. On the night of the tenth of October, towards morning, I heard in the distance the roar of heavy engines. It was a low thunder, which seemed to be violently stifling some mounting energy. Tanks started up inside the walls of the Schneller Barracks near where we live. They rumbled dully on their tracks. I imagined them as filthy, angry hounds straining furiously at their restraining chains.

The wind is also in it. The wind picks up scraps of garbage, makes a dirty vortex, and hurls them at the ancient shutters. It lifts up pieces of yellowing newspaper and forms ghostly shapes in the darkness. It clutches at the street lamps and sets sickly shadows dancing. Passers-by walk stooped against its harsh gusts. Now and again the wind catches an abandoned door and bangs it until breaking glass tinkles in the distance. Our heater burns all day. We even leave it on at night. The radio announcers' voices are stern and solemn. A bitter, prolonged restraint on the verge of bursting into violent fury.

In the middle of October our Persian greengrocer, Mr. Elijah Mossiah, was called up. His daughter Levana ran the shop in his absence. Her face was pale and her voice was very soft. Levana was a bashful girl. Her shy efforts to please pleased me. She was so nervous that she chewed her blond plait. The gesture was touching. In the night I dreamed of Michael Strogoff. He stood before shaven-headed Tartar notables, whose faces bore an expression of brutish cruelty. He endured his tortures in silence and did not betray his secret. His mouth was tight-shut and magnificent. Bluish steel glinted in his eyes.

At lunchtime Michael commented on the radio news: There is a well-known rule, established—if his memory did not deceive him—by the German Iron Chancellor, Bismarck, according to which, when one is faced by an alliance of enemy forces, one should turn and crush the strongest. So it would be this time, my husband declared with conviction. First of all we would scare Jordan and Iraq to death, then we would suddenly turn round and smash Egypt.

I stared at my husband as if he had suddenly started talking Sanskrit.

CHAPTER
31

 Autumn in Jerusalem.

Each morning I sweep the dead leaves from the kitchen balcony. New leaves fall to take their place. They crumble to dust between my fingers. They crackle drily.

The rain held off. Once or twice I thought the first drops had begun to fall. I rushed downstairs to bring the washing in from the line. But no rain came. Only a damp wind which ruffled my skin. I had a cold and a sore throat. My throat was most painful in the mornings. A certain tension had made itself felt in the city. A new stillness took hold of familiar objects.

Housewives in the shops said that the Arab Legion was installing gun batteries around Jerusalem. Canned foods, candles, and paraffin lamps vanished from the shops. I bought a large box of cookies.

In the district of Sanhedriya sentries fired at night. Artillery units were stationed in the woods at Tel Arza. I watched reservists spreading camouflage nets in a field behind the Biblical Zoo. My best friend Hadassah came round to tell me that according to her husband the Cabinet had sat in conference till dawn, and that when they came out the ministers had seemed agitated. By night trainloads of soldiers were coming up to Jerusalem. In Cafe Allenby in King George Street I saw four handsome French officers. They were wearing peaked caps, and purple stripes gleamed on their epaulettes. Only in films had I seen such a sight before.

In David Yelin Street, as I was staggering home with my shopping, I passed three paratroopers in mottled battle dress. Submachine guns hung from their shoulders. They were waiting at the Number 15 bus stop. One of them, dark and lean, called after me, "Sweetheart." His comrades joined in his laughter. I reveled in their laughter.

At first light on Wednesday an icy breeze swept through the house, colder than anything we had had that winter. I got up barefoot to cover Yair. I enjoyed the biting cold under the soles of my feet. Michael sighed heavily in his sleep. The table and armchairs were blocks of shadow. I stood at the window. I remembered fondly the attack of diphtheria I had suffered as a child of nine. The power to make my dreams carry me over the line that divides sleeping from waking. The cool mastery. The interplay of shapes in an expanse ranging in color from light to dark gray.

I stood at the window shivering with joy and expectation. Through the shutters I watched the sun, swathed in reddish clouds, struggling to penetrate a fine layer of bright mist. After a while the sun burst through, setting the treetops ablaze and flaming on tin basins hung out on rear balconies. I was enthralled. Barefoot I stood in my nightdress pressing my forehead to the glass. Frost patterns flowered on the windowpane.

A woman in a dressing gown came out to empty her garbage can. Her hair, like mine, was unkempt.

The alarm clock rang.

Michael pulled down the bedclothes. His eyelids were gummed together. His face looked rumpled. He spoke to himself in a cracked voice.

"It's cold. What a foul day."

Then, as his eyes opened, he caught sight of me in amazement.

"Have you gone out of your mind, Hannah?"

I turned to face him, but was unable to speak. I had lost my voice again. I tried to say so, but all my throat would yield was agonizing pain. Michael seized my arm and pulled me forcefully onto the bed.

"You've gone out of your mind, Hannah," he repeated in horror. "You're not well."

Gently his lips touched my forehead, and he added:

"Your hands are like ice and your forehead's burning. You're not well, Hannah."

Under the covers I continued to shiver violently. But I was also on fire with a fervid excitement I had not felt since I was a child. I was gripped by a fever of joy. I laughed and laughed without producing a sound.

Michael dressed. He tied his checkered tie and secured it with a small clip. He went out to the kitchen to heat me a cup of milk. He sweetened it with two spoonfuls of honey. I could not swallow. My throat was on fire. The pain was a new one. I savored the new pain as it grew stronger.

Michael put the milk down on a stool by my bed. My lips smiled at him. I visualized myself as a squirrel throwing pine cones at a dirty bear. The new pain was mine and I tried it on.

Michael stood and shaved. He turned the radio up so as to

be able to hear the news headlines over the buzz of the electric razor. Then he blew into the razor to clean it and switched off the radio. He went out to the drugstore to phone our doctor, Dr. Urbach of Alfandari Street. When he came in again he hurriedly dressed Yair and sent him off to kindergarten. His movements were as precise as those of a well-drilled soldier. He said:

"It's terribly cold outside. Please don't get out of bed. I rang Hadassah, too. She promised to send her maid round to look after you and do the cooking. Dr. Urbach promised to call at nine or half past. Hannah, do please try just once more to drink your milk before it gets cold."

My husband stood stiffly before me like a young waiter, and the cup was steady in his hand. I pushed away the cup and took hold of Michael's other hand. I kissed his fingers. I didn't want to stop laughing inwardly. Michael suggested I take an aspirin. I shook my head. He shrugged his shoulders—such a studied movement. Now he had put his hat and coat on. As he went out he said:

"Remember, Hannah, you're to stay in bed till Dr. Urbach comes. I'll try to come home early. You must keep quiet. You've caught cold, Hannah, that's all. It's cold in this house. I'll bring the heater nearer the bed."

No sooner had my husband shut the door behind him than I leaped barefoot out of bed and across to the window again. I was a wild, disobedient child. I strained my vocal cords like a drunkard, singing and shouting. The pain and the pleasure enflamed each other. The pain was delicious and exhilarating. I filled my lungs with air. I roared, I howled, I mimicked birds and animals as Emanuel and I had adored doing as children.

But still not a sound could be heard. It was pure magic. I was simply swept away by the violent floods of pleasure and pain. I was cold but my forehead was burning. Barefoot I stood and naked in the bath like a child on a stifling hot day. I turned the tap full on. I wallowed in the icy water. I splashed water all around, on the glazed tiles on the walls on the ceiling and the towels and on Michael's bathrobe hanging on a hook on the back of the door. I filled my mouth full of water and squirted jet after jet at my face reflected in the mirror. I turned blue with cold. The warm pain spread down my back, trickled down my spine. My nipples stiffened. My toes turned to stone. Only my head was burning, and I never stopped singing without making a sound. A violent yearning spread deep down in the caverns of my body, in my most sensitive joints and recesses which are mine even though I can never see them till the day I die. I had a body and it was mine and it throbbed and thrilled and was alive. Like a madwoman I roamed from room to room to the kitchen to the vestibule and the water dripped and dripped. Naked and wet I fell on the bed and hugged the pillows and bedclothes with my arms and knees. Crowds of friendly people reached out gently to touch me. As their fingers touched my skin I was washed by a blazing wave. Silently the twins clasped my arms to tie them behind my back. The poet Saul leaned over to intoxicate me with his mustache and his warm odor. Rahamim Rahamimov the handsome taxi driver came too and clasped me round the waist like a wild man. In the frenzy of the dance he lifted my body high in the air. The distant music blared and roared. Hands pressed my body. Kneaded. Pounded. Probed. I laughed and screamed with all my strength. Soundlessly. The soldiers thronged and closed round me in their mottled battle dress. A furious masculine smell exuded from them in waves. I was all theirs. I was

Yvonne Azulai. Yvonne Azulai, the opposite of Hannah Gonen. I was cold. Flooded. Men are born for water, to flood cold and violent in the depths on the plains on snowy open steppes and among the stars. Men are born for snow. To be and not to rest to shout and not to whisper to touch and not to watch to flood and not to yearn. I am made of ice, my city is made of ice, and my subjects too shall be of ice. Every one. The Princess has spoken. There will be a hailstorm in Danzig which will smite the whole city, violent, crystalline, and clear. Down, rebellious subjects, down, rub your noses in the snow. You shall all be clear, you shall all be white for I am a white princess. We must all be white and clear and cold else we shall crumble away. All the city will turn to crystal. Not a leaf shall fall not a bird shall soar not a woman tremble. I have spoken.

It was night in Danzig. Tel Arza and its woods stood in the snow. A great steppe stretched over Mahane Yehuda, Agrippa, Sheikh Bader, Rehavia, Beit Hakerem, Kiryat Shmuel, Talpiot, Givat Shaul to the slopes of Kfar Lifta. Steppe fog and darkness. This was my Danzig. An islet sprouted in the middle of the pool at the end of Mamillah Road. Upon it stood the statue of the Princess. Inside the stone was I.

But inside the walls of Schneller Barracks a secret plot was being hatched. Subdued rebellion was in the air. The two dark destroyers *Dragon* and *Tigress* weighed anchor. Their noble prows sliced through the crust of ice. A muffled sailor stood in the crow's nest atop the swaying mast. His body was made of snow like the High Commissioner of snow we made, Halil, Hannah and Aziz, in the great snow in the winter of '41.

Squat tanks rolled heavily in the darkness down the icy slope of Geula Street towards the quarter of Mea Shearim. At the gate of Schneller Barracks a group of officers in rough wind-breakers conspired in whispers. It was not I who had ordered this movement. My orders were to freeze. This was a plot. Urgent commands were communicated in strained whispers. Light snowflakes drifted in the black air. Short, sharp bursts of gunfire sounded. And at the tips of thick mustaches glistened icicles.

Massive and efficient, the squat tanks penetrated the outskirts of my sleeping city. I was alone. The moment had come for the twins to steal into the Russian Compound. Barefoot and silent they came. Noiselessly they crawled the last part of their way. To stab from behind the watchmen I had posted to guard the prison. All the scum of the city was set loose, and a violent shout erupted from their throats. Floods seethed into the narrow streets. The heavy breathing of a brooding evil.

Meanwhile the last pockets of resistance were broken. Key points were occupied. My faithful Strogoff was taken. But in the outlying sections the discipline of the rebellion was slacker. Burly, drunken soldiers, loyal and mutinous, burst into the homes of citizens and merchants. Their eyes were suffused with blood. Leather-gloved hands reached out to rape and pillage. Vile forces overran the city. The poet Saul was incarcerated in the cellar of the broadcasting station in Melisanda Street. He was abused by the rabble. I could not bear it. I wept.

Gun carriages rolled on silent rubber wheels beyond the city's elevated areas. I saw a bareheaded rebel climb up and silently change the flag on top of the Terra Sancta building. His locks were disheveled. He was a handsome, exultant rebel.

The freed prisoners laughed yellow laughter. They dispersed through the city in their prison uniforms. Knives were produced. They spread into outlying areas to settle a cruel score. Eminent scholars were imprisoned in their place. Still half-asleep, bewildered, and indignant, they protested in my name. Mentioned their good connections. Stood on their dignity. Already some of them fawned, and swore to their long-standing hatred of me. Gun butts in their backs urged them on or silenced them. A new, base power ruled the city.

The tanks surrounded the Princess's palace in accordance with a secretly prearranged plan. They carved deep scars in the smooth snow. The Princess stood at the window and called with all her might on Strogoff and Captain Nemo, but her voice was taken away and only her lips moved mechanically, as if she were trying to entertain the cheering troops. I could not guess the thoughts of the officers of my bodyguard. Perhaps they too were involved in the plot. They kept glancing at their watches. Were they waiting for a time fixed in advance?

Dragon and *Tigress* were at the gates of the palace. Their guns revolved slowly on their massive mountings. Like a monster's fingers the guns pointed at my window. At me. I am unwell, the Princess tried to whisper. She could see reddish flickers in the east beyond Mount Zion, towards the Judean Desert. The first sparks of a celebration which was not in her honor. Eagerly the two assassins leaned over her. The Princess saw pity, desire, and mockery in their eyes. They were both so young. Swarthy and dangerously handsome. Proudly and silently I tried to stand and face them, but my body, too, betrayed me. In her flimsy nightdress the Princess groveled on the icy tiles. She was exposed to their feverish glances. Twin smiled to twin. Their teeth shone white. A shudder which boded no good passed through their bodies. Like the twisted smiles of youths watching a woman's skirt lift suddenly in the wind.

On the outskirts of the city an armored car patrolled with a loudspeaker. A clear, calm voice announced a summary of the orders of the new regime. It warned of lightning trials and merciless executions. Anyone who resisted would be shot like a dog. The rule of the lunatic Ice Princess was over forever. Not even the white whale would escape. A new era had dawned in the city.

I only half-hear; the assassins' hands are already reaching out towards me. They both grunt hoarsely like a trussed animal's groaning. Their eyes are flashing with lust. The thrill of the pain shivers, sluices, scalds down my back to the tips of my toes, sending searing sparks and sensual shudders across my back, to my neck, my shoulders, everywhere. The scream bursts inward silently. My husband's fingers half-touch my face. He wants me to open my eyes. Can't he see how wide open they are? He wants me to listen to him. Who could be more attentive than I am? He shakes and shakes my shoulders. Touches my forehead with his lips. I still belong to the ice, yet already an alien power clutches.

CHAPTER
32

Our doctor, Dr. Urbach of Al-
fandari Street, was tiny and delicately sculpted like a china
figurine. He had high cheekbones, and the look in his eyes was
sad and sympathetic. During his examination he was in the
habit of delivering a little speech.

"We will be well again in another week. Perfectly well again.
We have simply caught cold and done what we should not
have done. The body is trying to get well, the mind perhaps is
causing us delay. The relations of the mind and the body is not
like the driver in the automobile but like, for instance, the vita-
mins in the food, so to say. My dear Mrs. Gonen, remember
you are a mother already. Please to take into consideration also
the young child. Mr. Gonen, we need complete rest for the
body, and for the nerves and the mind too. That is first of all.
We must also take an aspirin three times daily. For the throat
honey is good. And also to keep warm the room where we
sleep. And we must not argue with the lady. Only to say yes,
yes, and again yes. We need rest. Relaxation. All talking is
causing complications and mental sufferings. Please to talk as

little as possible. Only to use neutral and elementary words. We are not calm, not calm at all. You can call me on the telephone at once if there is any complications. But if there is signs of hysterics then it is necessary to keep quiet and wait with patience. Not to increase the drama. A passive audience kills the drama just like antibiotics kills the virus. We need complete calm, inner calm. I wish you better. Please."

Towards evening I felt easier. Michael brought Yair into the room to say good night from a distance. I forced myself to whisper, "Good night, both of you." Michael put his finger to his lips: You mustn't talk. Don't strain your voice.

He gave Yair his supper and put him to bed. Then he came back into our room. He switched on the radio. An excited newscaster spoke of an ultimatum issued by the President of the United States. The President called on all parties to exercise restraint and to avoid incidents. Unconfirmed reports of Iraqi troops moving into Jordan. A political commentator is skeptical. The government appeals for alertness and calm. Military experts are reticent. In France, Guy Mollet's cabinet has held two special sessions. A well-known actress has committed suicide. Frost is forecast again for Jerusalem.

Michael said:

"Simcha, Hadassah's maid, will come again tomorrow. And I shall take the day off. I'll talk to *you,* Hannah, but don't answer because you mustn't talk."

"It's not difficult, Michael, it doesn't hurt," I whispered.

Michael got up from the armchair and came over to sit on the end of my bed. He carefully drew back the corner of the bedclothes and sat on the mattress. He slowly nodded his head a few times, as if he had finally managed to solve a difficult mental equation and was now checking the calculations. He gazed at me for a while. Then he buried his face in his hands. Eventually he said, to himself more than to me:

"I was very frightened, Hannah, when I came home at lunchtime and found you like that."

Michael flinched as he spoke, as if he had hurt himself by saying this. He stood up, straightened the covers, turned on my bedside lamp, and put out the ceiling light. He took my hand in his. He set the hands of my wristwatch, which had stopped in the morning. He wound the watch. His fingers were warm, the nails flat. Inside his fingers there were sinews, flesh, nerves, muscles, bones, and blood vessels. When I studied literature I had to learn by heart a poem by ibn Gabirol which says that we are made of putrid humors. How pure, by comparison, is chemical poison: clear white crystals. The earth is merely a green crust overlaid on a suppressed volcano. I held my husband's fingers between my hands. The gesture produced a smile on Michael's face, as if he had sought my forgiveness and received it. I burst into tears. Michael stroked my cheeks. Bit his lip. Decided to say nothing. He stroked me exactly as he often stroked Yair's head. The comparison saddened me, for no reason I can explain, perhaps for no reason at all.

"When you're better we'll go somewhere far away," Michael said, "perhaps to Kibbutz Nof Harim. We could leave the boy there with your mother and your brother, and go to a sanatorium. Perhaps to Eilat. Or Nahariya. Good night, Hannah. I'll turn the light off and put the heater out in the vestibule. I seem to have made some sort of mistake. And I don't know what it is. I mean, what should I have done to prevent this happening or what should I not have done to avoid putting you in this state? At school in Holon I had a gym teacher called Yehiam Peled who always called me 'Goofy Ganz,' because my reflexes were rather slow. I was very good at English and math, but in P.T. I was Goofy Ganz. Everyone has strong and weak points. How trite! And anyway, it's beside the point. What I wanted to say, Hannah, is that, for my part, I'm glad we're married to each other and not anyone else. And I try to do everything I can to adapt to your needs. Please, Hannah, don't ever frighten me again as you did today when I came home at lunchtime and found you like that. Please, Hannah. I'm not made of iron, after all. There, I'm being trite again. Good night. Tomorrow I'll take the washing round to the laundry. If you need anything in the night don't shout, because of your throat. You can tap on the wall; I'll be sitting in the study and I'll come at once. I've put a thermos of hot tea on the stool, here. And here there's a sleeping pill. Don't take it if you can possibly get to sleep without it. It's much better for you to sleep without a pill. Please, Hannah, I beg you. It's not often I ask you for anything. Now, for the third time—what an old bore I'm getting to be suddenly—good night, Hannah."

Next morning Yair asked:

"Mummy, is it true if Daddy was a king I'd be a duke?"

I smiled and whispered hoarsely:

" 'If Grandma had wings and she could fly, she'd be an eagle in the sky.' "

Yair fell silent. Perhaps he was trying to visualize the effect of the rhyme. Translating it into picture-language. Rejecting the image. Finally he declared calmly:

"No. Grandma with wings is Grandma, not an eagle. You just say things without thinking about them. Like when you said about Red Riding Hood that they took the grandmother out of the wolf's tummy. A wolf's tummy isn't a storeroom.

And wolves chew when they eat. For you everything is possible. Daddy takes care what he says and he doesn't talk from his thoughts. Only from his brains."

Michael, above the whistle of the kettle boiling on the gas stove:

"Yair, into the kitchen with you this minute, please. Sit down and start eating. Mummy's not well. Stop being a nuisance, if you don't mind. I've warned you."

Hadassah's maid, Simcha, hung the bedclothes out of the window to air. I sat in the armchair. My hair was unkempt. Michael went out to the grocer clutching a shopping list I had given him: bread, cheese, olives, sour cream. He had taken the day off from work. Yair stood at the mirror in the vestibule, messing up his hair, combing it, and then messing it up again. Finally he stood making faces at himself in the mirror.

Simcha beats the mattress. I look and see a stream of golden flecks dancing up a ray of sunlight towards the corner of the window. A delicious limpness has taken hold of my body. No suffering, no longing. A lazy, hazy thought: to buy a lovely big Persian rug soon.

The doorbell rings. Yair answers it. The postman refuses to hand him the registered letter because it needs a signature. Meanwhile Michael comes up the stairs carrying the shopping basket. He takes the call-up papers from the postman and signs the receipt. His face when he comes into the room is solemn and serious.

When will this man lose his self-control? Oh, to see him just once in a panic. Shouting for joy. Running wild.

Michael explained tersely that no war was likely to last longer than three weeks. "The talk is of a limited, local war, of course.

Times have changed. There won't be another 1948. The balance between the Great Powers is very unsteady. Now that America is in the throes of elections and the Russians are busy in Hungary, there's a fleeting opportunity. No, this war won't drag on, for certain. Incidentally, I'm in Signals. I'm not a pilot and I'm not a paratrooper. So why are you crying? I'll be back in a few days and I'll bring you a genuine Arab coffeepot. That was a joke—why are you crying? When I get back we'll take a holiday, as I promised. We'll go to Upper Galilee. Or to Eilat. What are you doing, mourning for me? I'll be back almost before I've gone. Perhaps I've jumped to the wrong conclusion. It may just be a matter of general maneuvers, not a war at all. If I get a chance I'll write you a letter on the way. I don't want to disappoint you, though; I'd better warn you in advance that I'm not much of a hand at letter-writing. Now, I'll just get into my uniform and pack my rucksack. Shall I phone Nof Harim and ask your mother to come and keep an eye on you while I'm away?

"I feel so strange in khaki. I haven't put on any weight all these years. Do you remember, Hannah, how my father looked when he put on his watchman's uniform over his pajamas and played with Yair? Oh, I'm terribly sorry. It was stupid of me to mention that now of all times. Now I've hurt us both. We mustn't hunt for omens in every stray word. Words are just words, that's all. Here, I'm leaving you a hundred pounds in the drawer. And I've written down my army number and unit number. I've put the piece of paper under the vase. I paid the water, electricity, and gas bills at the beginning of the month. The war won't last long at all. That's my considered opinion, at least. You see, the Americans . . . never mind. Hannah, don't look at me like that. You're just making it harder for yourself. And for me. Hadassah's Simcha will work here till I get back.

I'll ring Hadassah. I'll ring Sarah Zeldin, too. Now you're looking at me like that again. It's not my fault, Hannah. Remember, I'm not a pilot and I'm not a paratrooper. What have you done with my sweater? Thanks. Oh yes, I think I'll take a scarf, too. It may be cold at night. Tell me truly, Hannah, how do I look in uniform? Don't I look like a professor in costume? Corporal Goofy Ganz, Signal Corps. I'm only joking, Hannah; you ought to be laughing, not crying again. Don't keep on crying like that. I'm not going on holiday, you know. Don't cry. It doesn't do any good. I . . . I'll be thinking of you. I'll write, provided the field post works. I'll take care of myself. You too . . . No, Hannah, this isn't the moment to talk about feelings. What's the use of statements? Sentiment is only painful. And I . . . I'm not a pilot or a paratrooper. I've said that several times already. When I come back I hope I'll find you well and happy. I'd like to hope that you won't think ill of me while I'm far away. I'll be thinking fondly of you. That way we won't be entirely apart. And . . . anyway."

Just as if I were only a figment of his imagination. How can anyone expect to be more than just a figment of someone else's imagination? I'm real, Michael. I'm not just a figment of your imagination.

33

Hadassah's Simcha is washing up in the kitchen. She hums Shoshana Damari songs to herself: *I am a loving hind, a pleasant roe. A star shines in the sky, in the woods jackals cry, come back, Hephzibah's waiting for you.*

I lie in bed, holding a novel by John Steinbeck which my best friend Hadassah brought me when she came to visit me last night. I am not reading. My icy feet nestle against a hot-water bottle. I am calm and wide awake. Yair has gone to the kindergarten. From Michael there is no word, nor could there be any yet. The paraffin-seller goes down the street with his cart, ringing and ringing his handbell. Jerusalem is awake. A fly dashes itself against the windowpane. A fly, not a sign and not an omen. Just a fly. I am not thirsty. I notice that the book I am holding is well thumbed. Its cover is held together with scotch tape. The vase is standing in its usual place. Beneath it is a piece of paper on which Michael has written down his army number and the number of his unit. *Nautilus* is lying quietly deep down below the crust of ice in the Bering Straits. Mr. Glick is sitting in his shop reading a religious daily. A cold autumn wind is blowing through the city. Tranquillity.

At nine o'clock the radio announced:

Last night the Israel Defense Forces penetrated the Sinai Desert, captured Kuntilla and Ras en-Naqeb, and have occupied positions in the vicinity of Nahel, sixty kilometers east of the Suez Canal. A military commentator explains. While from the political point of view. Repeated provocations. Flagrant violation of freedom of navigation. The moral justification. Terrorism and sabotage. Defenseless women and children. Mounting tension. Innocent civilians. Enlightened public opinion at home and abroad. Essentially a defensive operation. Keep calm. Stay indoors. Blackout. No hoarding. Obey instructions. The public is requested. No panic. The whole country is the front. The whole nation is an army. On hearing the warning signal. So far events have proceeded according to plan.

At a quarter past nine:

The armistice agreement is dead and buried and will never be revived. Our forces are overrunning. Enemy opposition is giving ground.

Till half past ten the radio played marching songs from my youth: *From Dan to Beersheba we'll never forget. Believe me, the day will come.*

Why should I believe you? And if you don't forget, what of it?

At half past ten:

The Sinai Desert, historic cradle of the Israelite nation.

As opposed to Jerusalem. I try my hardest to be proud and interested. I wonder if Michael has remembered to take his heartburn tablets. Always tidy, always neat. Well, he has danced his five years away; now he must "bid his pet dove farewell."

A deserted alley in New Beit Yisrael, on the edge of Jerusalem, breathes a new air. The alley is paved with stones. The paving stones are cracked but highly polished. Heavy arches stand between the alley and the low clouds. The alley is a blind alley. Time condenses and collects in the hollows of the stones. A drowsy watchman, an elderly civilian called up for civil defense, stands propped against a wall. Shuttered houses. Muted chimes echo from a distant bell. Down from the hills comes the wind. It splits and eddies in the winding alley. As it swirls along the alley it touches the iron shutters and the iron doors secured with rusting bolts. An Orthodox boy stands at a window, his earlocks flowing down his pallid cheeks. There is an apple in his hand. He stares at the birds in the branches of the aspen in the yard. The boy stands motionless. The ancient watchman tries to catch his eye through the glass. In his deep loneliness he smiles at the boy. Nothing melts. The boy is mine. Blue-gray light is trapped in the curls of the aspen. The hills far off, and here deep quiet and drifting chimes. The stillness has settled on birds and alley cats. Large carriages will come will pass will travel far away. Would I were of stone. Hard and at rest. Cold and present.

Perhaps the British High Commissioner was also wrong. In the High Commissioner's palace on the Hill of Evil Counsel to the southeast of Jerusalem a secret session is prolonged till sunrise. Pale day is dawning at the windows, but the lights still burn. Stenographers work in two-hour shifts. The guards are tired and restless.

Michael Strogoff bearing a secret message committed to

memory presses on determined and solitary through the night in the High Commissioner's service. Cold strong Michael Strogoff surrounded by brutish savages. The dazzling flash of daggers. A spurting laugh. Wordless. Like Aziz and Yehuda Gottlieb from Ussishkin Street fighting on the empty building site. I am the umpire. I am the prize. Both their faces are contorted. Their eyes flooded with stagnant hatred. They aim at the belly because it is softest. They flail wildly. They kick. They bite. One of them turns and runs. In mid-flight he turns to pursue. Picks up a heavy stone, throws, and misses narrowly. His opponent spits with vehement fury. On a spiky coil of rusty barbed wire the two of them roll interlocked grinding their teeth. Scratching one another. Bleeding. Reaching out to grab at throat or privates. Cursing from between pressed lips. As one man they both suddenly collapse exhausted. For an instant the foes lie wrapped in each other's arms like a pair of lovers. Like a pair of panting lovers Aziz and Yehuda Gottlieb lie gasping for air. Next moment dark energy courses through them once again. Skull beats against skull. Hands claw at eyes. Fist against chin. Knee into groin. Their backs ripped by the spikes on the rusty wire. Lips tight-pressed. Soundless. No cry, no sigh is heard. Peaceful and quiet. But both are crying without a sound. Crying in unison. Their cheeks are wet. I am the umpire and I am the prize. I laugh maliciously. I thirst to see blood, to hear wild shrieks. In Emek Refaim a freight train will whistle. The storm and the fury will silently fuse. And the tears.

Very late the rain will come. A rain not of words will lash the British armored cars. Down the alley at twilight terrorists steal, slipping past the arch in Mousrara. Slipping past pressing close to the stone wall in the darkness silencing the solitary street lamp fixing a fuse to the detonator and the detonator is still cold iron, an electric spark will jump and the volcano is hidden deep down under the surface of dust and slate and granite. It is cold.

The rain will come.

Gentle mists will wander in the wooded Valley of the Cross. On Mount Scopus a bird will cry. A stormy wind will lash the pine treetops into submission. The earth will not hold back, the earth will show no restraint. To the east is the desert. From the edge of Talpiot can be seen places which the rain cannot touch, the Mountains of Moab, the Dead Sea far below. Torrents of rain will pound Arnona opposite the gray village of Sur Baher. Fierce streams will assault the minarets. And in Bethlehem the players will shut themselves up in the coffee-house, backgammon boards will be opened, and from every corner will come the wailing music of Radio Amman. Enclosed and silent are the men at play. Desert robes and bushy mustaches. Scalding coffee. Smoke. Twins in commando uniforms armed with submachine guns.

After the rain, clear hail. Fine, sharp crystals. The old peddlers in Mahane Yehuda will crowd shivering under the shelter of overhanging balconies. In the hills of Abu Ghosh in Kiryat Yearim in Neve Ilan in Tirat Yaar thick woods intertwined pines shrouded in white fog. There fugitives from the law take refuge. Silently bitter deserters trudge along waterlogged paths, wandering on through the rain.

Low lies the sky over the North Sea *Dragon* and *Tigress* patrol side by side among massive icebergs prowling and searching for the sea-monster Moby Dick or *Nautilus* on the radar screen. Ahoy, ahoy, a muffled seaman will shout from the masthead. Ahoy there Captain, unidentified object sighted in the fog six miles east four knots, two degrees to port of the northern lights, the radio operator will transmit metallically to

Allied headquarters in a far-off underwater hideout. Palestine too will grow dark for there is rain and fog on the Hebron Hills up to Talpiot to Augusta Victoria to the desert's edge which the rain may never cross to the High Commissioner's palace.

Alone at the darkening window frail and tall stands the British High Commissioner, a gaunt man his hands joined behind his back a pipe between his teeth his eyes blue and clouded. Into two goblets he will pour a clear sharp potion one glass for himself and the other for short thickset Michael Strogoff sent to fight his way in the darkness through enemy territory blockaded by barbaric armies to the coast then over the main to the Mysterious Island where scanning the sea horizon with eagle eyes waits engineer Cyrus Smith gripping a powerful spyglass and never knowing despair. We had thought we were all alone here on the desert island. Surely our senses deluded us. We are not alone on the island. Someone sinister lurks in the depths of the mountain. We have searched the whole island most thoroughly and systematically and have not discovered who it is who is watching us out of the darkness with pale laughter on his face a silent presence watching unsensed behind our backs only his footprints appearing on the spongy pathway at dawn. Lurking and lying in wait in the murky shadow in the fog in the rain in the storm in the dark forest lurking beneath the surface of the earth lying hidden in wait behind convent walls in the village of Ein Kerem a strange man lurking relentlessly lying in wait. Let him come live and snarling hurl me to the ground and thrust into my body he will growl and I shriek in reply in a rapture of horror and magic of horror and thrill I will scream burn and suck like a vampire a madly whirling drunken ship in the night will I be when he comes at me, singing and seething and floating I will be flooded I will be a foam-flecked mare gliding through the night in the rain the torrents will rush down to flood Jerusalem the sky will come low clouds touching the earth and the wild wind will ravage the city.

CHAPTER

34

 "Good morning, Mrs. Gonen."

"Good morning, Dr. Urbach."

"Are we still feeling distressed, Mrs. Gonen?"

"The fever has gone, Doctor. I hope in a couple of days I shall be back to normal."

" 'Normal,' Mrs. Gonen, is a relative expression, so to say. Is Mr. Gonen not at home?"

"My husband has been called up, Doctor. My husband is apparently in the Sinai Desert. I have not had any news as yet from my husband."

"These are important days, Mrs. Gonen, fateful days. At times such as these it is difficult to refrain from scriptural thoughts. Is our throat still inflamed? Let us look inside and find out. It was bad, very bad, dear lady, what you did when you poured on yourself cold water in the middle of winter, as if it is possible to bring peace to the mind by bringing afflictions to the body. If you excuse me, please, what is the chosen subject of Dr. Gonen? Biology? Ah, geology. Excuse me, please. We were mistaken. Well, today the news from the war is optimistic. The English and the French also will fight together with us against the Moslems. The radio this morning spoke even of 'the allies.' Almost like in Europe. Nonetheless, Mrs. Gonen, there is also something from Faust in this war. Closer, you see, than anybody to the truth was little Gretchen. And how faithful was Gretchen, and not at all naïve, as she is usually depicted. Please, Mrs. Gonen, give me now your arm, I must measure your blood pressure. A simple test. Not painful in the slightest. There is a serious defect of the intellect in some Jews; we are not able to hate those who hate us. Some mental disorder. Well, yesterday the Israel army climbed up Mount Sinai with tanks. Almost apocalyptic, I would say, but only almost. Now I must beg very much your pardon but I must ask you a rather intimate question. Have you noticed any irregularity recently in your monthly cycle, Mrs. Gonen? No? That is a good sign. A very good sign. It is a sign that the body has not begun also to participate in the drama. So your husband is a geologist, not an anthropologist. We were somewhat mistaken. Now, we must continue to rest still for some days more. And to rest thoroughly. Not to tire ourselves out with thinking. Sleep is the best remedy. Sleep, in a sense, is the most natural condition for a human being. And the headache must not frighten us. Against the migraine we will arm ourselves with aspirin. Migraine is not an independent disease. And by the way, human beings do not die so easily as perhaps in an extreme moment we might imagine. I wish you better."

Dr. Urbach left and Simcha, Hadassah's maid, arrived. She took off her coat and stood warming her hands at the fire. She asked, how are you today, ma'am. I asked, what's the news in my friend Hadassah's house. Simcha had read in the paper that morning that the Arabs had lost and we were victorious. Well, she said, they certainly deserved it; one can only endure so much in silence.

Simcha went into the kitchen. She warmed me some milk. Then she opened a window in the study to air the room. Biting cold air came streaming in. Simcha polished the windows with old newspaper. She dusted the furniture. She went out to shop. When she came back she had news to tell of an Arab warship burning alive in the sea off Haifa. Should she make a start on the ironing?

My whole body felt good today. I was ill. I needn't concentrate. Burning alive at sea—all this had happened before in the distant past. This wasn't the first time.

"Your face is very pale today, ma'am," Simcha remarked anxiously. "The Master said before he went away not to talk to Madam a lot because of Madam's health."

"You talk to me, Simcha," I begged her. "Tell me about yourself. Keep talking. Don't stop."

"I'm not married yet, ma'am, but I'm engaged. When my man Bechor comes back from the army we're going to buy one of those new apartments in Beit Mazmil. We're going to have the wedding in the spring. My man Bechor has plenty of money put by. He works as a taxi driver for Kesher Taxis. He's a bit shy, but he's educated. I've noticed something, that most of my girl friends, they marry men like their pas. Bechor he's like my pa too. It's a rule, I read it once explained in *Woman* magazine: the husband is always like the father. I suppose if you love someone you want him to be at least a bit like someone you already loved to start with. That's funny, I was waiting and waiting for the iron to warm up, and I clean forgot the power's been cut off in Jerusalem."

.   .   .

I thought to myself.

A young man in a story by Somerset Maugham or Stefan Zweig has come from a small town to play roulette in an international casino. Since the beginning of the evening he has lost two-thirds of his money. The sum he finds himself left with after a careful calculation will just suffice to pay his hotel bill and to buy him a railway ticket so that he can leave town decently. It is two o'clock in the morning. Can the young man get up and leave now? The brightly lit wheel is still spinning and the chandeliers are sparkling. Perhaps the decisive win is waiting for him at the end of the very next spin? The Sheikh's son from the Hadhramaut sitting opposite has just collected a cool ten thousand in one go. No, he cannot get up and leave now. Especially since the elderly English lady who has been peering owl-eyed all evening at him through her pince-nez will be bound to flash him a look of cold irony. And outside in the dark, snow is falling as far as the eye can see. And the dim sound of the roaring sea, outside. No, the young man cannot get up and leave. He buys chips with the last of his money. Presses his eyes tight shut, then opens them. Opens them, and immediately blinks as if the light is blinding them. And outside in the dark is the muffled roar of the sea and the silently falling snow.

We have been married now for more than six years. If your work takes you to Tel Aviv, you always come back the same evening. We have never been apart for more than two nights since the day we were married. For six years we have been married and living in this apartment, and I have still not learned how to open and close the balcony shutters, because that is your job. Now that you have been called up, the shutters stand open day and night. I have been thinking about you. You knew in advance that you were being called up for a war, not for maneuvers. That the war would be in Egypt and not in the east. That the war would be a short one. All this you deduced with the aid of a well-balanced inner mechanism by means of which you continually produce thoroughly reasoned ideas. I have to present you with an equation on whose solution I depend in the way that a man standing on the edge of a precipice depends on the strength of the railing.

This morning I sat in the armchair and altered the buttons on the cuffs of your dark suit to make them more fashionable. As I sewed I asked myself, what is this impenetrable glass dome which has fallen on us to separate our lives from objects, places, people, opinions? Of course, Michael, there are friends, visitors, colleagues, neighbors, relatives. But when they are sitting in our living room talking to us their words are always indistinct because of the glass, which is not even transparent. It is only from their expressions that I manage to guess something of their meaning. Sometimes their shapes dissolve: vague masses without outlines. Objects, places, people, opinions, I need them and I can't keep going without them. What about you, Michael, are you contented or not? How can I find out? Sometimes you seem sad. Are you contented or not? What if I were to die? What if you were to die? I am merely groping my way through an introduction, a preliminary, still learning and rehearsing a complicated role which I shall have to act out in days yet to come. Packing. Preparing. Practicing. When will the journey begin, Michael? I have grown tired of waiting and waiting. You are resting your arms on the steering wheel. Are you dozing or thinking? I cannot tell; you are always so calm and controlled. Start up, Michael, start off; I have been ready and waiting for years.

CHAPTER

35

Simcha brought Yair home
from kindergarten. His fingers were blue with cold. In the
street they had met the postman, who had handed them a
military postcard from Sinai: My brother Emanuel says that
he is well and that he is doing and seeing great wonders. He
will send us another card from Cairo, capital of Egypt. He
hopes that all is well with us in Jerusalem. He has not met
Michael: the desert is vast; by comparison our Negev seems like
a tiny sand-pit. Do I remember the trip we made to Jericho
with Father when we were little? Next time we'll push down
to the Jordan, and then we'll be able to go down to Jericho to
buy rush mats again. "Kiss Yair from me," he concluded. "I
hope one day he'll grow, to fight against the foe. With love
and fond farewell—Yours, Emanuel."

From Michael there was not a word.

An image:

By the light of the field radio his carved features suggest
weary responsibility. His shoulders are hunched. His lips
pressed tightly together. He is bent over the radio. Huddled.

His back turned, no doubt, to the crescent moon which rises pale and thin behind him.

Two visitors came to see how I was that evening.

In the afternoon Mr. Kadishman and Mr. Glick had met in Haturim Street. It was from Mr. Glick that Mr. Kadishman had learned that Mrs. Gonen was ill and that Mr. Gonen had been called up. At once they had both determined to look in that evening and offer their assistance. So they had both come to visit me together: if one man had come alone it might have given rise to untoward gossip.

Mr. Glick said:

"It must be very hard for you, Mrs. Gonen. These are tense times, the weather is cold, and you are all alone."

Mr. Kadishman, in the meantime, had been feeling the cup of tea by my bedside with his large, fleshy fingers.

"Cold," he announced mournfully, "ice cold. Will you permit me, dear lady, to invade your kitchen, invade in quotation marks, of course, and make you a fresh cup of tea?"

"Certainly not," I said. "I'm allowed to get out of bed. I'll just slip my dressing gown on and make you both a cup of coffee or cocoa."

"Heaven forbid, Mrs. Gonen, Heaven forbid!" Mr. Glick was startled, and blinked as though I had outraged his sense of decency. His mouth twitched nervously. Like a hare twitching at an unfamiliar sound.

Mr. Kadishman registered interest:

"What does our friend write from the front?"

"I haven't had a letter from him yet," I said, smiling.

"The fighting is over," Mr. Kadishman interposed hastily, beaming with happiness. "The fighting is over and there is not a foe left in the Wilderness of Horeb."

"May I trouble you to turn on the light?" I asked. "There, to your left. Why should we sit here in the dark?"

Mr. Glick rolled his lower lip between his thumb and forefinger. His eyes seemed to follow the path of the electric current from the switch to the light bulb on the ceiling. Perhaps he felt he was superfluous. He asked:

"Is there anything I can do to help?"

"Thank you very much, my dear Mr. Glick, but I don't need any help."

It suddenly occurred to me to add:

"It must be hard for you, too, Mr. Glick, without your wife and . . . all alone."

Mr. Kadishman stood standing by the light switch for a moment, as if he had doubted the outcome of his action and could not believe in his complete success. Then he came back and sat down. As he did so he seemed rather ponderous, like those prehistoric creatures with gigantic bodies and tiny skulls. I suddenly noticed something Mongolian in Mr. Kadishman's face: broad, flat cheekbones, his features at the same time coarse and the opposite, amazingly refined. A Tartar face. Michael Strogoff's cunning interrogator. I smiled at him.

"Mrs. Gonen," Mr. Kadishman began after sitting down ponderously, "Mrs. Gonen, in these historic days I have been pondering at great length the fact that whereas Vladimir Jabotinsky's disciples have been swept into the corner, yet his doctrines are enjoying a great success. A very great success indeed."

He seemed to be speaking with secret inner relief. I loved what he said: There are setbacks and tribulations, but after prolonged tribulations due recompense will come. Thus I translated it in my mind from his Tartar tongue into my own language. So as not to offend him by my silence, I said:

"Time will tell."

"It already is telling," Mr. Kadishman said, with a triumphant expression on his outlandish face. "The message of these historic days is clear and unambiguous."

Meanwhile Mr. Glick had succeeded in formulating the answer to a question which I, who had asked it, had by now quite forgotten:

"My poor dear Duba, they are giving her electric shock treatment. They say there is still hope. One mustn't despair, they say. If God wills . . ."

His great hands crushed and kneaded a battered hat. His thin mustache quivered like a tiny living animal. His voice was anxious, pleading for a clemency he did not deserve: despair is a mortal sin.

"It will turn out all right," I said.

Mr. Glick:

"Amen. Amen selah. Oh, what a calamity. And all for what?"

Mr. Kadishman:

"From now on the State of Israel will change. This time the hand which wields the axe, in Bialik's phrase, is ours. Now it is the turn of the Gentile world to howl aloud and ask if there is justice in the world, and if so, when it will appear. Israel is no longer 'a scattered sheep'; we are no longer a ewe among seventy wolves, or a lamb being led to the slaughter. We have had enough. 'Among wolves, be a wolf.' It has all happened as Jabotinsky foretold in his prophetic novel, *Prelude to Delilah*. Have you read Jabotinsky's *Prelude to Delilah*, Mrs. Gonen? It is well worth reading. And especially now that our army is pursuing the routed forces of Pharaoh and the sea is not divided for the fleeing Egyptians."

"But why are you both sitting in your overcoats? I'll get up and put the heat on. I'll make something to drink. Please take off your coats."

As if reprimanded, Mr. Glick hurriedly rose to his feet:

"No, please, Mrs. Gonen, don't get out of bed. There's absolutely no need. We simply . . . looked in to see how you were. We must be off directly. Please don't get up. There's no need to put the heat on."

Mr. Kadishman:

"I, too, must take my leave. I merely called in on my way to a committee meeting, to see if there was anything I could do to help."

"To help, Mr. Kadishman?"

"In case you needed anything. To deal with any business matters, perhaps, or . . ."

"Thank you for your good intentions, Mr. Kadishman. You belong to the dying race of true gentlemen."

His saurian features lit up. "I shall call again tomorrow or the day after to find out what our dear friend has to say in his letter," he promised.

"Pray do call, Mr. Kadishman," I said mockingly. My Michael's choice of friends amazed me.

Mr. Kadishman nodded emphatically. "Now that you have been kind enough to offer me an explicit invitation, I shall most certainly call."

"I wish you a speedy and complete recovery," said Mr. Glick. "And if there is anything I can do by way of shopping or any other kind of errand . . . Is there anything you might require?"

"So kind of you, Mr. Glick," I replied. He stared intently at his battered hat. Silence fell. The two elderly men were standing now at the other end of the room, edging towards the door, putting as much distance as possible between themselves and my bed. Mr. Glick spotted a white thread on the back of Mr. Kadishman's overcoat, and removed it. Outside a breeze blew up and died away. From the kitchen came the sound of the refrigerator motor, which seemed suddenly to have taken a new lease on life. Once again I was flooded by that same calm, lucid feeling that I should soon be dead. What a bleak thought. A well-balanced woman is not indifferent to the thought of death. Death and I are indifferent to one another. Close and yet remote. Distant acquaintances who are barely on nodding terms. I felt I ought to say something at once. I felt that I should not say good-bye to my friends and let them go now. Perhaps tonight the first rain would fall. Surely I was not an old woman yet. I could still be attractive. I must get up at once. Put on my dressing gown. I must make coffee and cocoa, serve some cakes, make conversation, be interested, be interesting; I too am educated, I too have views and ideas; there is something clutching at my throat.

"Are you in a very great hurry?" I asked.

"Regretfully I must take my leave," said Mr. Kadishman. "Mr. Glick is at liberty to stay if he wishes."

Mr. Glick wrapped a thick scarf round his neck.

Don't go yet, old friends. She mustn't be left alone. Sit down in the armchairs. Take off your overcoats. Relax. We will discuss politics and philosophy. We will exchange views about religious faith and righteousness. We shall be fluent and friendly. We shall drink together. Don't go. She is afraid to be left alone in the house. Stay. Don't go.

"I wish you a speedy recovery, Mrs. Gonen, and a very good night."

"You're leaving, so soon. You must find me boring."

"Heaven forbid. Perish the thought." Their anxious voices converged.

Both these men had feeble gestures, being lonely and no longer young, and neither of them used to visiting the sick.

"The street is deserted," I said.

"I wish you better," replied Mr. Kadishman. He pressed his hat down onto his forehead as if suddenly shutting a skylight.

Mr. Glick said, as he left:

"Please do not be anxious, Mrs. Gonen. There is no sense in worrying. It will all be all right. Everything, absolutely everything will turn out for the best, as they say. Yes. You are smiling; how pleasant to see you smiling."

The visitors left.

Immediately I turned on the radio. Straightened the bed-clothes. Have I got a contagious disease? Why did the two old friends forget to shake hands with me when they arrived and again when they left?

The radio announced that the conquest of the peninsula was now complete. The Minister of Defense proclaimed that the Island of Jotbath, commonly known as Tiran, had returned to the possession of the Third Kingdom of Israel. Hannah Gonen will return to Yvonne Azulai. But our aim was peace, proclaimed the Minister, in his unique rhetorical style. If only the rational elements in the Arab camp would overcome their grim desire for vengeance, the long-awaited peace would come.

My twins, for instance.

In the suburb of Sanhedriya the cypresses bent and straightened, straightened and bent in the breeze. It is my humble opinion that all flexibility is witchcraft. It flows, yet it is cold and restful all at the same time. A few years ago, on a winter's day in Terra Sancta College, I copied down some remarks of the professor of Hebrew literature which were filled with sadness: From Abraham Mapu to Peretz Smolenskin the Hebrew Enlightenment underwent a painful transformation. A crisis of disappointment and disillusionment. When dreams are shat-

227

tered, sensitive men are not bent but broken. "Thy destroyers and they that lay thee waste shall go forth of thee." The implications of this verse of Isaiah are twofold, said the professor: First of all, the Hebrew Enlightenment nurtured in its own bosom the ideas which subsequently led to its destruction. Later on, many good men "went forth" to graze in alien pastures. The critic Abraham Uri Kovner was a tragic figure. He was like the scorpion, which when it is hemmed in by flames plants its sting in its own back. In the seventies and eighties of the last century there was an oppressive feeling of a vicious circle. Had it not been for a few dreamers and fighters, realists who rebelled against reality, we would have had no revival and would have been virtually doomed. But it is always the dreamers who achieve great things, the professor concluded. I have not forgotten. What an immense labor of translation awaits me! This too I have to translate into my own language. I do not want to die. Mrs. Hannah Greenbaum-Gonen: The initials *HG* spell the Hebrew for "festival"; if only the whole of her life could be one long festival. My friend the kind librarian from Terra Sancta, who used to wear a skullcap and exchange greetings and witticisms with me, has long been dead. What is left is words. I am tired of words. What a cheap lure.

CHAPTER

36

Next morning the radio announced that the Ninth Brigade had captured the shore batteries at Sharm el Sheikh. The prolonged blockade of our shipping had been shattered. From now on, new horizons were opened up to us.

Dr. Urbach, too, had an announcement to make that morning. He smiled his sad, sympathetic smile and shook his diminutive shoulders as if in contempt of the words he spoke:

"It is permissible now for us to walk a little and work a little. Provided we avoid all mental effort and also avoid straining the throat. And provided we come to terms with objective reality. I wish you a speedy recovery."

For the first time since Michael's departure I got up and went outside. It made a change. As if some shrill, piercing sound had suddenly stopped. As if a motor which had been trilling outside all day had suddenly been switched off towards evening. The sound had passed unnoticed all day; only when it stopped did it make itself felt. A sudden stillness. It had existed and now it had stopped. It had stopped, therefore it had existed.

. . .

I dismissed the maid. I wrote a reassuring letter to my mother and sister-in-law at Nof Harim. I baked a cheesecake. At noon I telephoned the military information office of Jerusalem. I asked where Michael's battalion was currently stationed. The reply was politely apologetic: Most of the army was still on the move. The field post was unreliable. There was no cause for alarm. The name "Michael Gonen" did not appear on any of their lists.

It was a wasted effort. When I got back from the drugstore I found a letter from Michael in the mailbox. The postmark showed that the letter had been delayed. Michael began by inquiring anxiously after my health and about the child and the house. Next he informed me that he was in good health, apart from the heartburn which was aggravated by the poor food, and apart from having broken his reading glasses on the first day out. Michael complied with military censorship regulations and did not reveal the whereabouts of his battalion, but he managed to hint indirectly that his unit had not been in action at all, but had been engaged in security duties inside the country. Finally, he reminded me that Yair was due to go for dental treatment that Thursday.

Thursday, that was tomorrow.

Next day I took Yair to the Strauss Medical Center, where the local dental clinic was. Yoram Kamnitzer, our neighbors' son, went with us part of the way because his youth club was near the clinic. Yoram explained awkwardly that he had been sorry to hear of my illness and was delighted to see me well again.

We stopped at a stall selling hot corn on the cob, and I offered to buy some for Yair and Yoram. Yoram thought it right to refuse. His refusal was faint and almost inaudible. I was unkind to him. I asked him why he seemed so dreamy and vacant today. Had he fallen in love with one of the girls in his class?

My question brought out large beads of perspiration on Yoram's brow. He wanted to wipe his face but could not because his hands were dirty and sticky from the corn I had bought him. I looked at him fixedly so as to increase his embarrassment. Humiliation and despair inspired a wave of nervous audacity in the youth. He turned a gloomy, tormented face on me and muttered:

"I'm not involved with any girl in my class, Mrs. Gonen, or with any girl at all. I'm sorry, I don't want to be rude, but you really shouldn't have asked me that question. I don't ask. Love and things like that are . . . private."

A late autumn was reigning in Jerusalem. The sky was not cloudy, but neither was it bright. Its color was autumnal: blue-gray, like the road and like the old stone buildings. It was a fitting hue. Once again I felt that this was by no means the first time. I had been here and now before.

I said:

"I'm sorry, Yoram. I forgot for a moment that you go to an Orthodox school. I was curious. There's no reason why you should share your secrets with me. You are seventeen and I am twenty-seven. Naturally I seem like an old hag to you."

I was now causing the boy worse torment than he had undergone before. And deliberately. He looked away. In his nervous state he bumped into Yair and almost sent him flying. He started to speak, failed to find the right words, and eventually gave up the attempt.

"Old—you? On the contrary, Mrs. Gonen, on the contrary . . . What I was trying to say was . . . You take an interest in

231

my problem, and . . . with you I can sometimes . . . No. When I try to put it into words, it comes out all back to front. All I meant was . . ."

"Relax, Yoram. You don't have to say it."

He was mine. All mine. He was at my mercy. I could paint any expression I liked on his face. Like on a sheet of paper. It was years since I had last enjoyed this grim game. I turned the screw further, relishing with cautious sips the laughter welling inside me.

"No, Yoram, you don't have to say it. You can write me a letter. In any case, you've already said nearly everything. By the way, has anyone ever told you you've got beautiful eyes? If you had more self-confidence, you'd be a real heart-throb. If I were your age instead of an old hag, I don't know how I could resist falling for you. You're a lovely boy."

I did not take my cold eyes off his face for a moment. I absorbed the astonishment, the longing, the suffering, the mad hope. I was intoxicated.

Yoram stammered:

"Please, Mrs. Gonen . . ."

"Hannah. You can call me Hannah."

"I . . . I feel respect for you, and . . . no, respect isn't the right word . . . regard, and . . . interest."

"Why apologize, Yoram? I like you. It's not a sin to be liked."

"You make me regret, Mrs. Gonen, Hannah . . . I won't say anything else, or I'll regret it later. I'm sorry, Mrs. Gonen."

"Keep talking, Yoram. I'm not so sure you'll regret it."

At that moment Yair intervened. With his mouth crammed full of corn he exclaimed:

"Regret—that's the British. In the War of Independence they were on the Arab side, and now they regret it already."

Yoram said:

232

"This is where I turn off, Mrs. Gonen. I take back everything I said just now and I beg your pardon."

"Wait a moment, Yoram. There's something I'd like to ask you to do."

"When we were in Holon, when Grandpa Zalman was alive, he told me the British are cold-blooded like snakes."

"Yes, Mrs. Gonen. What can I do for you?"

"Mummy, what does it mean that snakes are cold-blooded?"

"It means that their blood isn't warm. What I wanted to ask you . . ."

"But why isn't snakes' blood warm? And why do people have warm blood, except the British?"

"Say you're not cross with me, Mrs. Gonen. Perhaps I said something silly."

"In some animals the heart pumps the blood and warms it. I can't explain exactly. Don't torture yourself, Yoram. When I was your age I had a lot of strength to love. I'd like to have another chat with you. Today or tomorrow. Be quiet for a moment, Yair, stop nagging. How often has your father told you not to interrupt when people are talking? Today or tomorrow. That's what I wanted to ask you. I'd like to have a chat with you. I'd like to give you some advice."

"I didn't interrupt. Maybe only after Yoram interrupted me when I was talking."

"Meanwhile, don't torture yourself unnecessarily. Good-bye, Yoram. I'm not cross with you, and don't be cross with yourself. Yair, I've answered your question. That's the way it is. I can't explain everything in the world. How, why, where, when. 'If Grandma had wings and she could fly, she'd be an eagle in the sky.' When your father comes back he'll explain everything, because he's cleverer than I am and he knows everything."

"Daddy doesn't know everything, but when Daddy doesn't know he says he doesn't know. He doesn't say he knows but he can't explain. That's impossible. If you know something then you can explain it. I've finished."

"Thank goodness for that, Yair."

Yair threw away his chewed corncob. Carefully wiped his hands on his handkerchief. He refrained from taking offense. He did not speak. Even when I asked him in a sudden panic if we had turned off the gas before we left the house, he didn't say a word. I hated his stubborn pride. When we got to the clinic I sat him down forcibly in the dentist's chair, even though he had made no attempt to resist. Ever since Michael had explained to him how rot attacks the roots of the teeth he had proved understanding and thoroughly cooperative. Dentists were always amazed at him. Moreover, the drill and the other dental instruments aroused in the child a lively curiosity which I found revolting: a child of five who was fascinated by tooth-rot would grow up to be a disgusting person. I hated myself for the thought, but I could not dismiss it.

While the dentist attended to Yair's teeth I sat on a low stool in the corridor and arranged in my mind the things I intended to say to Yoram Kamnitzer.

First of all, I would extract the confession which was preying on him. I would easily succeed in this, I knew, and so I would revel once more in the powers which I had not lost entirely, even though time was attacking them, ravaging, rotting and wrecking them with pale, precise fingers.

Then, when I had achieved the mastery I longed for, I meant to induce Yoram to choose a precipitous life. That is, encourage him to be, say, a poet instead of a Bible teacher. That is, hurl him to the opposite bank. That is, subjugate a last Michael Strogoff for the last time to the will, to the mission, of a deposed princess.

I intended to offer him nothing more than a handful of friendly words couched in fairly general terms, because he was a gentle boy and I had not discovered in him the magical power of flexibility or the floods of deep-flowing energy.

All my plans came to nothing. The boy did not keep his agonized promise to come and see me. I must have stirred up in him a panic which was stronger than he was.

At the end of that month an obscure magazine published a love poem by Yoram. In contrast to his earlier poems, this time he dared to name parts of a woman's body. The woman was Potiphar's wife, exposing parts of her body to ensnare the righteous Joseph.

Mr. and Mrs. Kamnitzer were immediately summoned to a conference with the headmaster of the Orthodox high school. They decided to avoid making a fuss, provided Yoram completed his final year in an educational institute on an Orthodox kibbutz in the south. I only found out the details later. It was only later, too, that I read the daring poem about the plight of the righteous Joseph. It was sent to me by mail, in a plain cover with my name printed in block capitals. It was a flowery, high-flown poem: an outcry of a tortured body through a veil of low spirits.

I acknowledged my defeat. So Yoram would go to university. He would end up teaching Bible and Hebrew. He would not be a poet. He might manage to compose occasional pedantic verses, on the colored greeting card, for instance, which he would send us each New Year. We, the Gonen family, would respond with a New Year's card to Yoram and his young family. Time would be ever-present; a tall, freezing, transparent presence hostile to Yoram and hostile to me, boding no good.

In fact, it had all been decided by Mrs. Glick, our hysterical neighbor, who had attacked Yoram in the yard shortly before she was committed. She had torn his shirt open, slapped his face, and called him lecher, voyeur, peeping Tom.

But the defeat was mine. This was my last attempt. The menacing presence was stronger than I. From now on I would allow myself to float downstream, borne by the current, in passive repose.

CHAPTER

37

The following evening, as I was bathing Yair and washing his hair, a gaunt, dusty figure stood framed in the doorway. Because of the running water and Yair's talking, I had not heard him come in. He stood in his stocking feet in the bathroom doorway. He might have been standing staring silently at me for several minutes before I noticed him and let out a low cry of shock and surprise. He had removed his shoes in the hall so as not to bring mud into the apartment.

"Michael," I meant to say with a tender smile. But the name came hurtling out of my throat with a sob.

"Yair. Hannah. Good evening to you both. It's good to see you looking well. I'm back."

"Daddy, did you kill any Arabs?"

"No, my boy. On the contrary. The Jewish army nearly killed me. I'll tell you all about it later. Hannah, you'd better dry the boy and dress him before he catches his death. The water's ice cold."

. . .

The reserve battalion in which Michael was serving had not been demobilized yet, but they had released Michael early because they had inadvertently called up two radio operators too many, because his broken glasses rendered him all but useless at the radio, because in any case the whole battalion was due to be demobilized within a couple of days, and also because he was slightly ill.

"You, ill." I raised my voice as if I were reprimanding him.

"I said slightly. There's no need to shout, Hannah. You can see that I'm walking, talking, and breathing. Only slightly ill. Some sort of stomach poisoning, apparently."

"It was just the shock, Michael. I'll stop at once. I've stopped. There. No tears. I've got over it. I've missed you. When you left I was ill and bad-tempered. I'm not ill now, and I'll try to be nicer to you. I want you. You get washed and meanwhile I'll put Yair to bed. I'll make you a supper fit for a king. With a white tablecloth. A bottle of wine. And that's just to begin with. There, how silly of me; I've spoiled the surprise."

"I don't think I'm supposed to drink wine this evening," Michael said apologetically, and a calm smile spread over his face. "I'm not feeling too well."

When he had washed up, Michael unpacked his rucksack, threw his dirty clothes in the laundry basket, put everything away in its place. He wrapped himself up in a thick blanket. His teeth were chattering. He asked me to forgive him for spoiling his first evening home with his troubles.

His face looked strange. Without his glasses he had difficulty reading the newspaper. He switched off the light and turned his face to the wall. Several times during the night I woke up, thinking I heard Michael groaning, or perhaps just belching. I asked him if he wanted me to make him a glass of tea. He thanked me and refused. I got up and made some tea. I told him to drink it. He obeyed and gulped it down. Again he let out a sound which was neither a groan nor a belch. He seemed to be suffering a serious attack of nausea.

"Does it hurt, Michael?"

"No, it doesn't hurt. Go to sleep, Hannah. We'll talk about it tomorrow."

Next morning I sent Yair off to kindergarten and summoned Dr. Urbach. The doctor came in with china footsteps, smiled wistfully, and declared that we must go into the hospital for an urgent examination. He ended with his customary formula of reassurance:

"Human beings do not die so easily as perhaps in an extreme moment we might imagine. I wish you better."

In the taxi on the way to Shaare Zedek Hospital, Michael tried to dispel my anxiety with a joke:

"I feel like a war hero in a Soviet film. Almost."

Then, after a pause, he asked me to ring his Aunt Jenia in Tel Aviv if he got any worse and to tell her he was ill.

I still remember. When I was thirteen my father, Yosef Greenbaum, came down with his last illness. He died of a malignant growth. During the weeks preceding his death his features progressively decayed. His skin grew shriveled and sallow, his cheeks sank, his hair fell out in handfuls, his teeth rotted; he seemed to be shrinking hour by hour. The most frightening thing was the inward sinking of his mouth, giving the impression of a perpetual cunning smile. As if his illness were a practical joke which had come off. In fact, my father clung in his last days to a kind of forced jocularity. He told us that the problem of survival after death was one which had always exercised his curiosity ever since he was a young man in Cracow. Once he had even written a letter in German to Professor Martin Buber inquiring about the question. And once he had had a reply on the subject published in the correspondence column of a leading newspaper. And now in a few days he would have access to a reliable and authoritative solution to the mystery of life after death. Father had in his possession a reply written in German in Professor Buber's own hand-writing, in which he said that we live on in our children and our works.

"I can't lay claim to any works," his sunken mouth grinned, "but I do have children. Hannah, do you feel like a continuation of my soul or my body?"

And at once he added:

"I was only joking. Your personal feelings are your own personal feelings. It was of questions such as these that the ancients long ago said that they have no answer."

Father died at home. The doctors did not think it right to move him to the hospital, because there was no hope left, and he knew, and they knew that he knew. The doctors gave him medicines to relieve the pain, and expressed amazement at the composure he displayed in his last days. Father had been preparing all his life for the day of his death. He spent his last morning sitting in an armchair in his brown dressing gown, doing the prize crossword in the English-language newspaper, the *Palestine Post*. At noon he went out to the mailbox to send off his completed solution. When he came back he retired to his room and closed the door behind him, leaving it unlocked. He turned his back on the room, leaned on the window sill, and passed away. It was his intention to spare his loved ones the unpleasant sight. At that time my brother Emanuel was already a member of an underground group in a kibbutz a long way from Jerusalem. Mother and I were out at the hairdresser's. Unconfirmed reports had arrived that morning from the front of a dramatic change in the course of the war, at the Battle of Stalingrad. In his will Father left me three thousand pounds for my wedding day. I was to give half the sum to Emanuel in the event of his giving up kibbutz life. Father had been a thrifty man. He also left a file containing a dozen or so letters from eminent men who had deigned to answer his inquiries on a number of theoretical topics. Two or three of them were in the actual handwriting of world-famous personalities. Father also left behind a notebook filled with jottings. At first, I supposed he had been in the habit of secretly noting down his thoughts and observations. Later I realized that these were in fact remarks he had heard over the years from important men. Once, for example, he had conversed with the famous Menahem Ussishkin, with whom he was sharing a compartment in a train going from Jerusalem to Tel Aviv, and had heard him say: "Although in every action it is necessary to exercise doubt, yet one should also act as if doubt did not exist." I found these words recorded in Father's notebook, with the source, date, and other circumstances added in brackets. Father was an attentive man, always on the alert for hints and omens. He did not regard it as beneath his dignity to spend his whole life kowtowing to powerful forces whose nature remained hidden from him. I loved him more than I have ever loved anyone else in the world.

. . .

Michael spent three days in Shaare Zedek Hospital. He showed the early symptoms of a stomach disease. Thanks to Dr. Urbach's alertness, the disease was diagnosed in its early stages. From now on certain foods would be forbidden him. Within a week he would be able to go back to work as usual.

On one of our visits to the hospital Michael managed to keep his promise to tell Yair about the war. He told of patrols, ambushes, and alarms. No, he could not answer questions about the fighting itself: "Unfortunately, Daddy didn't capture the Egyptian destroyer in Haifa Bay or visit Gaza. He wasn't parachuted near the Suez Canal, either. Daddy isn't a pilot or a paratrooper."

Yair showed understanding:

"You weren't too fit. That's why they left you behind."

"Who do you think *is* fit for war, Yair?"

"Me."

"You?"

"When I grow up. I'm going to be a big strong soldier. I'm stronger than lots of bigger boys in the playground. It's no good to be weak. Just like in our playground. I've finished speaking."

Michael said:

"You need to be sensible, Yair."

Yair pondered this statement silently. Compared, contrasted, connected. He was serious. Thoughtful. Finally he pronounced sentence:

"Sensible isn't the opposite of strong."

I said:

"Strong, sensible men are my favorite people. I'd like to meet a strong, sensible man some day."

Michael replied, of course, with a smile. And silence.

. . .

Our friends spared no effort. We had frequent visitors. Mr. Glick. Mr. Kadishman. The geologists. My best friend Hadassah and her husband, Abba. And finally, Yardena, Michael's blonde friend. She arrived with an officer of the United Nations Emergency Force. He was a Canadian giant, and I could not keep my eyes off him, even though Yardena caught me looking at him and smiled at me twice. She bent over the bed, kissed Michael's lean hand as though he were dying, and said:

"Snap out of it, Micha. It doesn't suit you, all this illness. I'm surprised at you. Believe it or not, I've already handed in my paper and I've even registered for the final exams. Slow but sure, that's me. You'll be an angel, won't you, Micha, and give me a hand with the work for the exams?"

"Sure," Michael replied, laughing. "Of course I will. I'm delighted for you, Yardena."

Yardena said:

"Micha, you're great. I've never met anybody as clever or sweet as you. Get better now, there's a good boy."

Michael recovered and went back to work. He also went back, after a long break, to working on his thesis. Once more his silhouette moving about at night beyond the frosted glass which divides his study from the room where I sleep. At ten o'clock I make him a glass of tea, without lemon. At eleven he takes a few moments off to listen to the final news broadcast. After that, shadows dancing and writhing on the wall with every movement of his in the night: Opening a drawer. Turning a page. Resting his head on his arms. Reaching out for a book.

Michael's glasses came back from being mended. His Aunt Leah sent him a new pipe. My brother Emanuel sent a crate of apples from Nof Harim. My mother knitted me a red muffler. And our Persian greengrocer, Mr. Elijah Mossiah, came back from the army.

Finally, halfway through November, the long-awaited rain arrived. Because of the war it was late that year. It fell with violence and fury. The city was shuttered. There was soft soaking all around. The gloomy gurgling of drainpipes. Our backyard was wet and abandoned. Fierce winds shook the shutters by night. The ancient fig tree stood bleak and bare outside our kitchen balcony. But the pines turned rich and verdant. They whispered sensuously. Never left me alone. Every car that passed in the street drew a long-drawn-out swish from the sodden asphalt.

Twice a week I attend advanced English classes arranged by the Working Mothers' Association. In the interlude between showers Yair floats battleships and destroyers in the puddle outside our house. He has a strange yearning for the sea now. When we are shut up indoors by the rain, the rug and armchair serve as ocean and harbor. The dominoes are his fleet. Great sea battles are fought out in our living room. An Egyptian destroyer blazes at sea. Guns spit fire. A captain makes a decision.

Sometimes, if I finish preparing supper early, I too join in the game. My powder compact is a submarine. I am an enemy. Once I suddenly clasped Yair in an affectionate embrace. I showered his head with rough kisses because for a moment Yair seemed to me like a real sea captain. As a result I was promptly banished from the game and the room. My son displayed once more his sullen pride: I could take part in his game only so long as I remained aloof and unemotional.

Perhaps I was wrong. Yair is showing signs of a cold authority. He does not get it from Michael. Or from me, either. His powers of memory repeatedly cause me amazement. He still remembers Hassan Salame's gang and its assault on Holon from Tel Arish, which he heard about from his grandfather a year and a half ago, when Yehezkel was still alive.

In a few months' time Yair will move on from kindergarten to school. Michael and I have decided to send him to Beit Hakerem School rather than to Tachkemoni Orthodox Boys' School, which is near where we live. Michael is determined that his son have a progressive education.

Our upstairs neighbors, the Kamnitzers, treat me with polite hostility. They still condescend to return my greeting, but they have stopped sending their little daughter down to ask for the loan of the iron or a baking dish.

Mr. Glick visits us regularly every five days. His reading in the *Encyclopaedia Hebraica* has progressed as far as the article on Belgium. His poor wife Duba's brother is a diamond merchant in Antwerp. Mrs. Glick herself is doing well. The doctors have promised to send her home in April or May. Our neighbor's gratitude knows no bounds. In addition to the weekend supplements of the religious daily *Hatsofeh,* he brings us presents of packets of pins, paper clips, stamp hinges, foreign stamps.

Michael has finally managed to arouse in Yair an active interest in stamp-collecting. Every Saturday morning they devote themselves to the collection. Yair soaks the stamps in water, carefully peels them off the paper, lays them out to dry on a large sheet of blotting paper which Mr. Glick has given him as a present. Michael sorts the dry stamps and sticks them in the album. Meanwhile I put a record on the phonograph, curl up in an armchair with my tired feet tucked underneath me, knit, and listen to the music. Relax. Through the window I can watch the woman next door hanging the bedclothes out on the balcony railings to air. I don't think and I don't feel. Time is powerfully present. I ignore it deliberately so as to confound it. I treat it in exactly the same way as I used to respond in my youth to the cheeky glances of rude men: I don't avert my eyes or turn away. I fix a smile of cold disdain on my face. Avoid panicking or feeling embarrassed. As if I were saying:

"So what?"

I know, I admit: this is a pathetic defense. But then the deception, too, is pathetic and ugly. I don't make excessive demands: only that the glass should remain transparent. A clever, pretty girl in a blue coat. A shriveled kindergarten teacher with varicose veins spreading on her thighs. In between, Yvonne Azulai drifts on a sea which has no shores. That the glass should remain transparent. Nothing more.

Jerusalem in winter knows bright, sun-drenched Saturdays when the sky takes on a hue which is not sky-blue but a deep, dark, concentrated blue, as if the sea had come up and settled upside down over the city. It is a limpid, radiant purity, pricked out with choirs of care-free birds, steeped in light. Distant objects, hills, buildings, woods seem to shimmer ceaselessly. The phenomenon is caused by the evaporating moisture, so Michael explained to me.

On Saturdays like this we generally have breakfast early and go out for a long walk. We leave the Orthodox neighborhoods behind us and wander as far afield as Talpiot, or Ein Kerem or Malcha, to Givat Shaul. At midday we sit down in one of the woods and eat a picnic lunch. We go home at nightfall on the first bus after the Sabbath. Such days are calm. At times I imagine that Jerusalem lies open before me with all its hidden places alight. I do not forget that the blue light is a fleeting vision. That the birds will fly away. But now I have learned to ignore it. To float along. Not to resist.

On one of our Saturday expeditions we happened to meet the

old professor under whom I had studied Hebrew literature when I was younger. With a touching effort the scholar managed to remember me and to fit my name to my face. He asked:

"What secret surprise are you planning for us, dear lady? A volume of poems?"

I denied the suggestion.

The professor thought for a moment, then smiled kindly and proffered the remark:

"What a wonderful city our Jerusalem is! It is not for nothing that it has been the object of the yearnings of countless generations in the gloomy depths of the Diaspora."

I agreed. We parted with a handshake. Michael wished the old man well. The professor bowed slightly and waved his hat in the air. The meeting made me happy.

We pick bunches of wild flowers: ranunculus, narcissus, cyclamen, anemones. On the way we cross abandoned building sites. Rest in the shade of a damp gray rock. Gaze into the distance to the coastal plain, the Hebron Hills, the Judean Desert. Sometimes we play hide-and-seek or catch. Slipping and laughing. Michael is gay and lighthearted. Once in a while he can express enthusiasm, saying, for instance:

"Jerusalem is the biggest city in the world. As soon as you cross two or three streets you are in a different continent, a different generation, even a different climate."

Or:

"How beautiful it is, Hannah, and how beautiful you are here, my sad Jerusalemite."

Yair is particularly interested in two subjects: the battles in the War of Independence and the network of public bus services.

On the former subject Michael is a mine of information. He points with his hand, identifies features in the landscape, draws plans in the dust, demonstrates with the help of twigs and stones: The Arabs were here, we were here. They were trying to break through here. We came round behind them there.

Michael also considers it right to explain to the boy about miscalculations, errors of strategy, failures. I, too, listen and learn. How little I knew about the battle for Jerusalem. The villa which belonged to Rashid Shahada, the twins' father, was handed over to the Health Organization, which turned it into a pre- and postnatal clinic. A housing project was built on the empty site. The Germans and the Greeks abandoned the German and Greek Colonies. New people moved in to take their places. New men, women, and children moved into Jerusalem. That would not be the last battle for Jerusalem. So I have heard our friend Mr. Kadishman say. I too can sense secret forces restlessly scheming, swelling and surging and bursting out through the surface.

I am amazed by Michael's ability to explain complicated things to Yair in very simple language, using hardly any adjectives. I am also amazed by the serious, intelligent questions which Yair occasionally asks.

Yair imagines war as an extraordinarily complex game, which displays a whole fascinating world of system and logic. My husband and my son both see time as a succession of equal squares on a sheet of graph paper, which provide a structure to support the lines and shapes.

There was never any need to explain to Yair the conflicting motives in the war. They were self-evident: conquest and domination. The boy's questions turned solely on the order of events: Arabs, Jews, hill, valley, ruins, trenches, armor, movement, surprise.

The bus company's network also fascinated our son, because

of the complex interrelations of the lines joining different destinations. The filigree of routes afforded him cold-blooded pleasure: the distances between the stops, the overlapping of the various routes, the convergence on the city center, the dispersal outwards.

On this subject Yair could enlighten us both. Michael foretold a future for him as a route-controller for the bus company. He hastened to stress that he was only joking, naturally.

Yair knew the makes of the buses operating on each route by heart. He enjoyed explaining the reasons for the use of the different makes: Here a steep hill, there a sharp bend or a poor road surface. The child's style of explanation closely resembled his father's. Both of them made frequent use of such words as "thus," "whereas," "in conclusion," and also "remote possibility."

I made an effort to listen to both of them quietly and attentively.

An image:

My son and my husband poring over a huge map spread out on a large desk. Various markers scattered over the map. Colored pins stuck in according to a plan concerted between the two of them, which seems to me like total chaos. They are arguing politely in German. They are both wearing gray suits, and sober ties secured with silver clips. I am there, clad in a flimsy, shabby nightdress. They are completely absorbed in their task. Bathed in white light but casting no shadow. Their attitudes suggest concentration and cautious responsibility. I cut in with some remark or request. They are both sympathetic and affable, not irritated at my interruption. They are at my service. Delighted to be of assistance. Could I possibly wait just five minutes?

. . .

There are also rather different Saturday expeditions.

We walk through the most fashionable parts of the city, Rehavia or Beit Hakerem. We pick out a house for ourselves. Inspect half-finished buildings. Discuss the advantages and disadvantages of different kinds of apartment. Distribute the rooms among ourselves. Decide where to put everything: Yair's toys will go here. This will be the study. The sofa here. The bookshelves. The armchairs. The rug.

Michael says:

"We ought to start saving, Hannah. We can't go on living from hand to mouth forever."

Yair suggests:

"We could get some money for the phonograph and the records. The radio makes enough music. And besides I'm sick of hearing it."

Myself:

"I'd like to travel in Europe. Have a telephone. Buy a small car so we could go to the seaside on weekends. When I was a child we had an Arab neighbor called Rashid Shahada. He was a very rich Arab. I expect they live in a refugee camp now. They had a house in Katamon. It was a villa built round a courtyard. The courtyard was completely enclosed by the house. You could sit outside and be shut off and private. I'd like to have a house just like that. In a district of rocks and pine trees. Wait a minute, Michael, I haven't finished making my list. I'd like to have a daily maid, too. And a big garden."

"And a liveried chauffeur." Michael smiled.

"And a private submarine." Yair plodded along behind him with short, loyal steps.

"And a prince-poet-boxer-pilot husband," Michael added.

Yair's brow wrinkled like his father's when he was thinking out complicated thoughts. He paused for a moment or two, then exclaimed:

"And I want a little brother. Aron is the same age as me exactly, and he's already got two brothers. I deserve to have a brother."

Michael said:

"An apartment here in Rehavia or in Beit Hakerem costs a small fortune these days. But if we started saving systematically, we could borrow a little from Aunt Jenia, a little from the University Assistance Fund, a little from Mr. Kadishman. It's not entirely a castle in the air."

"No," I said, "it's not entirely that. But what about us?"

"What about us?"

"In the air, Michael. Not just me. You too. You're not just in the air, you're in outer space. All except Yair, our little realist."

"Hannah, you're a pessimist."

"I'm tired, Michael. Let's go home. I've just remembered the ironing. I've got piles of it waiting to be done. And tomorrow the decorators are coming."

"Daddy, what's a realist?"

"It's a word with a lot of meanings, my boy. Mummy meant someone who always behaves reasonably and doesn't live in a world of dreams."

"But I have dreams at night, too."

I asked with a faint laugh:

"What sort of dreams do you have, Yair?"

"Dreams."

"What sort?"

"All sorts."

"Such as?"

"Just dreams."

That night I did the ironing. Next day the whole apartment was whitewashed. My best friend Hadassah lent me her maid,

252

Simcha, again for a couple of days. The winter rain started again in the middle of the week. The drainpipes grumbled. Their music was sad and angry. There were frequent, prolonged power failures. The street was muddy.

After the whitewashing and the cleaning-up, I took forty-five pounds from Michael's wallet. I went into town in a lull between two cloudbursts. I bought chandeliers for all the lights. Now I would have glittering cut glass in my living room. Crystal. I liked the word "crystal." And I liked the crystal.

CHAPTER

39

There is a sameness in the days and a sameness in me. There is something which is not the same. I do not know its name.

My husband and I are like two strangers who happen to meet coming out of a clinic where they have received treatment involving some physical unpleasantness. Both embarrassed, reading each other's minds, conscious of an uneasy, embarrassing intimacy, wearily groping for the right tone in which to address each other now.

Michael's doctoral dissertation was approaching its final chapters. Next year he had a distinct hope of advancement on the academic scale. In the early summer of 1957 he spent ten days in the Negev, carrying out certain observations and experiments which were essential for his research. He brought us back a bottle filled with different-colored sands.

From one of Michael's colleagues I learned that after submitting his dissertation my husband intended to compete for a

254

fellowship which would allow him a lengthy period of advanced study in theoretical geology at an American university. Michael himself had chosen not to tell me of this intention, because he knew my weaknesses. He did not want to cause me fresh dreams. Dreams may be shattered. Disappointment might ensue.

Gradual changes had made themselves felt over the years in Mekor Baruch. New apartment blocks had been built to the west. Roads were paved. Top stories in a modern style were added to buildings of the Turkish period. The municipality put up green benches and trash cans in the side streets. A small public garden was opened. Workshops and printing presses sprang up on vacant sites previously overgrown with weeds.

The older inhabitants gradually left the district. The civil servants and Agency employees moved to Rehavia or Kiryat Shmuel. The clerks and cashiers bought cheap apartments in the government housing developments in the south of the city. The dealers in textiles and fashion accessories moved to Romema. We were left behind to keep watch over dying streets. It was a continuous, insensible decay. Shutters and iron railings gradually rusted away. An Orthodox contractor dug foundations opposite our home, unloaded heaps of sand and gravel, then suddenly abandoned his project. Perhaps he had changed his mind, perhaps he had died. The Kamnitzer family left our house and Jerusalem, and went to live in a suburb of Tel Aviv. Yoram came home on special leave from his army unit to help with the packing. He waved to me from a distance. He looked bronzed and fit in his uniform. I could not talk to him because his father was standing sternly by. And what had I left to say to Yoram—now?

Orthodox families moved into the numerous vacant apartments in the neighborhood. Recent immigrants, too, who had begun to get established, mainly from Iraq and Romania. It was a gradual process. More and more washlines came to be strung across the street from balcony to balcony. At night I could hear shouts in a guttural language. Our Persian greengrocer, Mr. Elijah Mossiah, sold his store to a pair of perpetually bad-tempered brothers. Even the children at Tachkemoni Orthodox Boys' School seemed to me to be wilder and more violent than in the old days.

At the end of May our friend Mr. Kadishman died of a kidney disease. He bequeathed a small sum to the Jerusalem branch of the National Party. To Michael and me he left all his books: the works of Herzl, Nordau, Jabotinsky, and Klausner. His lawyer was requested in the will to call on us and thank us for the warm atmosphere in which we had received the deceased. Mr. Kadishman had been a lonely man.

That same summer of 1957 the old kindergarten teacher Sarah Zeldin also died, after being hit by an army truck in Malachi Street. The kindergarten was closed down. I found a part-time job as a filing clerk in the Ministry of Trade and Industry. It was Abba, my best friend Hadassah's husband, who secured me the job. And in the autumn three Jerusalemites who had been close friends of my parents when I was a child also died. I have not mentioned them before because forgetfulness managed to pierce my defenses. The greatest effort cannot withstand it. I meant to write down everything. It is impossible to write everything. Most things slip away to perish in silence.

In September our son Yair started at Beit Hakerem Elementary School. Michael bought him a brown satchel. I bought him a pencil case, pencil sharpener, pencils, and a ruler. Aunt Leah sent a huge box of water colors. From Nof Harim came D'Amicis' *The Heart,* beautifully bound.

In October our neighbor, Mrs. Glick, was sent home from the institution. She displayed a silent resignation, seeming quieter and more peaceful now. She had also aged and put on a great deal of weight. She had lost that rich, ripe beauty with which she had been compensated for not having had children. We never heard again those hysterical outbursts and cries of despair. Mrs. Glick came back from her prolonged treatment apathetic and submissive. She sat for hours on end on the low wall by our front gate, looking out into the street. Looking and soundlessly laughing, as if our street had become a happy, amusing place.

Michael compared Mrs. Glick to the actor Albert Crispin, Aunt Jenia's second husband. Like her he had had a nervous breakdown, and when he recovered he succumbed to total apathy. He had been kept for sixteen years in a boarding-house in Nahariya where he did nothing all day but sleep, eat, and stare into space. Aunt Jenia was still supporting him at her own expense.

Aunt Jenia left her job in the children's department of the general hospital after a serious quarrel. After several attempts she managed to find another job, as a doctor in a private institution in Ramat Gan for old people with chronic complaints.

When she came to stay with us for the Feast of Succot, Aunt Jenia terrified me. Heavy smoking had made her voice coarser and deeper. Each time she lit a cigarette she cursed herself in Polish. When she coughed badly she muttered to herself through pursed lips: "Shut up, idiot. *Cholera.*" Her hair had become thin and gray. Her face was like the face of a bad-tempered old man. She was often at a loss for a Hebrew word.

She would light a fresh cigarette with a frantic gesture, spit out rather than blow out the match, mutter in Yiddish, curse herself in sibilant Polish. She accused me of dressing in clothes which did not become Michael's position in life. Charged Michael with giving in to me in everything, less like a man than a rag doll. Yair, in her view, was rude, insolent, and stupid. I dreamed of her after she left, and her image merged with the figures of those ancient Jerusalem ghosts, the itinerant craftsmen and peddlers, musty with age. I was afraid of her. I was afraid of dying young and afraid of dying old.

Dr. Urbach expressed anxiety about my vocal cords. I repeatedly lost my voice for a few hours at a time. The doctor instructed me to undergo a lengthy course of treatment, certain features of which caused me physical humiliation.

I would still wake before dawn, wide open to the evil voices and the recurrent nightmare which took on progressive, inexhaustible nuances. Sometimes a war. Sometimes a flood. A railway disaster. Being lost. Always I was rescued by powerful men, who saved me only to betray and abuse me.

I would wake my husband from his sleep. Burrow under his blanket. Cling to his body with all my might. Wring from his body the self-control I craved. Our nights became wilder than ever before. I made Michael amazed at my body and his own. Initiated him into colorful byways I had read of in novels. Tortuous paths half-learned in the cinema. Everything I had heard whispered in my adolescence by giggling schoolgirls. Everything I knew and guessed of a man's wildest and most tortured dreams. Everything my own dreams had taught me. Flashes of quivering ecstasy. Floods of blazing spasms in the depths of an icy pool. Deliciously gentle collapse.

And yet I evaded him. I made contact only with his body: muscles, limbs, hair. In my heart I knew that I deceived him again and again. With his own body. It was a blind plunge into the depths of a warm abyss. No other opening was left me. Soon even this would be blocked.

Michael could not take this feverish, stormy abundance lavished on him before dawn. He generally yielded and collapsed with my first stirrings. Could Michael feel beyond the flood of wild sensations the humiliation I inflicted on him? Once he dared to ask in a whisper whether I had fallen in love with him again. He asked with such evident apprehension that both of us knew there was nothing more to be said.

In the morning Michael gave no sign. There was his restrained sympathy, as usual. Less like a man who has been humiliated in the night than a tender youth courting for the first time a haughty, experienced girl. Will we die, Michael, you and I, without touching each other so much as once? Touching. Merging. You don't understand. Losing ourselves in each other. Melting. Fusing. Growing into one another. Helplessly coalescing. I can't explain. Even words are against me. What a deception, Michael. What a despicable snare. I'm worn out. Oh, to sleep and sleep.

Once I proposed playing a game: each of us was to tell everything about his first love.

Michael refused to understand: I was his first and last love.

I tried to explain: You must have been a child once. A young man. You read novels. There were girls in your class. Talk. Tell me. Have you lost your memory and all your feelings?

Speak. Say something. You never say anything. Stop keeping quiet, stop ticking on from day to day like an alarm clock, and stop driving me mad.

Finally a forced understanding dawned in Michael's eyes.

He started describing in carefully chosen words, without using adjectives, a long-forgotten summer camp at Kibbutz Ein Harod. His friend Liora who now lived in Kibbutz Tirat Yaar. A mock trial in which he was the prosecutor and Liora the defendant. A veiled insult. An old gym teacher called Yehiam Peled who called Michael "Goofy Ganz" because of his slow reflexes. A letter. A personal explanation to the youth leader. Liora again. An apology. And so on.

It was a dismal story. If I had to lecture even on geology, I wouldn't get so confused. Like most optimists, Michael regarded the present as a soft, shapeless substance from which one has to mold the future by dint of responsible hard work. He viewed the past with suspicion. An incubus. Somehow unnecessary. The past appeared to Michael like a pile of orange peels which must be disposed of, not by scattering them along the way, because they would make a mess; they must be collected up and destroyed. To be free and unburdened. To be responsible only for the plans which have been set before him for the future.

"Tell me something, Michael," I said, not troubling to hide my disgust. "What on earth do you think you're living for?"

Michael did not answer immediately. He considered the question. Meanwhile he collected some crumbs on the table and piled them into a heap in front of him. Finally he declared:

"Your question is meaningless. People don't live *for* anything. They live, period."

"Micha Ganz, you will die as you were born, an utter nonentity. Period."

"Everybody has strong and weak points. You would probably call that a trite remark. You'd be right. But trite isn't the opposite of true. 'Two times two is four' is a trite remark, but nevertheless . . ."

"Nevertheless, Michael, trite *is* the opposite of true, and one of these days I shall go mad just like Duba Glick and it'll be your fault, Doctor Goofy Ganz."

"Calm down, Hannah," Michael said.

In the evening we made up. Each of us blamed himself for the quarrel. We both said we were sorry, and went out together to visit Abba and Hadassah in their new apartment in Rehavia.

I must also record the following:

Michael and myself going down into the yard to shake out the bedspread. We manage after a bit to coordinate our movements so as to shake it together. The dust rises.

Then we fold the bedspread: Michael comes towards me with arms outstretched, as if he has suddenly decided to embrace me. He holds out his two corners. He walks back, takes hold of the new corners. Stretches out his arms. Comes towards me. Holds out. Walks back. Takes hold. Comes towards me. Holds out.

"That's enough, Michael. We've finished."

"Yes, Hannah."

"Thank you, Michael."

"There's no need to thank me, Hannah. The bedspread belongs to both of us."

As darkness falls on the yard. Evening. The first stars. A vague, distant howl—a woman screaming or a tune on the radio. It is cold.

CHAPTER

40

My new work in the Ministry of Trade and Industry suits me much better than my previous job in Sarah Zeldin's kindergarten. I sit from nine to one in the building which used to house the Palace Hotel. My room used to be the chambermaids' dressing room. Reports arrive on my desk from various projects up and down the country. My job is to extract certain information from these reports, compare it with other information contained in files on a shelf by my side, record the results of the comparison, copy out the remarks in the margin of the reports on a special form, and then send my work on to another department.

I enjoy the work, and particularly because of the endless fascination of such terms as "experimental engineering project," "chemical conglomerate," "shipyards," "heavy-metal workshops," "steel construction consortium."

These terms bear witness to me of the existence of a certain solid reality. I do not know and I do not wish to know these far-off enterprises. I am satisfied with the concrete certainty of the fact of their existence somewhere far away. They exist.

They function. Undergo changes. Calculations. Raw materials. Profitability. Planning. A powerful stream of objects, places, people, opinions.

Very far away, I know. But not beyond the rainbow. Not lost in a dream world.

In January 1958 we had a telephone installed in our apartment. Michael received priority as an academic. Our connection with Abba was also useful. Abba gave us important help, too, in the matter of moving to a new apartment. He arranged for us to be put high up on the waiting list for one of the government housing developments. We were to live in a new suburb which was about to be built on a hill behind Bayit Vagan, with a view of the Bethlehem hills and the edge of Emek Refaim. We put down a deposit, and contracted to pay the remainder in installments. Under the terms of the agreement we were to receive the keys of our new apartment in 1961.

That evening Michael produced a bottle of red wine. He also gave me a large bunch of chrysanthemums to mark the occasion. He poured two glasses half-full of wine, and said:

"To us, Hannah. I am sure the new neighborhood will have a calming effect on you. Mekor Baruch is a gloomy place."

"Yes, Michael," I said.

"All these years we've dreamed of moving to a new apartment. We'll have three whole rooms, plus a small study. I expected you to be happy this evening."

"I am happy, Michael," I said. "We're going to have a new apartment with three whole rooms. We've always dreamed of moving. Mekor Baruch is a gloomy place."

"But that's what I've just said," Michael exclaimed in amazement.

"That's what you've just said." I smiled. "After eight years of married life people are bound to think alike."

"Time and hard work will bring us everything, Hannah. You'll see. In time we may be able to travel to Europe, or even further. In time we may be able to afford a small car. In time you'll feel better."

"In time and with hard work everything will be better, Michael. Did you notice just now that it was your father speaking, not you?"

"No," Michael said, "actually I didn't. But it's not impossible. In fact it's only natural. After all, I am my father's son."

"Absolutely. Not impossible. Only natural. You are his son. It's horrible, Michael. Horrible."

"What's horrible about it, Hannah?" Michael asked sadly. "It's not right for you to make fun of my father. He was a pure soul. It was wrong of you to speak like that. You shouldn't have done it."

"You misunderstand me, Michael. It's not the fact that you're your father's son that's horrible, it's that you've started talking like your father. And your Grandfather Zalman. And my grandfather. And my father. And my mother. And after us Yair. All of us. As if one human being after another after another is nothing but a reject. One fresh draft is made after another, and each in turn is rejected and crumpled up and thrown in the wastebasket, to be replaced by a new, slightly improved version. How futile it all seems. How dull. What a pointless joke."

Michael accorded this thought a moment's silent reflection. Absent-mindedly he took a paper napkin out of the holder. Folded it meticulously into a little boat, examined it intently, and set it down very gently on the table. Finally he remarked that I had a rather imaginative view of life. His father had once made the comment that Hannah seemed to him to be a poetess, even though she did not write poetry.

Then Michael showed me the plan of the new apartment, which he had been given that morning when we signed the agreement. He explained it in his usual clear, factual manner. I asked him to elaborate on a detail. Michael repeated his explanation. For a moment I was gripped by that powerful sensation that this was by no means the first time. I had already known this moment and this place long before. All the words had already been spoken in the distant past. Even the paper boat was not new. Even the tobacco smoke, reaching up towards the light bulb. The hum of the refrigerator. Michael. Myself. Everything. It was all far away and yet clear as crystal.

In the spring of 1958 we took on a daily maid. From now on, another woman would run my kitchen. There would be no need now to come home tired from the office and frantically set to work opening cans and grating vegetables, relying on Michael's and Yair's good nature not to grumble at the monotony of the meals.

Every morning I gave Fortuna a written list of instructions. She crossed each one off as she finished. I found her satisfactory: hard-working, honest, unintelligent.

But once or twice I noticed on my husband's face a new expression, which I had never observed before in all the years we had been married. When Michael looked at the girl's figure his face expressed a kind of embarrassed tension. His mouth hung slightly open, his head inclined at an angle, his knife and fork froze for an instant in his hands. His expression was one of complete stupidity, of utter inanity, like a child who thinks he has been caught cheating in an examination. As a result I stopped letting Fortuna eat her lunch with us. I would give her some ironing to do, or dusting, or tell her to fold the linen. She would have her lunch alone, when we had finished.

Michael remarked:

"I'm sorry to see, Hannah, that you treat Fortuna in the way that ladies used to treat their maids. Fortuna isn't a servant. She doesn't belong to us. She's a workingwoman. Just like you."

I made fun of him:

"Aye aye, sir, Comrade Ganz."

Michael said:

"Now you're being unreasonable."

I said:

"Fortuna isn't a servant and she doesn't belong to us. She's a workingwoman. It's unreasonable of you to sit there in front of me and the child feasting your popping calf's-eyes on her body. It's unreasonable, and it's downright idiotic."

Michael was taken aback. He blanched. Started to say something. Thought better of it. Kept quiet. He opened a bottle of mineral water and carefully poured out three glasses.

One day, as I was coming home from the clinic I was going to for a lengthy course of treatment for my throat and vocal cords, Michael came out of the house and advanced towards me. We met outside the store which used to belong to Mr. Elijah Mossiah and was now run by the two bad-tempered brothers. There was bad news on his face. He had suffered a minor disaster, he said.

"Disaster, Michael?"

"A minor disaster."

Apparently he had just seen the latest issue of the official journal of the Royal Geological Society of Great Britain, which contained an article by a well-known professor from Cambridge, propounding a new and rather startling theory about erosion. Certain assumptions which were fundamental to Michael's thesis had been brilliantly disproved.

"That's marvelous," I said. "Now's your chance, Michael Gonen. You show this Englishman what's what. Pulverize him. Don't give in."

"I can't," Michael said sheepishly. "It's out of the question. He's right. I'm convinced."

Like most humanities students, I had always imagined that all facts are susceptible of different interpretations, and that a sharp-witted and determined interpreter could always adapt them and shape them to his will. Provided he was forceful and aggressive enough. I said:

"So you're giving in without a struggle, Michael. I should have liked to see you struggle and win. I'd have been very proud of you."

Michael smiled. He did not reply. If I had been Yair, he would have taken the trouble to answer me. I was offended, and made fun of him:

"Poor old Michael. Now you'll have to tear up all your work and start again from scratch."

"As a matter of fact, that's a slight exaggeration. The situation is not as desperate as you make out. I had a chat with my professor this morning. I shall have to rewrite the opening chapters and make some changes in three places in the body of the work. The final section isn't finished yet anyway, and I'll be able to take the new theory into account when I write it. The descriptive chapters are unaffected, and they'll stand as they are. I'll need an extra year, possibly even less. My professor agreed immediately to grant me an extension."

I thought to myself: When Strogoff was captured by the cruel Tartars they planned to put out his eyes with red-hot irons. Strogoff was a hard man, but he also had abounding love. Because of his love his eyes filled with tears. These tears of love saved him, because they cooled the red-hot irons. Willpower and cunning enabled him to pose as a blind man until he had completed the difficult mission entrusted to him by the Czar in St. Petersburg. The mission and the agent alike were saved by love and strength.

And perhaps in the distance he could hear the faint echo of a long-drawn-out melody. The vague sounds could only be detected with an effort of concentration. A far-off band played and played beyond the woods beyond the hills beyond the meadow. Young people marching and chanting. Powerful policemen on strong, disciplined horses. A military band in white uniforms with gold braid. A princess. A ceremony. Far away.

In May I went to Beit Hakerem School to meet Yair's teacher. She was young, fair-haired, blue-eyed, and attractive, like a princess in a children's picture book. She was a student. Jerusalem was suddenly full of lovely girls. Of course I had known some pretty girls when I'd been a student ten years before. I'd been one of them. But this new generation possessed something different, a floating quality, a light, effortless beauty. I disliked them. And I disliked the childish clothes they chose to wear.

From Yair's teacher I learned that young Gonen was gifted with a sharp and systematic mind and strong powers of memory and concentration, but that he lacked sensitivity. For instance, they had discussed the Exodus from Egypt and the Ten Plagues in class. The other children had been rather upset by the cruelty of the Egyptians and the sufferings of the Hebrews. Gonen, on the other hand, had questioned the Biblical account of the division of the Red Sea. He had given a rational explanation of the rise and fall of the tides. As if he was not interested in the Egyptians or the Hebrews.

The young teacher shed a fresh, light gaiety on everything around her. As she described little Zalman she smiled. And as she smiled, her face lit up as though there was no part of it which did not share in her smile. I hated with a sudden disgust the brown dress I was wearing.

Later, in the street, two girls walked past me. They were students. They were laughing gaily and both of them exuded a heady, overpowering beauty. They were wearing skirts with a deep slit up the side and carried straw handbags. I found their billowing laughter vulgar. As if they owned the whole of Jerusalem. As they went past me, one said:

"They're wild. They drive me crazy."

Her friend gave a laugh:

"It's a free country. They can please themselves. As far as I'm concerned, they can go jump in the lake."

Jerusalem is spreading and developing. Roads. Modern sewers. Public buildings. There are even some spots which convey for an instant an impression of an ordinary city: straight, paved avenues punctuated with public benches. But the impression is fleeting. If you turn your head you can see in the midst of all the frantic building a rocky field. Olive trees. A barren wilderness. Thick overgrown valleys. Crisscrossing paths worn by the tread of myriad feet. Herds grazing round the newly built Prime Minister's office. Sheep peacefully nibbling. An ancient shepherd frozen on a rock opposite. And all around, the hills. The ruins. The wind in the pine trees. The inhabitants.

In Herzl Street I saw a swarthy workman stripped to the waist, digging a trench across the road with a heavy mechanical drill. He was soaked in sweat. His skin gleamed like copper. And his shoulders shook and shook with the bouncing of the heavy drill, as if he could not restrain his rising tides of energy, and must suddenly roar and pounce.

An obituary notice stuck to the wall of the old people's home at the end of Jaffa Road informed me of the death of the pious Mrs. Tarnopoler, who had been my landlady before I was married. It was Mrs. Tarnopoler who had taught me to brew mint tea as a balm for a troubled soul. I was sorry to learn of her death. Sorry for myself. And for sorely troubled souls.

I told Yair at bedtime a story I had learned by heart in the far-off days of my childhood. It was the charming story of little David, who was "always tidy, always neat." I loved that story. I wanted to make my son love it too.

In the summer we all went to Tel Aviv for a holiday by the sea. We stayed with Aunt Leah again, in her apartment in an old house on Rothschild Avenue. Five days. Every morning we went to the beach south of Tel Aviv, by Bat Yam. In the afternoon we jostled our way to the zoo, the amusement park, the cinema. One evening Aunt Leah dragged us to the opera. It was full of elderly Polish ladies, heavily bedecked with gold. They sailed regally about like massive battleships.

Michael and I slunk off during an intermission. We went down to the sea. We walked north along the sands until we came to the harbor wall. It flooded me suddenly to the tips of my toes. Like a pain. Like a shudder. Michael refused and tried to explain. I didn't listen to him. With a strength which surprised me I tore his shirt off him. Threw him down in the sand. There was a bite. A sob. I bore him down with every part of my body as if I was heavier than he was. This was how a girl in a blue coat used to wrestle, years ago, in the break between lessons, with boys who were much stronger than she was. Cold and blazing. Crying and mocking.

The sea joined in. And the sand. There were fine lashes of rough pleasure, piercing and searing. Michael was frightened. He didn't recognize me, he mumbled, I was unfamiliar again, and he didn't like me. I was glad I was unfamiliar. I didn't want him to like me.

When we got back to Aunt Leah's apartment at midnight, Michael had to explain, red-faced, to his anxious aunt why his shirt was torn and his face scratched.

"We went for a walk, and . . . some hoodlums tried to attack us, and . . . it was rather unpleasant."

Aunt Leah said:

"You must always remember your position in life, Micha. A man of your sort must never be involved in any scandal."

I burst out laughing. I went on laughing silently till dawn.

Next day we took Yair to the circus in Ramat Gan. At the end of the week we went home. Michael learned that his friend Liora from Kibbutz Tirat Yaar had left her husband. She had taken the children and gone to live as a divorcee in a young kibbutz in the Negev, the kibbutz which was founded after the War of Independence by her schoolfriends and Michael's. This news made a powerful impression on Michael. Ill-suppressed fear showed on his face. He was subdued and silent. More so even than usual. At one point that Saturday afternoon, as he was changing the water in a vase, he displayed a sudden hesitation. A slow movement was succeeded by one which was too fast. I jumped up and caught the vase in mid-air. Next day I went into town to buy him the most expensive fountain pen I could find.

CHAPTER

41

In the spring of 1959, three weeks before Passover, Michael's doctoral thesis was completed. It was a thorough study of the effects of erosion in the ravines of the Wilderness of Paran. The work was carried out in accordance with the latest theories on erosion of scientists all over the world. The morphotectonic structure of the area was examined in detail. The *cuestas,* the exogenic and endogenic elements, the effects of climate, and the tectonic factors were all studied. The concluding chapters even hinted at some practical applications of the results. The argument was closely reasoned. Michael had mastered a very complex subject. He had devoted four years to his research. The thesis was written in a responsible manner. He had not been spared delays and obstacles, both inherent difficulties and also personal problems.

After Passover Michael would give his manuscript to a typist who would prepare a fair copy. Then he would submit his work to the scrutiny of the leading geologists. He would have to defend his conclusions in the course of a lecture and free discussion in the usual scientific forum. He intended to dedicate the thesis to the beloved memory of the late Yehezkel Gonen, a serious, upright, and modest man, in commemoration of his hopes, his love, and his devotion.

It was at this time too that we bade farewell to my best friend Hadassah and her husband Abba. Abba was being sent to Switzerland for two years as an economic attaché. He confided to us that in his heart of hearts he looked forward to the day when he would be offered a suitable official position that would allow him to live permanently in Jerusalem, instead of dashing off to foreign capitals like an errand boy. He had not, however, abandoned his idea of leaving the civil service and making his own way in the great world of finance.

Hadassah said:

"You'll be happy one day too, Hannah. I'm sure of it. One day you'll reach your goal. Michael is a hard-working lad and you were always a clever girl."

Hadassah's departure and her parting words moved me. I cried when I heard her say that one day we too would reach our goal. Was it possible that everyone except me had come to terms with time, with dedication, perseverance, effort, ambition, and achievement? I do not use the words loneliness, despair. I feel depressed. Humiliated. There has been a deception. My late father warned me when I was thirteen against wicked men who seduce women with sweet words and then abandon them to their fate. He formulated his remarks as if the very existence of two distinct sexes was a disorder which multiplied agony in the world, a disorder whose results men and women must do everything in their power to mitigate. I have not been seduced by a lewd and loutish man. Nor am I opposed to the existence of two distinct sexes. But there has been a deception, and it is humiliating. Farewell, Hadassah. Write often to Jerusalem to Hannah to far-away Palestine. Stick pretty stamps on the covers for my husband and son. Write and tell me all about the mountains and the snow. About inns. About abandoned cottages scattered in the valley, ancient cottages whose doors the wind lashes till the hinges screech. I don't mind, Hadassah. There is no sea in Switzerland, *Dragon* and *Tigress* are laid up in dry dock in a harbor in the St. Pierre and Miquelon Islands. Their crews are roaming the valleys in search of new girls. I am not jealous. I am not involved. I am at rest. The middle of March. In Jerusalem it is still drizzling.

Our neighbor Mr. Glick passed away ten days before Passover. He died of an internal hemorrhage. Michael and I attended the funeral. Orthodox tradesmen from David Yelin Street discussed in furious Yiddish the opening of a non-kosher butcher shop in Jerusalem. A lean hired cantor in a black frock coat read the service by the open grave, and the heavens responded with a heavy downpour. Mrs. Duba Glick found the conjunction of prayer and rain somehow amusing. She burst into hoarse laughter. Mr. Glick and his wife Duba had no family. Michael owed them nothing. But he owed loyalty to the principles and character of his late father Yehezkel. Hence he shouldered the responsibility of the funeral arrangements. And thanks to the influence of Aunt Jenia he managed to arrange for Mrs. Glick to be accommodated in a home for elderly people suffering from chronic diseases. It was the same institution where Aunt Jenia herself now worked.

We went to spend the festival in Galilee.

We were invited to join in the Passover celebrations at Kibbutz Nof Harim, with my mother and my brother's family.

Away from Jerusalem. Far from the back streets. Far from the elderly Orthodox women shriveling in the sun like evil birds on low stools scanning the horizon with their eyes as though they were looking out over a vast expanse of plain instead of a cramped town.

It was spring in the country. Wild flowers bloomed by the roadside. Flights of migrating birds streamed through blue space. There were stiff cypresses, and leafy eucalyptus trees restfully shading the road. There were whitewashed villages. There were red roofs. No more dreary stone buildings and crumbling balconies fenced with rusty iron railings. It was a white world. Green. Red. All the roads were thronged. Crowds of people traveling far and wide. The passengers in our bus sang and sang. They were a party of young people from a youth movement. They laughed and sang songs translated from Russian about love and the open fields. The driver held onto the wheel with one hand. In the other he clasped the ticket punch, and beat a tattoo on the dashboard. The rhythm was merry. At times he twirled his mustache and turned on the loudspeaker. He told us all funny stories. He was blessed with a lively, throaty voice.

All along the way we were bathed in warm sunlight. The sun's rays made every scrap of metal sparkle, every splinter of glass glitter. Shades of green and sky-blue merged at the edge of the vast plain. At each stop people got on and off, carrying suitcases, rucksacks, shotguns, bunches of cyclamens and anemones, ranunculus, marigolds, orchids. When we got to Ramla, Michael bought us each a lemon ice popsicle. At Beit Lod Junction we bought lemonades and peanuts. On both sides of the road stretched plots of land crisscrossed with irrigation pipes. The warm sunlight blazed on the pipes, turning them all to strips of flickering dazzle.

The hills were very far away, blue-tinged, swathed in a shimmering haze. The air was warm and moist. Michael and his son talked all the way about battles in the War of Independence and about the irrigation works the government was planning. I put on the prettiest smile I had. I had every confidence that the government would bring to fruition all the great works of irrigation it was planning. I peeled orange after orange for my husband and my son, separating the segments, removing the white pith, wiping Yair's mouth with a handkerchief.

In the villages along Wadi Ara the inhabitants stood along the road and waved to us. I took off my green silk kerchief and waved back until the people vanished from sight, and still I did not stop.

In Afula some important date was being celebrated. The town was draped with blue and white flags. Colored light bulbs were stretched across the streets. A decorated iron gateway had been erected at the western approach to the town, and an exultant greeting waved in the breeze. My hair was also waving.

Michael bought the Passover Eve edition of a newspaper. There was some good political news. Michael explained. I put my arm round his shoulder and blew into his close-cropped hair. Between Afula and Tiberias Yair dozed on our laps. I gazed at my son's square head, at his firm jawline and high, pale brow. For an instant I knew through the waves of blue light that my son would grow into a handsome, powerful man. His officer's uniform would cling tightly to his body. Yellow down would sprout on his forearms. I would lean on his arm in the street and there would be no prouder mother than I in the whole of Jerusalem. Why Jerusalem? We would live in Ashkelon. In Netanya. By the seaside, looking out over the foam-capped waves. We would live in a little white bungalow, with a red-tiled roof and four identical windows. Michael would be a mechanic. There would be a flower bed in front of the house. Every morning we would go out and gather seashells on the beach. The salt breeze would blow all day through the window. We would be salty and sun-tanned all the time. The hot sunshine would beat down on us every day. And the radio would sing and sing in every room in the house.

At Tiberias the driver announced a stop of half an hour. Yair woke up. We ate a falafel and walked down to the lakeside. All three of us took off our shoes and paddled in the water. The water was warm. The lake shimmered and sparkled. We saw shoals of fish swimming silently in the deep water. Fishermen stood leaning idly on the jetty rail. They were rugged men, with strong, hairy arms. I waved to them with my green silk kerchief, and not in vain. One of them spotted me and called out "darling."

The next stretch of our journey took us along the verdant valleys flanked by sheer hills. To the right of the road the fishponds shone like blue-gray squares of brightness. The reflections of the great hills trembled in the water. Their trembling was gentle and subdued, like the trembling of bodies in love. Black basalt blocks lay scattered around. Ancient settlements radiated a gray tranquillity: Migdal, Rosh Pinah, Yisud Hamaalah, Mahanayim. The whole land whirled and reeled drunkenly, as if overflowing with some teeming inner madness.

Outside Kiryat Shmoneh an elderly conductor, who looked like a pioneer from the thirties, climbed aboard. The driver was apparently an old friend of his. They chatted merrily about a deer hunt in the Hills of Naphtali which was planned for the middle days of the approaching festival. All the drivers from the old gang would be invited to take part. All those in the old gang who were still going strong: Chita, Abu Masri, Moskovitch, Zambezi. No wives allowed. Three days and three nights. And a famous trail guide from the paratroopers would be there. A hunt whose like the world had not yet known. From Manarah by way of Bar'am to Hanita and Rosh Hanikrah. Three great days. No wives and no crybabies. Only the old gang. The guns were all ready, and American-style bivouac-tents. Who wouldn't be there! All the old wolves and lions who still had strength left in their loins. Just like the grand old days. "Everybody will be there, but everybody. To a man. We'll run and jump over those old hills till the sparks start flying."

From Kiryat Shmoneh the bus started climbing up into the Hills of Naphtali. The road was narrow and uneven. Sharp bends were carved out of the mountain rock. It was a wild, dizzy whirl. The bus filled with screams of joy and fear. The driver added to the excitement by twisting the wheel sharply and letting the bus graze the very brink of the precipice. Then he pretended to dash us against the mountain wall. I too screamed with joy and fear.

We reached Nof Harim with the last light of day. People in clean clothes were coming out of the showers, their hair wet and combed. A towel over every arm. Fair-haired children romped on the lawns. There was a smell of new-mown grass. Sprinklers scattered showers of droplets. The glow of evening twilight flickered in the droplets like a fountain of rainbow-colored pearls.

Kibbutz Nof Harim is often nicknamed "the eagle's aerie." The buildings cling to the craggy hilltop as if floating in mid-air. At the foot of the hill can be seen the spreading valley divided up into a patchwork of squares. Looking down I was thrilled by the view. I could see distant villages half-submerged in woods and fishponds. Solid blocks of lush orchard. Slender paths flanked by columns of cypress. White water towers. And the far-off hills deep blue.

The members of Nof Harim, my brother's contemporaries, were mostly in their middle thirties. They were an exuberant crowd who hid the signs of earnest responsibility behind a gay façade. I noticed a solid, self-restrained quality in them. As if they were perpetually being amused and entertained in obedience to a grimly accepted resolution. I liked them. I liked the high place.

Then, Emanuel's small house overlooking the kibbutz fence which was also the Lebanese border. A cold shower. Orange juice and cakes baked by my mother. A summer frock. A short rest. The smiling attentions of my sister-in-law, Rina. Emanuel imitating bears for the benefit of my son Yair. It was the same clumsy imitation which Emanuel used to perform so well when we were children that we would both burst into tears of laughter. Even now we laughed and laughed.

My nephew Yosi offered to entertain Yair. They strolled hand in hand to see the cows and the sheep. It was a time of long shadows and dim light. We lay down on the lawn. When night fell, Emanuel brought out an electric light on a long wire and hung it on a tree branch. There was a slight, good-natured difference of opinion between my brother and my husband, which was soon resolved in almost complete agreement.

Afterwards, the tearful happiness of my mother, Malka. Her kisses. Her questions. The broken Hebrew in which she congratulated Michael on completing his doctoral dissertation.

My mother had been suffering recently from serious disorders of the circulation. She seemed to be nearing the end.

What a small place my mother occupied in my thoughts. She was Father's wife. That was all. On the few occasions when she had raised her voice against Father, I had hated her. Apart from that, I had made no room for her in my heart. I knew deep down inside me that I must talk to her sometime about myself. About her. About Father's youth. And I knew that I would not broach the subject this time. And I also knew that there might not be another opportunity because my mother already seemed to be nearing the end. But these thoughts did not detract from my happiness. My happiness surged within me as if it had an independent life of its own.

I have not forgotten. The Passover Eve Party. The arc lamps. The wine. The kibbutz choir. The ceremony, of waving the wheat sheaf. The barbecue round the campfire in the small hours of the morning. The dancing. I joined in every single dance. I sang. I whirled hefty dancers round and round. I even dragged Michael, alarmed, into the center of the ring. Jerusalem was far away and could not haunt me here. Perhaps she had been conquered in the meantime by the enemy who hemmed her in on three sides. Perhaps she had finally crumbled to dust. As she deserved. I did not love Jerusalem from a distance. She wished me ill. I wished her ill. I had a wild, lively night in Kibbutz Nof Harim. The dining hall was filled with smells of smoke, sweat, and tobacco. The harmonicas never stopped playing. I reveled. I was swept away. I belonged.

But towards dawn I went out and stood all alone on the balcony of Emanuel's small house. I saw coils of barbed wire. I saw dark bushes. The sky lightened. I was facing north. I could make out the silhouettes of a mountainous landscape: the Lebanese border. Tired lights shone yellow in the ancient stone-built villages. Unapproachable valleys. Distant snow-capped peaks. Lonely buildings on the hilltops, monasteries or forts. A boulder-strewn expanse scarred with deep wadis. A chill breeze blew. I shivered. I longed to leave. What a powerful yearning.

Close on five o'clock the sun burst out. It rose shrouded in thick mist. Low scrub lay hazily on the face of the earth. On the opposite slope stood a young Arab shepherd boy surrounded by gray goats furiously munching. I could hear the chimes of distant bells stirring ripples in the sky. As if the other Jerusalem had come up and appeared out of a melancholy dream. It was a dark, terrifying reflection. Jerusalem was haunting me. Headlights shone from a car on a road I could not see. Great, solitary, ancient trees grew vigorously. Stray wisps of mist wandered in the deserted valleys. The spectacle was frozen and turbid. An alien land was being washed with cold light.

CHAPTER

42

I have written somewhere in these pages: "There is an alchemy in things which is also the inner melody of my life." I am inclined to reject this statement now because it is too high-flown. "Alchemy." "Inner melody." Something did finally happen, in May of 1959, but it happened in a cheap way. It was a sordid, grotesque travesty.

At the beginning of May I conceived. A medical examination was necessary because of the slight complications I had suffered during my first pregnancy. The examination was carried out by a Dr. Lombrozo, because our family doctor, Dr. Urbach, had died of a heart attack early in the previous winter. The new doctor could discover no cause for anxiety. Nevertheless, he said, a woman of thirty is not quite the same as a girl of twenty. I must avoid excessive strain, heavily spiced foods, and physical relations with my husband from now until the end of the pregnancy. The veins in my legs began to swell again. Dark rings appeared once more around my eyes. And the nausea. The perpetual tiredness. Several times in the course of the month of May I forgot where I had put some object or article of clothing. I took this as a sign. Up till then I had never forgotten a thing.

Meanwhile, Yardena volunteered to type out Michael's doctoral thesis. Michael, in return, offered to prepare her for her final examinations, which she had already deferred to the last date permitted. So every evening Michael, tidy and neat, went off to Yardena's room on the edge of the university campus.

I admit it: the whole thing verged on the ridiculous. And deep down inside me I had expected it all along. I was not disturbed. Over supper Michael would appear to me to be nervous and distracted. He would keep fidgeting with his tie, his sober tie secured with a silver clip. His smile was elusive and guilty. His pipe refused to light. He was forever fussing over me with offers of help: to carry, shake out, sweep, serve. I no longer felt any need to torture myself by detecting signs.

Let me speak quite frankly: I do not suppose that Michael went any further than shy thoughts and speculations. I can see no reason why Yardena should have given herself to him. On the other hand, I can see no reason why she should have refused him. But the word "reason" is meaningless to me. I do not know and I do not care to know. I am closer to inner laughter than to jealousy. At most, Michael is like our kitten, Snowy, who once struggled with pathetic leaps to catch a moth fluttering just below the ceiling. Ten years ago Michael and I saw a Greta Garbo film at the Edison Cinema. The heroine of the film sacrificed her body and her soul for a worthless man. I recall that her suffering and his worthlessness seemed to me like two terms in a simple mathematical equation. I watched the screen sideways, until the pictures turned into a capering succession of different tones graded between black and white, but principally various shades of gray. So too, now, I do not take the trouble to unravel or solve. I watch sideways. Only I am much more tired now. And yet, surely something has changed after all these dreary years.

For some years now Michael has been resting with his arms on the steering wheel, thinking or dozing. I bid him farewell. I am not involved. I have given in. When I was a girl of eight I believed that if I behaved exactly like a boy I would grow up to be a man instead of a woman. What a wasted effort. I do not have to rush up panting like a madwoman. My eyes are opened. Farewell, Michael. I shall stand at the window and trace shapes with my finger on the misty pane. You may suppose, if you like, that I am waving to you. I shall not disillusion you. I am not with you. We are two people, not one. You couldn't go on being my thoughtful elder son. Fare you well. Perhaps it is not too late to tell you that nothing depended on you. Or on me. Have you forgotten, Michael, how you said once, many years ago, when we were sitting together in Cafe Atara, that it might be nice if our parents could meet. Try to visualize it now in your own mind. Our dead parents. Yosef. Yehezkel. Please, Michael, stop smiling for once. Make an effort. Concentrate. Try to imagine the picture: You and me as brother and sister. There are so many possible relationships. A mother and her son. A hill and woods. A stone and water. A lake and a boat. Movement and shadow. Pine tree and wind.

But I have more left than mere words. I am still able to unfasten a heavy padlock. To part the iron gates. To set free two twin brothers, who will slip out into the vast night to do my bidding. I shall urge them on.

At dusk they will crouch on the ground to prepare their

equipment. Faded army rucksacks. A box of explosives. Detonators. Fuses. Ammunition. Hand grenades. Glittering knives. In the ruined hut thick darkness reigns. Halil and Aziz the beautiful pair whom I called by the name of Halziz. They will have no words. Guttural sounds will emerge. Their movements controlled. Their fingers supple and strong. They form one body. It rises firm and gentle like a palm. A submachine gun suspended from the shoulder. The shoulder square and brown. They move on rubber soles. Dark khaki tight to the body. Their heads bare to the wind. In the last twilight glimmer they will rise as one man. From the hut they will glide down the steep slope. Their soles treading a path the eye cannot see. Theirs is a language of simple signs: light touches, hushed murmurs, like a man and a woman at love. Finger to shoulder. Hand to neck. A bird's cry. A secret whistle. Tall thorns in the gulley. The shade of ancient olives. Silent the earth surrenders. Lean and grimly gaunt they will trickle down the winding wadi. The tension lurks gnawing deep within. Their movements bowed and curved, like tender saplings swaying in the breeze. Night will clutch and veil and swallow them in his folds. The chirp of crickets. A distant fox's cackle.

A road crossed in a crouched leap. Their movement approaches a weightless glide. The rustling of shadowy groves. Barbed wire severed by savage shears. The stars are their accomplices. They flash instructions. In the distance, the mountains like masses of darkening clouds. Villages glimmer below on the plain. The swish of the water in serpentine pipes. Sprinklers splash. They sense sound in their skins, in their soles and their palms, in the roots of their hair. Soundlessly circling an ambush secreted in the folds of the gulley. Slantwise they cut through pitch-black orchards. A small stone clatters. A sign. Aziz darts ahead. Halil crouches behind a low stone wall. A jackal shrieks shrilly, falls silent. The submachine guns loaded, sprung, and cocked. A vicious dagger flashes. A stifled groan. Unbending. The chill of salty sweat. Noiseless onward flow.

A weary woman leans out of a lighted window, closes it, and vanishes. A sleepy watchman coughs hoarsely. They crawl winding among spiked shrubs. White teeth bared to bite out the pin of a grenade. The hoarse watchman belches. Turns back. Walks away.

The huge water tower rests heavily on its concrete legs. Its angles soften in the darkness, curving into shadow. Four lithe arms reach out. Matching as in a dance. As in love. As if all four spring from a single body. Cable. Timing device. Fuse. Detonator. Igniter. Bodies surge down the hill and away, softly padding. And on the slope below the skyline a stealthy run, a longing caress. The undergrowth flattens and straightens as they pass. Like a light skiff edging through still, calm waters. The rocky ground. The mouth of the wadi. Round the lurking ambush. Quivering black cypresses. The orchards. The winding path. Cunningly clinging to the cliff face. Nostrils flared and sniffing. Fingers groping for a hold. Far-away wistful crickets. The damp of the dew and the wind. Then, suddenly, not suddenly, the dim thunder of the blast. A flash of light capers on the western skyline. Shreds of low echoes resound in the mountain caves.

Then spurting laughter bursts. Wild and throaty and stifled. A rapid hand-clasp. The shade of a lonely carob up the hill. The hut. A sooty lamp. The first words. A cry of joy. Then sleep. The night outside is purple. A heavy fall of dew in every valley. A star. The massive mountain range.

I sent them. To me towards dawn they will return. Come battered and warm. Exuding a smell of sweat and foam.

A peaceful breeze touches and stirs the pines. Slowly the far sky pales. And on the vast expanses quiet cold calm descends.

___ The Ark Sakura by Kobo Abe	$8.95	0-679-72161-4
___ The Woman in the Dunes by Kobo Abe	$10.00	0-679-73378-7
___ Chromos by Felipe Alfau	$11.00	0-679-73443-0
___ Locos: A Comedy of Gestures by Felipe Alfau	$8.95	0-679-72846-5
___ Dead Babies by Martin Amis	$10.00	0-679-73449-X
___ Einstein's Monsters by Martin Amis	$8.95	0-679-72996-8
___ London Fields by Martin Amis	$11.00	0-679-73034-6
___ Success by Martin Amis	$10.00	0-679-73448-1
___ For Every Sin by Aharon Appelfeld	$9.95	0-679-72758-2
___ One Day of Life by Manlio Argueta	$10.00	0-679-73243-8
___ Collected Poems by W. H. Auden	$22.50	0-679-73197-0
___ The Dyer's Hand by W. H. Auden	$12.95	0-679-72484-2
___ Forewords and Afterwords by W. H. Auden	$12.95	0-679-72485-0
___ Selected Poems by W. H. Auden	$11.00	0-679-72483-4
___ Flaubert's Parrot by Julian Barnes	$8.95	0-679-73136-9
___ A History of the World in 10½ Chapters by Julian Barnes	$9.95	0-679-73137-7
___ The Tattered Cloak and Other Novels by Nina Berberova	$11.00	0-679-73366-3
___ About Looking by John Berger	$10.00	0-679-73655-7
___ And Our Faces, My Heart, Brief as Photos by John Berger	$9.00	0-679-73656-5
___ G. by John Berger	$11.00	0-679-73654-9
___ A Man for All Seasons by Robert Bolt	$7.95	0-679-72822-8
___ The Sheltering Sky by Paul Bowles	$9.95	0-679-72979-8
___ Possession by A. S. Byatt	$12.00	0-679-73590-9
___ The Virgin in the Garden by A. S. Byatt	$12.00	0-679-73829-0
___ Exile and the Kingdom by Albert Camus	$10.00	0-679-73385-X
___ The Fall by Albert Camus	$9.00	0-679-72022-7
___ The Myth of Sisyphus and Other Essays by Albert Camus	$9.00	0-679-73373-6
___ The Plague by Albert Camus	$10.00	0-679-72021-9
___ The Rebel by Albert Camus	$11.00	0-679-73384-1
___ The Stranger by Albert Camus	$7.95	0-679-72020-0
___ Bullet Park by John Cheever	$10.00	0-679-73787-1
___ Falconer by John Cheever	$10.00	0-679-73786-3
___ Oh What a Paradise It Seems by John Cheever	$8.00	0-679-73785-5
___ No Telephone to Heaven by Michelle Cliff	$11.00	0-679-73942-4
___ Age of Iron by J. M. Coetzee	$10.00	0-679-73292-6
___ Last Tales by Isak Dinesen	$12.00	0-679-73640-9
___ Out of Africa and Shadows on the Grass by Isak Dinesen	$12.00	0-679-72475-3
___ Seven Gothic Tales by Isak Dinesen	$12.00	0-679-73641-7
___ The Book of Daniel by E. L. Doctorow	$10.00	0-679-73657-3
___ Loon Lake by E. L. Doctorow	$10.00	0-679-73625-5
___ Ragtime by E. L. Doctorow	$10.00	0-679-73626-3
___ World's Fair by E. L. Doctorow	$11.00	0-679-73628-X
___ Love, Pain, and the Whole Damn Thing by Doris Dörrie	$9.00	0-679-72992-5
___ The Assignment by Friedrich Dürrenmatt	$7.95	0-679-72233-5

VINTAGE INTERNATIONAL

___ **Invisible Man** by Ralph Ellison	$10.00	0-679-72313-7
___ **Scandal** by Shusaku Endo	$8.95	0-679-72355-2
___ **Absalom, Absalom!** by William Faulkner	$9.95	0-679-73218-7
___ **As I Lay Dying** by William Faulkner	$8.95	0-679-73225-X
___ **Go Down, Moses** by William Faulkner	$9.95	0-679-73217-9
___ **The Hamlet** by William Faulkner	$10.00	0-679-73653-0
___ **Intruder in the Dust** by William Faulkner	$9.00	0-679-73651-4
___ **Light in August** by William Faulkner	$9.95	0-679-73226-8
___ **The Sound and the Fury** by William Faulkner	$8.95	0-679-73224-1
___ **The Unvanquished** by William Faulkner	$9.00	0-679-73652-2
___ **The Good Soldier** by Ford Madox Ford	$10.00	0-679-72218-1
___ **Howards End** by E. M. Forster	$8.95	0-679-72255-6
___ **A Room With a View** by E. M. Forster	$8.00	0-679-72476-1
___ **Where Angels Fear to Tread** by E. M. Forster	$9.00	0-679-73634-4
___ **Christopher Unborn** by Carlos Fuentes	$12.95	0-679-73222-5
___ **The Story of My Wife** by Milán Füst	$8.95	0-679-72217-3
___ **The Story of a Shipwrecked Sailor** by Gabriel García Márquez	$9.00	0-679-72205-X
___ **The Tin Drum** by Günter Grass	$15.00	0-679-72575-X
___ **Claudius the God** by Robert Graves	$14.00	0-679-72573-3
___ **I, Claudius** by Robert Graves	$11.00	0-679-72477-X
___ **Aurora's Motive** by Erich Hackl	$7.95	0-679-72435-4
___ **Dispatches** by Michael Herr	$10.00	0-679-73525-9
___ **Walter Winchell** by Michael Herr	$9.00	0-679-73393-0
___ **The Swimming-Pool Library** by Alan Hollinghurst	$12.00	0-679-72256-4
___ **I Served the King of England** by Bohumil Hrabal	$10.95	0-679-72786-8
___ **An Artist of the Floating World** by Kazuo Ishiguro	$9.00	0-679-72266-1
___ **A Pale View of Hills** by Kazuo Ishiguro	$9.00	0-679-72267-X
___ **The Remains of the Day** by Kazuo Ishiguro	$11.00	0-679-73172-5
___ **Dubliners** by James Joyce	$10.00	0-679-73990-4
___ **A Portrait of the Artist as a Young Man** by James Joyce	$9.00	0-679-73989-0
___ **Ulysses** by James Joyce	$14.95	0-679-72276-9
___ **The Emperor** by Ryszard Kapuściński	$9.00	0-679-72203-3
___ **Shah of Shahs** by Ryszard Kapuściński	$9.00	0-679-73801-0
___ **The Soccer War** by Ryszard Kapuściński	$10.00	0-679-73805-3
___ **China Men** by Maxine Hong Kingston	$9.95	0-679-72328-5
___ **Tripmaster Monkey** by Maxine Hong Kingston	$11.00	0-679-72789-2
___ **The Woman Warrior** by Maxine Hong Kingston	$10.00	0-679-72188-6
___ **Barabbas** by Pär Lagerkvist	$8.00	0-679-72544-X
___ **The Plumed Serpent** by D. H. Lawrence	$12.00	0-679-73493-7
___ **The Virgin & the Gipsy** by D. H. Lawrence	$10.00	0-679-74077-5
___ **The Radiance of the King** by Camara Laye	$9.95	0-679-72200-9
___ **The Fifth Child** by Doris Lessing	$8.00	0-679-72182-7
___ **The Drowned and the Saved** by Primo Levi	$10.00	0-679-72186-X
___ **The Real Life of Alejandro Mayta** by Mario Vargas Llosa	$11.00	0-679-72478-8
___ **My Traitor's Heart** by Rian Malan	$10.95	0-679-73215-2

VINTAGE INTERNATIONAL

___ Man's Fate by André Malraux	$9.95	0-679-72574-1
___ Buddenbrooks by Thomas Mann	$14.00	0-679-73646-8
___ Confessions of Felix Krull by Thomas Mann	$11.00	0-679-73904-1
___ Death in Venice and Seven Other Stories by Thomas Mann	$10.00	0-679-72206-8
___ Doctor Faustus by Thomas Mann	$13.00	0-679-73905-X
___ The Magic Mountain by Thomas Mann	$14.00	0-679-73645-X
___ Blood Meridian by Cormac McCarthy	$11.00	0-679-72875-9
___ Suttree by Cormac McCarthy	$12.00	0-679-73632-8
___ The Captive Mind by Czeslaw Milosz	$10.00	0-679-72856-2
___ The Decay of the Angel by Yukio Mishima	$10.95	0-679-72243-2
___ Runaway Horses by Yukio Mishima	$12.00	0-679-72240-8
___ Spring Snow by Yukio Mishima	$12.00	0-679-72241-6
___ The Temple of Dawn by Yukio Mishima	$12.00	0-679-72242-4
___ Such a Long Journey by Rohinton Mistry	$11.00	0-679-73871-1
___ Cities of Salt by Abdelrahman Munif	$16.00	0-394-75526-X
___ Ada, or Ardor by Vladimir Nabokov	$15.00	0-679-72522-9
___ Bend Sinister by Vladimir Nabokov	$11.00	0-679-72727-2
___ The Defense by Vladimir Nabokov	$8.95	0-679-72722-1
___ Despair by Vladimir Nabokov	$11.00	0-679-72343-9
___ The Enchanter by Vladimir Nabokov	$9.00	0-679-72886-4
___ The Eye by Vladimir Nabokov	$8.95	0-679-72723-X
___ The Gift by Vladimir Nabokov	$11.00	0-679-72725-6
___ Glory by Vladimir Nabokov	$10.00	0-679-72724-8
___ Invitation to a Beheading by Vladimir Nabokov	$7.95	0-679-72531-8
___ King, Queen, Knave by Vladimir Nabokov	$8.95	0-679-72340-4
___ Laughter in the Dark by Vladimir Nabokov	$8.95	0-679-72450-8
___ Lolita by Vladimir Nabokov	$9.00	0-679-72316-1
___ Look at the Harlequins! by Vladimir Nabokov	$9.95	0-679-72728-0
___ Mary by Vladimir Nabokov	$10.00	0-679-72620-9
___ Pale Fire by Vladimir Nabokov	$11.00	0-679-72342-0
___ Pnin by Vladimir Nabokov	$10.00	0-679-72341-2
___ The Real Life of Sebastian Knight by Vladimir Nabokov	$10.00	0-679-72726-4
___ Speak, Memory by Vladimir Nabokov	$12.00	0-679-72339-0
___ Strong Opinions by Vladimir Nabokov	$9.95	0-679-72609-8
___ Transparent Things by Vladimir Nabokov	$6.95	0-679-72541-5
___ A Bend in the River by V. S. Naipaul	$9.00	0-679-72202-5
___ Guerrillas by V. S. Naipaul	$10.95	0-679-73174-1
___ A Turn in the South by V. S. Naipaul	$11.00	0-679-72488-5
___ Black Box by Amos Oz	$10.00	0-679-72185-1
___ My Michael by Amos Oz	$11.00	0-679-72804-X
___ The Slopes of Lebanon by Amos Oz	$11.00	0-679-73144-X
___ Metaphor and Memory by Cynthia Ozick	$12.00	0-679-73425-2
___ The Shawl by Cynthia Ozick	$7.95	0-679-72926-7
___ Dictionary of the Khazars by Milorad Pavić		
male edition	$9.95	0-679-72461-3
female edition	$9.95	0-679-72754-X
___ Landscape Painted with Tea by Milorad Pavić	$12.00	0-679-73344-2
___ Swann's Way by Marcel Proust	$13.00	0-679-72009-X

VINTAGE INTERNATIONAL

___ Kiss of the Spider Woman by Manuel Puig	$10.00	0-679-72449-4
___ Grey Is the Color of Hope by Irina Ratushinskaya	$8.95	0-679-72447-8
___ Memoirs of an Anti-Semite by Gregor von Rezzori	$10.95	0-679-73182-2
___ The Snows of Yesteryear by Gregor von Rezzori	$10.95	0-679-73181-4
___ The Notebooks of Malte Laurids Brigge by Rainer Maria Rilke	$10.95	0-679-73245-4
___ Selected Poetry by Rainer Maria Rilke	$12.00	0-679-72201-7
___ The Age of Reason by Jean-Paul Sartre	$12.00	0-679-73895-9
___ No Exit and 3 Other Plays by Jean-Paul Sartre	$10.00	0-679-72516-4
___ The Reprieve by Jean-Paul Sartre	$12.00	0-679-74078-3
___ Troubled Sleep by Jean-Paul Sartre	$12.00	0-679-74079-1
___ All You Who Sleep Tonight by Vikram Seth	$7.00	0-679-73025-7
___ The Golden Gate by Vikram Seth	$11.00	0-679-73457-0
___ And Quiet Flows the Don by Mikhail Sholokhov	$12.95	0-679-72521-0
___ By Grand Central Station I Sat Down and Wept by Elizabeth Smart	$10.00	0-679-73804-5
___ Ake: The Years of Childhood by Wole Soyinka	$11.00	0-679-72540-7
___ Ìsarà: A Voyage Around "Essay" by Wole Soyinka	$9.95	0-679-73246-2
___ Children of Light by Robert Stone	$10.00	0-679-73593-3
___ A Flag for Sunrise by Robert Stone	$12.00	0-679-73762-6
___ Lie Down in Darkness by William Styron	$12.00	0-679-73597-6
___ Sophie's Choice by William Styron	$13.00	0-679-73637-9
___ Confessions of Zeno by Italo Svevo	$12.00	0-679-72234-3
___ Learning to Swim by Graham Swift	$9.00	0-679-73978-5
___ Shuttlecock by Graham Swift	$10.00	0-679-73933-5
___ Waterland by Graham Swift	$11.00	0-679-73979-3
___ The Beautiful Mrs. Seidenman by Andrzej Szczypiorski	$9.95	0-679-73214-4
___ Diary of a Mad Old Man by Junichiro Tanizaki	$10.00	0-679-73024-9
___ The Key by Junichiro Tanizaki	$10.00	0-679-73023-0
___ On the Golden Porch by Tatyana Tolstaya	$8.95	0-679-72843-0
___ The Eye of the Story by Eudora Welty	$8.95	0-679-73004-4
___ Losing Battles by Eudora Welty	$8.95	0-679-72882-1
___ The Optimist's Daughter by Eudora Welty	$9.00	0-679-72883-X
___ The Passion by Jeanette Winterson	$10.00	0-679-72437-0
___ Sexing the Cherry by Jeanette Winterson	$9.00	0-679-73316-7

Available at your bookstore or call toll-free to order: 1-800-733-3000.
Credit cards only. Prices subject to change.